ON SECOND BASE

Enjoy!

Kathy Johncox

Kathy Johncox

For Tom ♥

Many Thanks

To all my family and friends for listening and giving feedback and encouragement to my seemingly endless plotting and revisions on this novel.

To my brother, Dr. Jim Herman, for his baseball knowledge, constant encouragement and willingness to listen.

To my pastor, Rev. Andrew Gookin, for making sure the story accurately follows pastoral life and practice.

To my Writers' Group, Laura Cummings and Deborah Benjamin, dedicated friends, who were always there to listen and read and who tossed around endless titles before finally homing in on "the one."

Chapter One

Grand Slam

Susan awoke to an empty bed. She rubbed the spot where Paul had slept restlessly, turning and moaning, creeping onto her territory, to be close, to be soothed. His absence was predictable, considering his nocturnal malaise. It was a sure sign he was in complete sermon distress and out searching for inspiration on the Little League field, always his idea of hallowed ground. She visualized him there in his Red Sox sweatshirt with the arms cut off at the shoulders, black running shorts, socks with tired elastic trying desperately to stay up as he jogged around the infield. After a few laps, he might crouch on second base in the early light, remembering things past, the thrills and accolades he'd amassed through his nearly 40 years of baseball participation—no, make that passion. Friends and strangers had told her how they had seen Paul on second base, so thoughtful and contemplative in those early morning times, but she'd never seen him herself. She had to imagine his lanky frame covering the canvas, leaning back against strong arms, blue eyes squinting against the sunrise, dark hair with emerging gray, tousled by the running. As it groped for a sermon topic, his brain might ignore many topics, but not baseball, the past glories of his baseball career having all the value these days.

Susan stretched her arms over her head and felt the sheets touch her softly in places where Paul hadn't in a very long time. In their 18 years of marriage, Susan Lombard had considered herself Paul's wife first, and minister's wife was a role that she, to herself, disavowed as much as she could, and got on with the life that would support a husband's calling and nurture two sons into men she would be proud to represent her in the world. She had always considered the three Lombard men a special gift. One she had chosen as a life partner. She had given birth to the other two. Amid their many positive qualities, they all loved baseball, and she

1

did, too.

As she sat up, she had one of those flutters in her chest, just a sprinkling of malaise, a head-to-toe warning that something wasn't right but she just couldn't put her finger on that something. So they forged ahead, he in his place, she in hers, trying to make some sense of whatever it was that was getting in the way of their collective safe place where they had been able to escape to together for so many years.

Sometimes she just wished for the good old days. She fondly remembered the college years when discussions were about thoughtful topics like faith and joy and forgiveness when Paul and his fellow-seminarian friends got together and then after they left, Paul and Susan were energized and could talk long into the night before they fell asleep in each other's arms. They had been married for three years before Joe was born, and after that much of the talk was about babies, but they still found time for thought-provoking exchanges that reminded them of what they loved and respected about each other. After Willie's birth, children's needs became consuming, usurping Paul-Susan time at every turn. They hadn't anticipated the intensity of two children but ultimately had to give in and that's when the growing apart began, Susan remembered. She would have moments when she felt being with Paul for a few quiet minutes was all she needed, but she hadn't grabbed the opportunities, few as they were, to exchange feelings with Paul, share thoughts, talk about problems, offer solutions and move on, or forward. Yes, she had contributed to this disconnect they seemed to be facing now, but so had Paul. They needed time to talk. Uninterrupted time to talk to keep this marriage vital. She had been sure Paul felt the same. But lately, not so much.

She arched her back, winding her arms around her knees, listening to the morning sounds of the house and of the kids tossing around in their beds. Joe's tall frame would be without covers, since at 16 he had recently grown too big for the bed. Willie, the 10-year-old, would be snuggled deeply into the mattress, wrapped mummy-like in the sheets, arms clutching his beat-up Mr. Puppy.

She swung her legs over the side of the bed and rubbed her eyes. Paul had probably made the coffee so long ago that it was burned by now. Probably hadn't put the clothes in the dryer either as he made his pre-dawn escape. These things were easy for her to remedy. Other things were more difficult. But there's always hope, she thought.

In the bathroom, she stepped out of her Red Sox nightshirt, a gift from Paul and the boys at Christmas. She ripped her towel off the rack and suddenly wadded it up to throw it across the room when she thought better of it. Why be upset, she asked herself. Certainly there was something better to think about than Paul's erratic behavior. Something that contained joy and excitement and some measure of passion. She would get some things done first, then take a leisurely shower and think about Joe's baseball practice of yesterday. There was joy in that still. Thankfully the league had let her co-coach the senior league team this year, and so far the hormonal boys were accepting a female coach. She had the skills after all, had been a softball coach for the local community college. And someone had to do it, since Paul didn't have time. Or the psychic energy either, for that matter. Someone had to step up to the plate and keep baseball alive in the Lombard family, and she was in the best place to do that now. She pulled on her Red Sox T-shirt and sweat pants, brushed her dark brown hair back into a ponytail and went downstairs.

She tossed the old coffee, set up some new and sat down to focus on the sports page in anticipation of any dugout discussion regarding the Red Sox later that day with the team and Greg Stone, her coaching partner. But, even the trickling sound of the coffee distracted her and she stared out the window over the sink at the April sunrise. Funny really, that she'd never actually seen Paul camped on second base. She hoped he would find inspiration there today.

On the Little League field near his home, the Reverend Paul Lombard crouched on the damp canvas of second base staring into the sunrise. He closed his eyes and murmured the mantra he had used to retreat when the seminarian's life of learning had become overwhelming. Grand slam. Grand slam. Grand slam.

They were not the most relaxing words, but certainly the most satisfying. Clearing the bases and bringing everyone home, back to the start, a new beginning, another chance. He shifted his weight until he felt just right. He was invulnerable here on the comfort of the canvas, in the green of the infield, a short toss from the pitcher's mound. Grand slam. Grand slam.

He opened his eyes and looked around. Here, he was surrounded by things he loved. He found comfort in the symmetry of the bases. He was grateful that the coaches had voted to keep the canvas bags on the field instead of lugging them home after every game. He liked the look of the gray wooden bleachers, always welcoming spectators, and the dugouts, always anticipating the players. He cherished the somewhat worn-out gray and brown hot dog stand that exuded the lingering odor of grease from frenzied grilling the evening before. And amid all this gray and brown, green was bursting forth, the first signs of spring, the season of baseball.

Groves of fir trees mixed with seedlings of oak and maple hid the baseball diamond from the highway to suburban Barnfield on one side, and from the housing development and convenience store and the Massachusetts Turnpike on the two others. The fourth side overlooked The Great Pond, now home to several herons. If Paul perched just right on the canvas, he could see the pond and beyond it, the cross on the steeple of St. Luke's Lutheran Church where he was pastor. No one could see him.

He closed his eyes again and, on his personal movie screen, he saw the people he loved. His wife, Susan, would be lying on her side, snuggled into the mattress. He wished he could tap her on the shoulder and do some early morning pillow-talk about his angst and dissatisfaction, talk the way they used to. But he hadn't. He had run to the ballfield instead. That was all right. Anyway she'd probably be dreaming in the moments that remained before the boys inevitably announced their Saturday needs: breakfast, socks, rides here and there and the other kid things Susan always made herself available to do. The boys would be lying on their backs, hands behind their heads, resting their brains before the daily onslaught of ideas on what to do and where to go. Joey's hormones would be revving up for a weekend of hanging out with girls and anyone but his parents. Willie's mind would be strategizing how to hang out with Joey and the older kids even though they considered him a pain. Even the cat and the dog rested in their predictable places, the cat napping on the leather chair in his study, the dog snoozing on the floor at its feet.

Paul found it disturbing that he could feel so restless amidst all that tranquility. But then on this Saturday morning, he wasn't home being his usual part of that family tableau. He was in his safe place on second base.

Thoughts of tomorrow's unwritten sermon intruded as Paul opened his eyes and saw the sun reaching over the tops of the fir trees. Peaceful, Paul thought, maybe like heaven. He strained to continue that thought, hoping it might lead toward tomorrow's message to the faithful.

It was sheer stupidity to have left this week's sermon until the last minute. Wednesday was his usual sermon-writing day. But this past week, Wednesday had come and gone, crammed full of hospital visits, and providing coverage for a colleague on vacation with her family. There had been Little League organizational meetings and a trip to the bank with Susan to apply for a home improvement loan to add a bathroom downstairs. They both knew Paul could do the work himself, given the time and a home improvement app on the Internet, not to mention the patience of Job, but both also realizing he possessed none of these, they had chosen to hire out the project. Susan and he used to be a great sermon-writing team. She wouldn't write it but just talking over his thoughts with her often clarified his thinking when he was stuck and gave him a new perspective when he wasn't. Like they did way back when. I miss that, he thought. Where did that go? Maybe we could talk tonight.

Ahh. But there could be no talking tonight and no sermon cramming either. That party at the Jensen's place was a command performance. Paul closed his eyes tightly once again and waited for divine inspiration. The baseball diamond seemed to change into the kind of soft focus that photographers use to capture the rings of newlyweds, a symbol of eternal devotion until death did them part. And then, the image of a woman appeared. He felt she was someone he'd seen before, he wasn't sure where, but it was recently, at the library or maybe at the ballfield. And now, Paul saw her long red hair blow in the breeze. He saw the sunlight reflect in the blond highlights. He saw her smile his way.

Her image stirred him. He felt lighter. He breathed more quickly, his thoughts seemed clearer, his energy felt stimulated. If she were real, she could be touched and cajoled and won over. She could be in his dugout.

He shook his head and blinked. The red-haired woman dissolved into several blurred words he took to be the awaited sign for his sermon topic. He blinked again, voluntarily this time, like a genie trying to retrieve something wonderful for a needy master. The words "fair play" now appeared before him in bold black and white so clearly he felt he could reach out and touch the letters.

He took a deep breath and shrugged. "So be it," he said, standing and sighing to the empty bleachers. He headed home to the computer.

Chapter Two

Discussion

"Don't you think you've had enough coffee, Hon?" Susan asked. "This is the third pot and it's only 9:30."

Paul watched her as she unloaded the dishwasher from the top first so that residual water from the bottoms of the cups and glasses dripped all over the dry dishes below. She was usually so logical and organized that this seemed just bizarre. Paul thought about the lineups and administrative work that accompanied her stint as coach of Joe's team. He was sure that every "I" was dotted and "t" crossed.

"I've got to stoke up for sermon writing, Suze," Paul said. "I got up early and went for a run but it didn't help. I'm still uninspired." He yawned and grabbed the white coffee mug with both hands, gulping the dregs in anticipation of the new pot she was making. "What are the boys up to? Nothing nefarious, I hope."

"Still sleeping," she said, turning to look at him. "And what does 'nefarious' mean anyway. And where did that come from?" She smoothed back the wisps of dark brown hair that had escaped her pre-shower ponytail. Getting no answer, she leaned against the counter waiting for the coffee to be ready and watched her husband scan the newspaper. His body still had a youthful look, abdominals fairly well-defined with just a tiny hint of middle-aged slippage. His angular, honest face was beginning to show at age 49 some of what her mother would call character wrinkles. He had on his reading glasses, those Susan called his Clark Kent glasses. When he put them on, they hid the scar along his right eyebrow where his college roommate and best friend, Jim Fuller, had clipped him with a baseball bat years earlier.

"Huh? What'd you say?" Paul snapped back from his daydream.

"I asked you what does 'nefarious' mean and where you got that word from anyway?"

"I don't know where that came from. I guess it means bad, or maybe a little worse than bad. Maybe wicked. You know I'm a word guy." He dropped the paper and stretched his arms over his head, his long legs under the table.

"Why would you use that word to describe the kids?" Susan, in cleanup mode, started moving around the kitchen with a sponge.

"It just came to mind that's all. Just kidding. We both know they're good kids." Paul stared, surprised at her serious expression, surprised at his own choice of vocabulary, dismayed that he had to walk on eggshells everywhere, at home, at church, at play. "Maybe you should lighten up."

Susan felt a seething begin, a seething she hadn't felt since she was much younger, living at home with her parents, and as she used to do then, she instinctively changed the subject. She picked up the coffee pot and moved toward Paul, speaking casually as though making light conversation. She tried not to take the accusatory tone she knew she was beginning to reserve for discussions about and comments on his work.

"You're writing your sermon today? What happened to Wednesdays?" she asked. She poured him some coffee and replaced the pot, then picked up the sponge to concentrate on a non-existent spot on the counter near him.

"Yeah. Too much going on last week," he said. "I wanted to make tomorrow's message really a good one, too. I've been skating for too long. I intended to put some real thought into it. I was hoping maybe you and I could brainstorm topics like we used to. Haven't done that for a while. Do you have time this afternoon for a session like we use to have? We can go to the coffee shop. I'll buy. Joey and Willie can hang out here."

"We'll see." Susan said. "We have a game in about an hour and then I have to primp for the party tonight. Why don't you mock something up for me to glance at and give you some feedback?

"Wait," Susan frowned. "It's tomorrow's sermon, right? Well, you could always default to baseball," Susan suggested. "At least all the men and boys over age 6 and your wife and children will be entertained." The thought of baseball relaxed her once again, as it always did. She grinned and took a batting stance by the sink, wiggling her bottom. "Do a sermon for the rest of the congregation next week."

"It's tempting, Suze." Paul stood up and moved behind her. He put his arms around her, correcting the height of her elbow just a little. "But I can't please everyone. If I have to concentrate on mass appeal, baseball sermons aren't going to do it."

"Maybe you should concentrate more on me." Susan made this comment softly, but Paul heard an edge in it. At another time, he would have kissed that tone of voice away. Her scent followed him as he moved to the center of the kitchen and went through the motions of winding up for the pitch. He was not stirred by his closeness to her, not energized, did not feel lighter, in fact quite the opposite, sluggish and immobile. He had to force himself to continue this play.

She did have a good stance. Her arms were strong and she knew how to hold a bat. And in her raggedy Red Sox T-shirt and torn jeans, she didn't look her 47 years.

"I know we've been through this before but I'll ask again. Why do you have to please everyone all the time?" Susan swung at the imaginary pitch, made a face and pretended to whack the bat on home plate, preparing for another swipe. "Strike one."

"It just makes everything easier," he said. "Elbow up."

"Yeah," she said, frowning but dutifully adjusting her elbow. "But it puts you at a disadvantage. You should do yourself a favor and take one of those how-to-win-friends-and-keep-them courses. Then you could preach about any old thing you wanted to." She swung hard and watched the imaginary ball go by. "Strike two. You might need all the friends you can get this year."

He hunkered down, taking aim at an imaginary catcher's glove. "What does that mean?"

"You know. You need a team behind you when you're in a slump," she said, turning to watch the pitch whiz by. "Strike three. Time to throw down the bat and head for the dugout."

He didn't know what she'd meant. She'd thrown him a curve, and he could only watch it sail by. And he didn't like the idea his finger may have slipped off the pulse of the congregation.

Paul booted up the computer and waited. He swiveled in his chair and surveyed the wreckage the boys had left in his study. Here, nothing was sacred. The binders containing his baseball card collection lay on the floor near the window and the baseball hats hanging on the wall were out of order. His framed copy of Martin Luther's *95 Theses* and his antique catechisms were thankfully untouched. When he swiveled back, the screen displayed a game with two monsters boxing and sparring. If it wouldn't have taken precious time, Paul would have yelled for the boys so he could once again read them the riot act about the need to leave his computer alone.

He cleared the screen and waited for the magic of the blank monitor to focus him on his necessary task. The temptation to retrieve sermons from two or three years ago was always great. Just a click of the mouse and a myriad of spiritual exhortations, and lectures about salvation and how to get it, would magically appear. Paragraphs containing pleas for people of good conscience to follow in Christ's footsteps and accept the poor, the disabled and the homeless would make themselves easily available. So far he had not given in. No. FAIR PLAY was definitely his subject. He typed it on the screen in bold and underlined the words. He swiveled absently around again, waiting for inspiration.

Lately, to try to focus, he had been reading treatises on morals and philosophical analyses about Christian values. And then there was his dog-eared paperback copy of John Updike's *A Month of Sundays*. This combination led him to theorize that maybe some works of fiction were inspired, that the authors were imbued with special introspection fueled by fantasy and imagination. The latter two characteristics were what separated them from clergymen whom he viewed as trapped between the spiritual and the earthly. He had remembered in seminary reading Updike's tale about a clergyman in pastoral rehabilitation for sexual indiscretions. He and his fellow students had read it with disbelief back then. Now, he considered it a possible metaphor for contemporary life.

He knew his congregation was looking for answers to some of the same life questions he himself was grappling with more and more frequently. From his parishioners he was learning that regardless of your sense of self and of your mission, dissatisfaction sneaks up on you and lurks around just waiting for the right time to make you aware of it.

An hour later, when the words FAIR PLAY were still the only characters on the screen, Paul pounded the roll top desk, and swiveled around angrily in his leather chair for the last time. He clicked to the message about the Sermon on the Mount from two years ago and made a few changes. The humdinger would have to wait until next week.

After spending the afternoon at baseball practice watching Susan and Greg Stone practice with Joe's team, Paul headed home to get ready for the Jensen's party. His self-evaluation in the bathroom mirror this day was more in depth than the usual hurried grooming on the way to a pastoral visit, his pastors' group meeting or a baseball practice. First of all, he had the luxury of extra time. Secondly, he realized with some dismay, he was looking for what a red-haired woman might see and like. He pushed the thought aside as an adolescent thought worthy of Joey, yet continued to enumerate his good points.

His quads were tight and strong, a tribute to his early morning runs past the baseball field and to the many years of crouching down in the waiting position of a second baseman, now long past. When he was Willie's age, he'd hoped to have huge forearms like Mickey Mantle but lack of time had developed only those muscles used in gesturing to make a salient point during Sunday sermons. He made a muscle with his right arm. The definition was obvious, a tribute to the making of many salient points. Not bad for 49 seasons, he thought. Not bad for a guy with a sedentary job and not a lot of spare time. Not bad at all.

Lately, though, when he looked in the mirror he saw not the Reverend Lombard. He saw just Paul. It was getting harder not to let loose from time to time. He couldn't prepare a sermon on baseball because of the comments the council would most certainly have at the next meeting. If he were invited to a parishioner's home, he had to conform to people's expectations of how he should behave. He couldn't drink much or stay as late as he wanted for the same reason. He couldn't wear what he would have liked because the white T-shirt, leather jacket James Dean look didn't fit his calling either.

After parishioner after parishioner had beleaguered him with their "mid-life crises," he had renamed them "changes in life direction" because it sounded less like a single event and more like the gradual process of self-discovery it really was. And there was nothing wrong with a change in direction, if you didn't throw away everything and everyone who had helped you get where you were so far. It was getting monotonous listening as people paraded through his office with litanies of concerns about their earthly lives, not their spiritual selves. When he had realized a few days ago that the phrase "patience is a virtue" was making him sick, he knew he'd better find someone to talk to.

He turned on the shower and stepped inside. He reached for the shampoo and began to lather up, closing his eyes against the suds. When the cleansing warmth of the water began to relax his muscles, he opened his eyes and nodded. He would call his fellow pastor and friend, Jim Fuller, as soon as he had a chance.

Chapter 3

Command Performance

Paul rang the bell at the Jensen house and waited. He could hear the sounds of fellowship inside. There's always the performance element to consider, he thought. Just being here is not enough. I have to be in a good mood and on my best behavior. Forget it for tonight, Reverend, he told himself as he rang the bell once more, but his neck was tightening already just thinking about it.

By the time Henry Jensen opened the door, Paul had decided that just one stiff drink wouldn't hurt, and when Henry offered him a scotch on the rocks, the golden glow of the liquid had a downright magical lure. Paul anticipated its cool smoothness and that familiar relaxation, the last memory of which was much too far away. Before he took the first taste, he saw Susan's face earlier that afternoon, intent on finding Joey's heel guards for his baseball cleats; at the same time intent on making Paul understand that he'd better use some self-control tonight.

He took a welcome first sip and looked around. As usual, the most active church people, the largest financial contributors, and the most ostensibly devout were all in attendance. All the people a pastor would most want to enfold in his sphere of influence were out in force to celebrate Henry's good fortune. It was Henry's 45th birthday and he had just married for the second time. His former wife, Pam, the church organist, was not at the party. His new bride Rachel, the mental health nurse who had supported him through his nervous breakdown last year, was flitting from group to group, chattering and being the good hostess. To make matters even better, Henry had landed a huge account for the business supply company where he worked and he was proclaiming to everyone who would listen that life was good. Paul remembered when it hadn't been so good, when Henry had been on both disability and medication, in agony over his crisis.

Leaving his wife and asking for only minimal custody of his two young children had worked well for Henry. Being left alone and having most of the responsibility for the children had not worked well for Pam. She was doing better, but it had taken many hours of Paul and Pam working together through her mixed up feelings.

Paul found himself an out-of-the-way chair and sat down. Even though he welcomed this quiet time to observe the flock, he half hoped he wouldn't be alone for long. He remembered Dr. Bill Wilhelm, his mentor in seminary, always said that the best pastors were people magnets, and the more de-magnetized they became, the more they were in danger of losing their core altogether.

His magnet was working. Jody Ellwanger caught his eye and moved tentatively to his side.

"Hello, Pastor. Good to see you." she said. She looked around. "Where's Susan tonight?" she asked.

"Hi, Jody. Oh Susan? Running late. Lots to do today." Paul said.

Jody seemed to be searching for another topic. Finally she settled on something she thought would interest him. "How's Joey's ball team doing?"

"It's shaping up nicely. Thanks for asking," Paul said.

"I heard Susan was coaching."

"Yes, and she's really doing an excellent job. Boys that age are not really into their mothers even being in the bleachers, so it isn't easy." He watched Jody sip her wine.

Susan **was** doing an excellent job and why not, he thought. She brought everything to it. Her father had been the manager for a minor league team in Rochester, New York and she had grown up in dugouts, living and breathing baseball. She'd even found a way to maneuver herself out of her part-time job every day, so she could share the coaching responsibilities with Greg, whose son Hunter was on the team as well.

15

"Super," Jody said, then more softly added, "Pastor, I need some time with you next week. When would be convenient?"

Paul studied her face. She didn't look like she was having problems in her marriage. It was his experience that when women had those problems, they almost always dropped some weight and got dark circles under their eyes. Sarcastic comments about their husbands frequently escaped their carefully glossed lips. They often couched their requests in mystery. But her request had been fairly direct, not embarrassed or flirtatious. He decided not to let it bother him. After all, she was the Christian education director and perhaps planning the fall curriculum was on her mind.

"How about Monday afternoon? I have about an hour at 3 o'clock." Paul had learned in pastoral time management to put limits on appointments.

"That'd be great. I won't take long. It's just not something I can talk about right here right, right now. You understand. Don't you?" She threw her blond mane over her shoulder and turned away to take a mini creme puff off a serving tray.

"Of course," Paul said, not really understanding anything.

He looked around, reviewing the individual secrets he knew about most of the people in the room. That one was depressed about a work problem, that one stressed out about teenage kids. The one in the corner was unhappy staying home, the one by the fireplace was unhappy working. The two talking in the hallway were unhappy in their respective marriages and looking for someone to save them. That one was an adulterer, that one an adulteress. Everyone seemed to have a need for something.

And then there were the women who seemed very flirtatious. There was the parishioner at the Little League banquet who, as they danced, placed her hand on his neck, idly caressing his hair, instead of putting her hand on his shoulder. There was Jocelyn who waited after meetings and sat knee to knee with him discussing her personal problems even though he had twice referred her for some professional counseling. Even one of the young girls from the youth group, who was a cashier at the grocery store, had flirted with him. He didn't think he imagined her touch on his hand longer than necessary when giving him change, or her frown when he refused a cup of coffee when she got off work. There were other incidents that would point to all this attention not being solely in his imagination. For a time there were so many occurrences that he was convinced that some women were just throwing themselves his way, that is, until he remembered that it was in his father's 49th year that similar problems boiled over for his parents. Paul had been away at seminary in Boston when his father succumbed to the charms of a woman at the perfume counter while buying a gift for Paul's mother. The woman was a member of the church where Paul's father was a deacon. He remembered telephone calls at college from his father, so confused by the level of his mother's outrage. Almost as confused as Paul was in trying, at age 20, to understand his father's need for what he called a "life change."

Perhaps all this perceived attention from women was a result of the fact that Paul was facing his own 49th in two months and approaching this birthday with more dread than he had any other. It was beginning to seem part of his birthright that his life would cease to be the way he had planned and thought he liked it. There were already signs of an unraveling. One in particular had red hair.

Susan arrived late, baseball getting in the way already and the season hadn't yet officially started. She looked good, probably had taken extra precious time to make sure she did. That navy silk dress always made her feel glamorous and sexy she said, feelings that she hoped separated her from your average minister's wife, a place he knew she always wanted to be. He saw her look for him, her antennae no doubt on damage control as they so often were these days. Two of the church ladies caught her attention and involved her in a conversation about herb gardens. She listened absently, smiling appropriately, still looking. She saw him, excused herself and moved to join him.

Paul watched her walking toward him. That dress fit just right.

The fabric pulled and touched in just the right places. It tightened across her breasts, still firm, and clung to her hips, still narrow. The length was demure when she stood but when she sat, it would show her sexy legs. Paul was proud of her for being so attractive, for being so well put together. He thought of her warmth in their bed, the comfort of her arms. Now, if only she had long, red hair. He found himself thinking back to the baseball diamond, warm breeze at his back, fantasy woman approaching. He shook himself free of the thought. The ice jingled in his glass as he looked around for another drink.

Susan had done everything right. When he had gotten the pastoral call from the congregation in Barnfield, she hadn't hesitated leaving Boston even though she loved the big city life. "Whither thou goest..." she'd quoted the book of Ruth in the Bible, and patted her pregnant belly. Willie was in there and Joey was six years old. In their 10 years at St. Luke's, she had always had energy for whatever he wanted to do, be it a trip to the amusement park with the boys or what he called comfort time early in the morning before their day began. She needed him when he felt useless and helped him when he didn't know he needed it. He felt she was his intellectual equal and his creative superior. She was strong and hopeful in her life and in her faith. Not a typical pastor's wife, not the Sunday-school-teaching, ladies'-guild-joining, potluck-supper-making typical pastor's wife, but then he hadn't wanted that.

"She sure looks great, doesn't she," said Henry, coming up behind him and poking Paul with his elbow.

"Even better now than when we were first married," Paul agreed.

"I'm talking about my wife, not yours." Henry said it proudly as though she were a hard-won prize. He nodded in Rachel's direction. She grinned and walked over to meet them. Paul thought her tousled dark hair, the aqua jump suit and the gold earrings nearly dragging on her shoulders made her look a lot more vital than she did at the hospital.

"Honey, the caterer needs you for a moment," she said as she rubbed

Henry's back.

"Probably wants to hand me the bill. That feels good." He closed his eyes and leaned back into her touch. "Maybe we should just disappear for awhile. No one will miss us."

"The caterer will," Rachel said, giving Henry a push in the right direction.

"Don't go away." He blew her a kiss and made for the kitchen.

"Isn't he great?" Rachel said. She stopped one of the servers for honeyed chicken pieces on a stick. "Um. Delicious. I'll try anything as long as I don't have to cook it," she added, leaning conspiratorially closer to Paul.

Paul watched Susan wave his way and walk toward Greg Stone, apparently the self appointed bartender, and suddenly remembered how she had let him know, in an uncharacteristic burst of cattiness, that Rachel's skills were not in the kitchen. He remembered it was that morning several months ago when they had last made love.

"Where are her skills then?" Paul had asked.

"Oh, here." Susan had kissed his neck. "And here." She'd brushed kisses across his cheek. "Oh, and here." She had wet his lips with her tongue and wrapped her arms around his neck.

"Could that possibly lead to this?" Paul had lifted Susan into his arms, tossed her on the bed and thrown himself down next to her.

"They say it does." She turned to fit herself to him, all the while listening for the school bus brakes to squeal as the bus stopped to scoop up the kids.

"Who's they?" Paul whispered.

"Who cares?" Susan had murmured.

The squealing of the bus brakes had been replaced by the squeaking of the bed. Her warmth had been comforting, her breath like toothpaste. Their passion had been abbreviated by the daily responsibilities calling to them both. And those responsibilities had been calling ever since, separating them from this method of comfort and sweetness for days, weeks, months—long enough for Paul to allow a fantasy woman to make her way between them.

Paul made his way toward the bar where Greg was putting on a show. He reached for the scotch and grabbed a few ice cubes. He tossed them in Paul's glass with great panache, then took the bottle and threw it from one hand to another twice before filling the glass. He looked like an all-American college kid except for the mustache, the longish, blond hair, the blue eyes that widened often in surprise, since for Greg many normal life happenings were unexpected. Paul knew all this and more since counseling Greg after his wife had suddenly left him for another man. The other man was in Nashville, a country-western singer-wanna-be up north for a brief tour. Greg said he had appealed to his wife's, now ex-wife's, dreams of singing at the Grand Ole Opry. Greg had shaken his head as he described her singing voice.

"You know I tended bar in college." Greg slid the glass down the counter to Paul. "That and baseball were my two loves. Well, actually, I had three loves if you include conquering women." He smiled slyly. Paul wondered if it was the same smile he had used for the conquerings.

"I played ball in college, you know." Paul said.

"No kidding. What position?"

"Mostly second base," Paul said, swirling the ice in the glass.

"Were you any good?" Greg wiped the counter.

"Not bad. Not many people know this but at one time, I thought about a career in baseball."

"Oh yeah. I guess Susan did tell me that. I was kind of surprised. I thought pastors knew they were going to be pastors even when they were kids. It's kind of strange to think of you wanting to be anything else."

Paul frowned. So Susan had shared some of his past with Greg. Disappointing. She knew he liked to keep parishioners guessing about some things. If they knew all his secrets, they would know him much more personally than the flock should know its shepherd.

Now Paul warmed to the topic. "I played on the varsity team at college and had minor league scouts looking at me."

"Whoa. Wait a minute. How far did you go?"

"Got to the advanced thinking stage. You know, the one where you begin to fantasize what your life will be like. You congratulate yourself on being able to do what you love for a living, unlike your parents who did what they had to do. You try to imagine what it will be like to live your passion every day." Paul meant to continue but Greg interrupted.

"Interesting fantasies you conjure up. I loved playing ball too but my fantasies more involved a huge desk in a corporate home office with plenty of secretaries to do my bidding. Now they'd be administrative assistants, of course." Greg smiled broadly.

Paul badly wanted yet another drink. This baseball talk had made him thirsty. He could see the dust on the hot, dry infield blowing in the warm summer breeze, feel it drying on his lips. His buddies were on the bleachers, drinking beers and accusing the batter of many forms of cowardice as he watched the balls whiz by. They leaned forward and pointed as Paul began his ritual dance around his assigned position at second base. This display had had two objectives, to kick up dust and to tempt the first base runner to take a chance. To gamble with the temptation to take the lead and win. To not be afraid to pay the price.

Susan watched Paul, frowning imperceptibly as he reached for the scotch and poured his own. Greg was watching Susan.

Chapter Four

Something Different

The next morning, the smell of the flowers cascading over the altar rail made Paul queasy. This reaction was definitely the result of overindulgence the night before. He didn't remember much of what had happened at the Jensen home last night and what he did recall wasn't pleasant. From the taste still in his mouth even after brushing his teeth three times, and the dull ache behind his eyes, he knew scotch was involved. From Susan's cool reception at breakfast, he assumed other aberrant behaviors had slipped past his pastoral guard, a facade that until recently had protected everyone against the real Paul.

He sat down on the bench facing the altar and began a prayer to provide the proper contemplative atmosphere in which to prepare for God's words. The sweet flower smell wafted in his direction and his stomach objected with a small jolt. Paul looked up to see Pam Jensen come out of the hidden door with the trays of wine for Holy Communion. She placed them reverently on the altar. He winced. Hung over or not, communion must go on.

"Good morning, Pastor," she said, smiling. "How's the head?"

"A little rough, Pamela. Take it easy on those high notes today, will you?"

Pam negotiated her way through the choir loft, her generous hips bumping one choir pew and then another. She reached into her pocket and tossed him two aspirin as she seated herself at the organ. "I'll do my best, but I hear you were the one who was holding forth last night about the need for 'a rousing chorus.'" She tucked her hair, blond and frizzy from a new color and perm, behind her ears, and began to flip pages in the nearest music book.

Teasing was her forte and she could jolly almost anyone into doing or admitting almost anything with a gentle comment or playful nudge from her elbow. Anyone except her ex-husband, Henry. Maybe it was too many years of teasing that made Henry opt out. Or maybe her desire to have more input into decisions for the family. At any rate, Henry had left her for Rachel beckoning from the wings. And Paul had been there for Pam, forging a strong friendship based on mutual need.

Paul smiled gratefully but grimaced as he swallowed the pills without water. He put his head in his hands and said into his lap, "Pam, could I talk to you after service?"

"Sure." She winked and turned to shuffle through the anthem music. Pam could be counted on to be in his corner should the need ever arise.

Paul moved through the door hidden in the woodwork to the left of the altar. Behind it was a room with a kneeling bench for private prayer and a hook holding Paul's pastoral robe and the green stole, color dictated by the church calendar. He slipped them on and sat down to await Pam's prelude. Although the rest of the music was chosen by committee, Pam insisted the prelude always be her choice. Most of the time she stuck to traditional prelude music, but she'd been known to sneak in Phil Collins tunes, Eric Clapton, and even some Beatles. Pam's exceptional talent made those popular tunes sound as beautiful as some of the classic opening religious music. She was smart to keep an unpredictable element in her music selection. Those in the know were never bored waiting for whatever pop-rock motif might appear. This day's opening notes sounded suspiciously like a Paul McCartney tune. Paul found himself humming along as he stepped from the room and walked down the aisle to join the choir. His headache was much better, but his sour stomach would still need some of the antacids he kept hidden behind the collection plates.

The choir members nodded to him as he joined them. As Pam began the processional, they arranged themselves in the rear of the church effectively blocking the entry of anyone who dared be late.

23

Paul liked the inside of the church. It was relatively modern but, because of a series of benefactors from New England, had elements of an old meeting house. Its dark rough-hewn beams and Tudor-style walls gave it a Hawthornian flavor. The windows were clear leaded glass with beveled diamond-shaped panes. The pews were of dark brown wood and would have been uncomfortably puritan, but in a concession to 20th century comfort, the Ladies' Guild had carefully created long soft seat coverings for all wooden seating areas except the Pastor's bench.

The organ was situated in the front of the church behind the altar and the choir sat to the left in elevated pews that faced the congregation. Maximum seating was about three hundred but only on holidays did St. Luke's even approach capacity. There were usually good seats available for every "performance," Paul thought.

It was always amazing to walk toward the altar and turn around to face the congregation. Not because of the people necessarily, but because of the glorious stained glass window that faced the altar and pulpit. The stained glass was a colorful mosaic of Jesus, the Shepherd surrounded by lambs, smiling beneficently over the men, women and children who every Sunday sat beneath his gaze. Only the pastor, organist and choir could see the colorful window during the service, as if they were the only ones in need of inspiration. The congregation could only see it walking back from communion or when they were leaving after service. If the sun hit it just right, the halo behind the head of Christ would glow and for a moment, for Paul, time would seem to stand still. He would pause in whatever he was saying, doing or celebrating and know that something was right.

It wasn't sunny today.

Paul waited as the faithful filled the pews. Attendance had been down for the past few months, probably a tribute to spring and sport practices. There were the Turners settling in the fourth pew from the back, like clockwork. The Sundstroms, complete with color books, magic markers, toddler twin sons and infant daughter marched down to the front pew. Paul guessed they chose that area so the kids could spread out in front of them and color. Henry and Pam's teenage daughter had charge of the nursery along with Joey today and Paul wondered why people didn't leave their kids there. It was hard enough to concentrate on his delivery without kids crying and Amy Sundstrom nursing her daughter literally in front of God and everyone. Then there were Mr. and Mrs. Phillips, an older couple who routinely fell asleep in the back pew. Paul couldn't believe that people didn't think he saw all these things. But then it's easy to let your mind wander when you could give sermons in your sleep. Looking out over the 30 rows of pews divided by the center aisle was like reading a familiar road map. All the landmarks were there with only an occasional detour, and not a very exciting one at that. There were certainly no women with red hair in sight, Paul thought, surprised by the persistence of that image. He pushed it away.

When the opening liturgy was finished, people began settling in for the sermon. In the hush that preceded his usual pre-sermon prayer, Paul moved to the pulpit and quietly arranged his sermon notes. Amy Sundstrom opened her blouse and covered up for the mid-morning feeding.

"Friends and followers in the teachings of Christ, welcome to God's words, through me, for you today," Paul began.

Then he stopped. His message about the Sermon on the Mount sat neatly before him, word-processed, spell-checked and triple-spaced. He stared at the words, but he couldn't read them. Not because they weren't clear, but because he wasn't sure they'd make a difference. How many times could people hear how blessed the meek are or how blessed the poor in spirit? What did it mean to them as they worked, played, loved, lived, died? Paul used to be able to find the words to bring the true import of this Bible lesson home, but not today. The words he had borrowed from the sermon were good ones, but unfair to these people looking expectantly at him for spiritual nourishment to sustain them for the week. What loaves or fish could he toss them that would multiply and satisfy their spiritual hunger? Would there be enough left over for him?

People were clearing their throats uncomfortably. They were looking around the sanctuary. They were nudging each other. Some were staring right at him.

It felt like the final pitch of the last inning and his team was down by two. Two men on and Paul, the game winning run, was at bat. He stepped up to the plate.

"Today I'd like to try something different." He paused. "I'd like you all to close your eyes and get as comfortable as you can. Even take your shoes off and put your feet up if that's what it takes." There were some chuckles. "Now give up all those things you usually fill your minds with on Sunday mornings. You know. Shall we stop at the store after church? Did I turn off the coffee pot before I left home? Did I take something out of the freezer for dinner?" There was some snickering. "Now, fill your minds only with the thoughts and images I give you." Paul waited. Some people were fidgeting but all of them had closed their eyes and all were waiting.

Paul tried desperately to remember exactly how that visualization process went. He had learned it at the synod's pastoral retreat in January and had been keeping this for an ace to use sometime when he needed it. He wasn't exactly prepared. He should've boned up on the how-to's. But sometime was now.

He prayed silently for his mind and mouth to work in concert and began slowly in a quiet and soothing voice.

"You're walking alone on a beach. The warm sea breeze is relaxing and the white sand is warm and comfortable under your feet. Waves lap quietly, soothingly as you continue down the beach for a while, revelling in the joy of a beautiful day." He paused.

"Soon you see a path to your left. You take it and it leads to some woods bordering the beach. You walk along the path savoring the coolness of the trees and the snapping of twigs and crackling of leaves as you walk. You arrive at a clearing. You see a small shovel there and some dirt that

26

has been tossed around. You pick up the shovel and start digging, first tentatively, then more confidently. You feel and hear the faint thud of metal on wood. You bend down and lift out a wooden chest. You gently brush off the dirt and prepare to open it. Now you open the chest to see what's inside."

He paused and continued in quieter tones. "That something inside can be whatever you want it to be, something you need, something you are searching for, something you have. You pick it up and examine it. It pleases you." Paul's voice broke as he choked back an unexpected sob. He had to clear his throat softly and compose himself before he could start again.

"Slowly, you begin to feel you're not alone. You turn and look and Jesus is with you in the clearing. He greets you by name with a welcoming smile and tells you that what you have just found is yours to keep. Then He says you may ask Him or tell Him anything you wish. He tells you He is there for you and you alone. You talk for quite a while. You share your worries and concerns, your hopes and dreams. He listens quietly but somehow you know he is not only listening because you feel lighter, like you could float or fly and there is joy in this freedom. He talks to you and He remains at your side as he gestures for you to place the empty chest back and cover it with dirt. You are puzzled as it feels heavier and it is a strain for you to place it deep in the hole, but you do it.

"You walk back down the path toward the beach, taking your treasure with you. Jesus walks with you. He puts His arm around your shoulders and you are filled with His presence. As you approach the beach, His touch becomes lighter and lighter, finally disappearing. You are alone, but left with a deep sense of well-being. You have shared some of your burden with the One who can help you carry it, if you let Him."

Paul stopped and looked out over the people gathered there, most of whom still had their eyes closed. Some of them were hunched forward with their elbows on their knees and their chins in palms of their hands.

Others had leaned back and sprawled out. Some sat with their arms folded across their chests. The kids were coloring and the baby had fallen asleep nursing. Without looking, he knew both Susan and Pam were watching him.

"You may open your eyes now."

Blinking against the daylight, the members of the congregation opened their eyes.

Paul moved through Holy Communion and the rest of the service on automatic, gave the Benediction, and then hurried to the back of the church. He watched eyes and body language, looking for any clues of joy or relief or displeasure. He wondered if he had struck out or cranked a grand slam.

"Nice job today, Pastor," Mrs. Phillips said. She grabbed Paul's hand with both of hers and shook it vigorously.

"Thank you, Mrs. P.," Paul patted her arm as she walked past him and out of the sanctuary.

Amy Sundstrom was full of praise. "What a nice change," she said. "The sermon was so short I actually got to listen to it. The kids just played for the whole brief time you talked. It was great, really great, Pastor. Someday I'd like to tell you what I found in the chest," she added, then dashed after one of her boys as he made a break for the door to the parking lot.

He shook almost all the hands and anyone who said anything about his message liked it. There were a number who said nothing, but that was expected. He was starting to feel like he was safe at home plate when Susan grabbed his elbow and walked with him toward his office door.

"We have to talk," she said.

"Okay," he said slowly, drawing out the word, welcoming her immediate comments.

"At home. After practice."

"Okay," he said again. "See you there." This time his spine was tingling, his body on full alert.

Paul went into his office. He smoothed his hair in the mirror behind the door and adjusted an imaginary baseball cap. Well, then it wasn't a strikeout, he assured himself as he took off his robe. But possibly not quite a grand slam either.

Pam peeked in the door. "You wanted to talk to me?"

"Yeah, thanks, I have something to run by you."

"Well, I'll just put the kids in the Sunday school room to play while we talk." She leaned a little farther into the room and whispered, "Does it have something to do with your binge at Henry's last night?" She turned to leave, grinning.

Susan appeared behind Pam and said, "Joey and I are going to baseball practice. You take Willie home with you, OK?"

"Sure. We'll see you at home later." He leaned forward for a kiss, a gesture which from the look on her face he figured she wouldn't even have acknowledged if it hadn't been for Pam. Susan took a deep breath, lent her cheek for a peck and hurried out looking for Joey. Pam left to place her children in protected territory and came back puffing.

"Come on in." He closed the door.

"Is Susan upset?" Pam studied his face.

"Yeah. I guess I overdid it with the drink last night like I haven't overdone it in years."

"So I heard."

"How? It was just last night."

"Word gets around when the fearless leader of the Christian soldiers moves onward into uncharted territory."

"Don't talk in riddles, please. And grab me two more aspirin out of that drawer, will you? My headache is revving up again."

Pam reached into his top drawer for the pills and handed them to Paul. Then she pulled out the Updike book. "Hey, I think I read this in college," she said. "I mean, I did read this in college," she repeated slowly. "This is the one about the minister in trouble." It was more a question than a comment.

The aspirin he had popped into his mouth without water were melting into disgusting bitterness on the back of his tongue. In desperation, he swigged them down with the morning's cold coffee.

"I was just going to look up something before I called Reverend Fuller tomorrow. We read it together in seminary and we used to joke about it a lot."

"Oh," she said.

"About that talk," Paul said.

"Okay. I've got a few minutes but I have to have the kids home in time for Henry and his bride to pick them up for a movie."

"Pam, I'll come right to the point. I just feel like recently I've moved from the center to the periphery of things here and I wonder if you or anyone else had noticed." He walked to the window and pretended to be looking for Willie outside. His eyes were moist and he couldn't look at her as he waited for her answer.

He thought he heard her sigh.

"Actually yes," she said carefully. "You do seem to have a lot on your mind." She paused. "But that's okay. Some of us are just waiting for you to jump back to the middle. The others, well, I'm not sure just what is happening. There's an undercurrent that I haven't been able to get a handle on yet. I'm working on it though."

"I've got eyes and I can see some things are a little off. But I need ears. You'll let me know what's going on?"

"Sure. Can't have the fearless leader getting lost now, can we?" He knew she was smiling.

He heard her take a few steps toward him and stop. He knew if he turned to look at her, she would want to touch him to reassure him of her pledge. He kept staring out the window because if she touched him, he felt he might begin to weep. It took a minute before he could turn to her and say, "Thanks for your help, Pam. You've always been a friend."

"Thank you, Paul, for what you do for all of us." She rushed on. "Like today. I really did for a moment feel peace at having that beautiful memory, sharing it with Jesus. It was so wonderful how you put us there in that place. Guess what I found in my chest?" She hurried on. "It was a cross, a beautiful one with sparkling stones set in shining gold. Actually my grandmother had one like it."

"What a terrific image. Just the kind of experience I was hoping for," Paul said, sincerely.

"It was wonderful." Her kind, round face was beaming with the memory. "What did you find in yours?"

Her kids had escaped from the Sunday School room and were at the door pounding on it, calling her name. "Got to go. You can tell me some other time. On that other matter, I'll let you know what I come up with." The kids tugged at her dress, pulling her out the door.

Paul put his glasses on the desk, closed and rubbed his eyes. The rubbing took him back to the beach, the woods, the chest, Jesus. There was no lightness, no freedom, no treasure for him, only emptiness.

Paul started when Pam stuck her head back inside his office.

"By the way, I still am," she said.

"Am what?"

"I am still your friend." And she was gone.

Chapter 5
Practice

After practice, Susan slammed the car door so hard that Joe looked up from the baseball cards he had just traded with a teammate in the dugout. His face, his sweatshirt and pants were covered with grit from plays practiced at his second base position. He was still irritated and embarrassed by the ugly scene he had just witnessed between his mother and Coach Stone.

"Now what?" he asked.

"What?" Susan hedged. He gave her an exasperated look.

"Oh, the door? The wind caught it," she said, trying to sound casual. He shook his head as she started the car, careful not to peel out of the parking lot.

But the slamming had felt good to Susan. Something physical always helped when she had a lot on her mind. What a show last night had been. Two scotches and Paul's innermost thoughts were a matter of public record. Still he swigged down a third drink and turned Susan's evening into a nightmare of marital babysitting. She pretended to hold his hands affectionately after he caressed Jody Ellwanger's long hair, but in reality she was trying to control him so he wouldn't grope anyone else. Then he spewed forth two jokes so lewd even Greg turned pale. When she finally got him to the door she had to reach in his pants pockets to grab the keys to his car so he couldn't drive. Thank God for Greg and Henry teaming up to get their other car home last night. She hoped the overcast and moonless night helped to hide her embarrassment and anger as she tried to thank them as though everything were fine, an attempt to dismiss Paul's behavior with a casual tone. Then, that sermon today. It was unbelievable that Paul would stoop to giving an unprepared sermon. It was like cheating on an exam or lying to a boss. He owed these people more respect.

And then there was Greg Stone today at practice. What a piece of work he could be.

"How'd practice go, Joe?" Paul flipped his son's cap off, intending to ruffle his hair.

Joe ducked away and sat down on the stool in the mudroom to remove his cleats.

"Just great," he muttered.

"Why do I think otherwise?"

"Nothing was good enough for her today. No one could pitch good enough or run hard enough or do anything enough." Joey pulled hard on his shoe and pitched backward. He caught himself and looked up at Paul. "And then Coach Stone said something about women sometimes having days when nothing pleases them. That's when she really freaked out."

Paul was about to try to offer an explanation for her behavior when Susan stormed in and slammed her clipboard on the kitchen table. "**I** freaked out!? All they were doing was trying to impress the girls. Maybe we could actually play ball if these guys ever get control of their hormones which is dubious since most of the MEN I know haven't even achieved that yet."

Susan paced back and forth in front of the kitchen sink. "Joe, you've got to decide—girls or baseball, because they both aren't going to fit into your life right now with school, homework and games to win."

"Playing ball used to be fun," Joe said, looking straight at his mother. "I'll get some pizza later." He stomped out the back door, punctuating his exit with a better-than-average slam. Susan glared at the vibrating screen door.

Paul wondered where Joe had gone. Somewhere to brood, no doubt. Maybe to smoke. Maybe to do some other forbidden thing. It amazed him how kid-like Joe could look with his dark brown hair sticking straight up because of the way he'd put his baseball cap on, and how adult he could seem, when his brown eyes bored straight into you if you tried to invade his emotional turf.

"I'm making peanut butter sandwiches for everyone," said Paul.

"Oh, and you," said Susan. "Just ignore the whole problem. If it were YOU sitting in the dugout watching nubile young girls distract your son and his teammates from the game at hand, I'm sure you'd be thrilled too. But you wouldn't have to listen to Stone's demeaning comments because he wouldn't be making them in front of you. I'm going to take a shower." She flounced up the stairs, her ponytail swinging violently.

Take a cold one, Paul thought.

Willie had been standing inside the back door. "What's 'nubile' mean?" he asked.

"Do you want strawberry or grape jam?" Paul asked.

"Grape."

"Grape it is."

"Fine." Willie went to the refrigerator for some milk. "It probably means something sexy, huh? That's why you won't tell me."

"Why don't you go look it up?"

"Kevin's waiting." Willie's mouth was full and milk clung to the top of his lip. Paul marveled that his 10-year-old innocence still surrounded him like a halo.

Paul sat down and took a bite of his sandwich. Joe's one good-looking kid when he's cleaned up, he thought. Girls would pay attention to him. How prudish Susan could be about this teen-age sex thing. She didn't approve of Joe's behavior, difficult though it was to handle sometimes, which was only natural—for a guy. Many conversations hadn't convinced

34

her of that and Paul felt he was always taking sides. Now, even early in the season, he felt his bad vibes about her coaching were becoming justified. Joe's heart was not in the game this season. And Susan didn't, wouldn't see it. As she wouldn't see so many other things lately.

The sound of the shower would not be the welcome soothing wake-up sound of the early morning shower, his family coming alive for a new day. The sound would be intense; drops of water beating like hailstones on the shower walls and on Susan.

Paul made a sandwich for her, put it on a tray with his own and filled two wine goblets with milk. He carried their lunch up to the bedroom.

Upstairs, Susan had undressed quickly, trying to relax, trying to push Paul, Joe, Greg and the practice out of her mind. She made herself think back to her few minutes of quiet time earlier that morning. The indentation on Paul's side of the bed described him well these days. An invisible weight, an off and on presence—not constant like he used to be. And his sense of humor, his wry comments, his jokes had become nearly nonexistent.

Through many good and bad times he had carried their family, carried her. Through various family emergencies, her difficult pregnancy with Willie, through uprooting their family and settling in a new area, he had been her rock. In those early years when money was tight, they had only half joked with each other that they lived on love. He couldn't quite make pleasure out of pain but with a touch or a murmur, rubbing her neck, her back, holding her hand, his strength was hers. They had agreed many times that together they were protected and strong against what life threw their way. What God thought they could handle, they could handle.

Suddenly, she missed the quirky games he used to create to make sadness less, to make happiness greater, to make the unknown not so frightening, to make a big thing, little. She looked forward to those, to the creativity he always denied having. But lately she hadn't seen any of it. Even in the kitchen this morning, his playing along with the baseball charade had been half-hearted, his mind mostly elsewhere. And this wasn't new, she realized as she shampooed her hair, the thick lather dropping in dollops on the shower floor.

Right before Christmas, she had felt something was different. She thought then that it was the stress of the holidays, but Paul hadn't exhibited his usual joy at each event nor had he brought the enthusiasm he seemed to find in previous years. She had been so busy herself that she had not focused on Paul's moods or harsh words to the kids or his lack of communication with her or his increasing gripes about the job. Only now did she see all that as the start of something bad. And it gave her a chill, right there under the warm water. It made the hair stand up on her neck to think she may have missed something big happening right under her very nose.

She fumbled for the soap, only now realizing that it was a tiny sliver, that once again Paul hadn't taken the time to replace it. She swore and slid the shower curtain away to reach for a new bar in the cabinet. She then noticed the toilet paper roll was empty too. She swore again and ripped the wrapper off the soap. She lathered up and scrubbed hard with the loofa, feeling layers of niceness peel away.

She was being too understanding about everything. He was keeping something from her. Their good lines of communication had broken down. He was not sharing something really important to him and it was being reflected in other ways. It was too much. In spite of the warm water, her neck was starting to hurt.

She soaped her legs, then, with a deep breath, reached for her razor. Somehow shaving her legs, the physical transformation from rough to smooth, always had a calming effect. She looked forward to indulging her favorite habit, sitting on the bed and applying lotion, slowly, pampering herself for the few moments it took to really soak in.

Men should have something like that, she thought as she roughly snapped the shower off. Something they didn't have to do routinely, like trim their nose hair or shave their stubble. Paul should have something that seemed luxurious and spoiling. A thing, a little thing that could take his mind off the big things for a moment. Maybe he would say that second base fulfilled that function. She'd have to ask him.

She toweled her hair first, then the rest of her. With a green bath sheet around her in case a kid had invaded her bedroom while she showered, she looked toward the bedroom door and saw it was ajar. She sighed. The lotion would have to wait.

Paul had placed the tray on the bedroom floor and sat next to it, leaning against the foot of the bed. When the door opened, he saw her wrapped in the large dark green bath sheet. There was a time not long ago when he would have looked into her eyes and moved closer to her. She might have teasingly peeled the towel slowly away, an act that would have led to locking the bedroom door.

Her neck grew tighter when she saw Paul. There was a time when he would have noticed her tension and offered a neck and shoulder massage. She'd be damned if she'd ask him to rub her neck now. She pulled the bath sheet tightly to her and grabbed her robe from the closet. She flopped on the bed, looking longingly at the bottle of lotion waiting on the nightstand.

They sat in their respective spaces, saying nothing for a few minutes. Paul cleared his throat. "So I can be callous. You know that about me. I'm sorry I wasn't more sympathetic." That got no response. "I'm saying I'm sorry. What else is there to say? I can't remember too much from last night."

You could tell me everything, she thought, like you used to, or like I think you used to. Focus, focus, she prompted herself. Deal with the situation at hand. Don't add all the stuff that's out there. He never responds well to that.

"Well, I can tell you some things. You were an ass last night." She perched on the side of the bed and held up her hand, ticking things off on her fingers. "After I watched you have several drinks, even though you know you're lousy at holding your liquor, I see the leader of the flock behaving like a sheep dog, separating sweet young lambs from the herd and taking them on, one by one." She poked with distaste at her sandwich, then picked up half of it.

Paul winced. "Could you be more specific?"

"Perfect," she grumbled. "Isn't it great to be able to make a fool of yourself and not remember a thing?" She slapped the bread down on the plate and resumed ticking off her points. "You don't remember the hair-stroking debacle with Jody? The lewd exchange with Greg? Greg finally helping me get you home?"

Paul paled. "I have a vague memory of seeing Jody there, but ..."

"What's gotten into you anyway? Remember who you are, for God's sake."

Paul winced again.

"I don't understand you anymore," she said. "You were always Mister Do-The-Right-Thing, Mister Live-By-The-Ten Commandments, not to mention Mr. Fun, Mr. Laughter. And now, you're Mister, Mister— Oh God, I don't know who you are. You insult your friends by flirting with their wives. You shirk your duties as their spiritual guide. I don't know who you are." She buried her head in part of the dark green terry cloth next to her.

"And then there's this morning," she started again, voice muffled by the cloth. "You go to church prepared with a sermon, I know you did. Then you do something completely inane like tell that stupid story and everyone loves it, proving what a luck-out you are. You even had me going for a while and imagining something in that chest until I reminded myself how this is so your style lately. Get them all to trust you, then leave them out there to fend for themselves. That sermon was idiotic. How do you think

38

that made you look?"

"No one else seemed to think it was so bad, or off kilter," he said. He stood up and began to pace. Susan said something in response but Paul didn't hear it. His mind was elsewhere. Where is all this coming from, he wondered. She needs to cool down and I need some time to think.

"Dad," Willie called from downstairs. "Can you go with Kevin and me to the park and play ball with us? We're bored."

Thank you, Paul offered silently. "I'll go with the kids and we'll talk when I get back, okay?"

Susan lifted her face from the towel and rolled her eyes. "A total luck-out," she repeated, shaking her head. She pushed the tray with her uneaten food toward Paul.

"Fine," she said.

———————

Susan was a master at saying the word "fine" and not meaning it, Paul thought. The boys were walking ahead of him, jostling each other in the way of 10-year-olds.

"Hey, Dad," Willie shouted. "No one's on the baseball diamond. Wanna play something with us there? We'd be all alone."

"Good idea," Paul hollered back, wishing he **were** all alone. What a weekend.

The second base canvas looked very tempting.

Paul had positioned himself on second base and Kevin at first with Willie running in between. About 20 minutes of hot box and everyone was sweating.

"Why don't you guys go swing for a while? I'm tired, too. I'll just rest here." Paul said. He collapsed on the canvas base, sitting down with a thud.

"You're gonna stay there?" Willie couldn't believe it. "We're dying of thirst."

"Here's some change for a soda from the store. Come back when you're ready to go. And be careful crossing the street," he yelled at their disappearing backs. His head was hurting again and he lay his head on the canvas, his hands behind his neck, eyes closed against the late afternoon sun. Some quiet time to think. Only the faraway sounds of traffic intruded. He needed to get straight in his mind what was going on with everyone— Susan, the boys, himself, Pam, Henry, everyone.

Things were all confused. He felt he was approaching the dreaded sustained low point, the kind that Dr. Bill Wilhelm, his spiritual advisor, had warned him about when he accepted his first pastoral call. He even remembered how Dr. Wilhelm had put it: "A pastor should above all else guard against the sustained low point and the temptation to despair." All the Lutheran teachings went against this kind of reaction to the Christian life. Despair was out. Justification by grace was in. Wilderness was everywhere. Paul dozed off.

The red-haired woman was passion personified. She was all the women he'd looked at twice but shrugged off like a good preacher, a good husband, should. She was the one that, if he wasn't careful, could creep under his skin like an itch that would never vanish, one that the salve of family life could keep at bay for a limited time only.

He took her in his arms, and they kissed passionately, reaching for the buttons and ties on each other's clothes. When they couldn't stand any longer, they fell to the moist grass of the infield, side by side and for a brief moment looked at each other under the stars, eyes sparkling and wide with the enormity of the commandments at least one of them knew they were about to shatter. They lost themselves quickly in each other in the splendor of the infield grass. Her hair shone in the moonlight. The shadows played on her shoulders as the straps of her tank top tumbled down. Their bodies felt red hot for the minutes they moaned and moved together. His thoughts were focused on the woman and he wondered at her desire to have sex on the baseball diamond where every time she came to a ball game, she could look at second base and remember the moonlight and the man with whom she had shared a physical communion there.

A woman's voice awakened him. When Paul opened his eyes he was looking straight up at the sky. The voice was saying "Excuse me. Hi. Is practice over?" He looked toward the sound. She was standing with her back to the fading sun and her face in shadow. Red hair blazed like a glorious halo around her head.

He sat up, feeling a little dizzy from that abrupt action, from the brief nap he'd stolen, from the disturbing dream.

"Pardon me?"

"There was supposed to be a practice here for the 16-year-olds and I came to watch. I'm Nicolette Stone, Hunter's mother." She moved a little to block the sun so he could stop squinting. "I've really never seen anyone sleeping on second base before. Sorry if I bothered you." She smiled as Paul stood and brushed the infield grit from his jeans. In that split second, he saw she had full lips and green eyes.

"No, that's all right. I'm Paul Lombard, Joey's dad. The other coach, Susan Lombard, is my wife. And actually practice was over several hours ago."

"My ex never tells me the right times for these things. This is the third practice I've missed. I can't wait until the games start. Not knowing when **they are** should be **really** fun." She laughed ruefully. "Well, thanks for the info. I guess I'll call your wife to find out the schedule since I'm avoiding Greg. Sorry to have bothered you," she said again, and smiling, turned around, hair framed once more by the sun, and sauntered off.

Paul was two blocks away before he remembered the boys.

41

Chapter 6

Fight That Night

"Mom, we're home," Willie called, running into the kitchen. "Can you believe Dad almost left us at the park?"

"I've been tempted to do that myself," Susan said, smiling. An hour by herself had given her some much needed space. She was at the counter by the sink packing lunches for the next day.

"Real funny, Mom!" Willie said.

Paul came in behind him, breathless from racing Willie the last 100 yards, breathless from his ballpark encounter. He hoped Willie wouldn't elaborate.

"Are these for lunches?" Willie asked as he grabbed a carrot stick, and before Susan could even respond, he began to whine. "None of the other kids have crude things for lunch. They have potato chips and crackers or something else crunchy."

"It's crudités," Susan corrected him. "And you'll thank me when you're lean and mean and the other kids are fat and lazy." Willie shrugged his shoulders and ran out to scour the neighborhood for playmates.

"Dinner in 45 minutes," Susan called after the puff of dust his sneakers left behind.

Good. Paul felt if he could finish their discussion now, it would be over and done before the week started. Lately on Sunday evenings, he felt surrounded by the week to come, engulfed by the many hours over which he had no control. He liked to start each week fresh, renewed, with new and different problems, challenges, issues. Things unresolved from the previous six days ceased to interest him, and try as he might to muster resources for a continuing problem, his heart often wasn't in it.

Paul noticed the pace of her carrot peeling, always vigorous, had been increasing since he'd arrived. "Got any extra for me?" Paul put his chin on her shoulder and peered into the sink.

She stepped away. "Help yourself."

"Maybe you should buy the kind that are cut up already. Or those baby carrots. It would save you time," Paul suggested, crunching the carrot and pulling a stool up to the island in the center of the kitchen.

"I don't because they cost more and they dry out." She cut the peeled carrot into thin sticks and flung them into the bowl of cold water on the counter.

Paul sighed.

"So, continuing our talk about last night," he said. "You could fill me in so I know whether to simply be embarrassed or to get the resume out. Got any aspirin?"

She opened the cabinet and pointed to the bottle. Paul grabbed it and reached around her for a drinking glass.

Susan went back to peeling. "You're starting to really worry me."

"Like how?" His senses were suddenly on full alert.

"Well. There are a couple of things." She turned around and wiped her forehead with the back of her hand.

"Okay." Paul perched on the stool, devoting his full attention. "Number one."

"If this is a joke to you..."

"It's not."

"All right. About the party last night."

"Fair. I don't like not remembering what happened. I haven't had so much to drink in years."

"Bingo. Why do you think you did that? I even warned you about it."

"Part of it was fatigue. Last week was rough covering for Sarah and

43

all. Her congregation is very needy."

"But you only got two calls," she reminded him.

"True. But being on call, well, it's like waiting for one more shoe to drop all week. Then," Paul continued, "I waited too long to get the sermon done. Procrastinating always haunts me."

"Why does the sermon always have to be so hard? How come after all these years you can't just get up there and say something from the heart?"

Paul took a deep breath. "I don't get why you can't understand how hard it is. Not only is it harder to put a new spin on the same problems, but **you** don't have to stand there and watch Mr. Phillips sleeping and catch Henry checking his watch. **You** don't have to watch their eyes glaze over, knowing they'll only regain consciousness when they hear the blessing."

He stood up and reached around Susan to fill his glass with water. "If I can't get them to think differently about something at least for a small period of time each week, I'm not much good at what I do." He paused. "At least if I were playing ball, they might remember some memorable play or miss or catch or strike out. At least then I might wow them with my effort."

"You used to say sermon-giving was one of your gifts," Susan said.

Paul took another bite of the carrot stick and crunched for a moment. "The other part was I just needed to relax. A few drinks always helps, you know that yourself."

"I've said this at least a hundred times. You, more than anyone, have to watch out that you don't get too relaxed that way. You always flirt when you drink. That goes back to college, I recall."

"If you mean Rachel, I'm sure I remember she was coming on to me."

"Oh, for God's sake. She's a newlywed."

"Come on. You know there are always women who try to catch my eye. It's the same thing that college professors go through with coeds. I figure there's some power thing involved, only in my case maybe it's the ultimate temptation. The course they should teach in seminary is how to repel unwanted advances." Paul stopped and stared out the window for a moment.

"They should all be unwanted," Susan said.

"You know what I mean."

"I know, Paul. But you have to be careful." She turned to face him. The white mini blind on the window over the sink clattered in the breeze. Carrot peelings clung to her T-shirt.

Paul suddenly realized that, right now, Susan was embarrassed… as a wife, as a pastor's wife, as a mother, and as a woman. His head felt swollen and tight, the ache creeping down into the back of his neck and top of his shoulders. Paul had heard this "be careful" warning a million times already: from his professors, his friends, his relatives, from Susan, from his mother and his father and from his conscience, and he had always been careful to protect himself, to keep the pedestal he knew people constructed for him, inviolate.

"Could we talk more later? I'm tired. I haven't been sleeping well and I really do have a killer headache," he said.

"I really hate having to always delay talking about anything important until the kids are in bed."

"Tell you what. Let's go out to dinner this week and talk."

"I'd rather finish this now."

Paul bent his head forward and began to massage his neck. "Okay. Well then, go on. Continue." He was tired and irritated at the prolonging of whatever this was going to evolve into this time—confrontation, confession, or knock-down-drag-out-emotionally-wrenching-yet-resolutionless discussion.

She wadded the dishtowel in front of her chest. "It's like you're not taking care of yourself. More like you're neglecting your soul or

45

something. And what you're not doing for yourself is affecting all of us."

"Excuse me?"

Over the next few seconds, Susan became aware that Paul's voice getting higher. It always did that when he got angry. And she knew he hadn't been able to sleep well. And his appetite seemed off. All more signs of something.

"What would you know about taking care of souls? Mine or anyone else's?" he said.

"Oh. So now I'm in charge of only the superficial, just the house, a job, and baseball. We used to share thoughts about these things. I guess now I need to just let you worry about the deeper things." Susan' s voice cracked and got husky when she cried. She wiped her eyes with the dishtowel and slapped the towel on the counter. She turned toward the sink to look out the window. "If I have to take care of everything else, then the least you can do is pay attention to your job. If you don't do a good job, we all suffer."

She whirled around to face him and she was blinking hard.

"Let me paint you a picture of what could happen," she said. "Rumors of shirked parish responsibilities could make their way to synod headquarters. The bishop's troubleshooting assistant would visit. Lines would be drawn. Some people would support you, others wouldn't. Some might comment on the way you have been looking at women, notably at Henry's party. Others may not appreciate your preaching style. Some might have imagined themselves singled out in your sermon topics. Others might have felt slighted in some imperceptible way. Everything you've ever done, good or bad, would be scrutinized and judgments made."

Paul knew Susan was right. Everyone would evaluate his performance as though he were someone special in spite of all his sermons to the contrary, despite his attempts to place himself with them in the middle of all their earthly wants, needs and temptations. It was on his behavior as a minister that they would pass judgment. They wouldn't allow any thought to his needs, his behavior as a man.

Like having too many parents or bosses or coaches, it was a strain to try to discern everyone's expectations, much less live up to them. What Susan didn't see was how tired he was. How much effort it took.

She turned slowly to look at him. "Paul, people look to you for ways to cope! How can you help us if you can't help yourself? You used to be much better at this."

He cleared his throat. "I've always thought the best teachers are those who learn along with their students. That could apply here."

"When you get flip like this, I know I've lost your attention." She sighed.

Paul put his elbows on the island and his head in his hands. "One of the things I'm tired of is trying live up to your expectations and anticipate your criticisms."

"I'm not trying to be critical. I'm trying to get at something here."

"What then?"

"I'm not sure what it is." She looked tired. "Maybe restlessness is the right word."

"Whose restlessness?"

"Yours. Maybe mine. The kids feel it, I know they do."

"I don't think the kids notice anything," Paul murmured. "And really," his voice grew louder, "if what you say is true, it's my problem. This is not about us. This is about me. It's not our job. It's my job."

They both were silent. The blinds clattered in the early evening breeze.

"I'd like to help," she said softly.

"What if I don't need any help?"

She turned, blinking to focus her teary eyes on him. "Any help, period? Or any help from me?"

Paul automatically crossed his fingers under the counter like he used to do when he was a teenager explaining away some exploit with the help of a tiny lie. "Any help, period."

The phone rang in Paul's study and he went to answer it. He knew the landline was old-fashioned but it worked better for the church; people could always leave a message and trust he would get it. The older folks were less trusting of cell phones, at least so far. It was the first of five phone calls from parishioners that evening, people in various states of need who picked Sunday night at dinnertime and later to act on those needs. Paul got less thankful as the evening wore on. Through dinner, the boys teased each other about their baseball prowess. Paul had to excuse himself three times for the phone. He met Susan's eye after the third, after he saw her shoulders tense and her grip tighten on the dinner knife. See, he willed her to hear his unspoken words, they want too much. The answering machine, she willed him to understand. Use the answering machine.

Chapter 7

Reverend Jim

O n Monday morning, Paul stepped out of his car in the crushed stone parking lot. Every time he walked across the lot, at least one irritating stone would find its way into his black wing-tips and cause discomfort for the rest of the day. The stones were a constant reminder of the financial hardships of St. Luke's. On one level, they symbolized the inability of the faithful to work together toward a common secular goal, like to make a decision on having the parking lot paved. On another level, they reflected Paul's disinterest in the whole process of the church's worldly needs. From the very beginning he'd decided that his responsibilities lay foremost in the spiritual well-being of his parishioners, that the maintenance of God's house fell to the property committee.

He stopped to empty his shoe in the narrow hallway leading to his office, and dumped the small pebble on the growing pile in the corner near the bottom step. That was a sure sermon topic someday.

Ellie was rustling around in her office, her way of letting him know she was there. A simple morning greeting was not her style. She always had the coffee made yet never emptied and cleaned the pot; that was Paul's job at the end of the day. As Paul's administrative assistant, she was extremely detail-oriented and kept close track of the weekly offerings of parishioners, notes for the newsletter, committee meetings, who was sick and who was better, who needed a visit, and all the things a church secretary is known for accomplishing for the good of the cause. This also included all gossip.

Five days a week Ellie wore V-necked knit dresses, every day a different color. Paul couldn't keep track of whether or not she wore the same color on the same day each week, but he thought she probably did.

Her husband was the church treasurer and a partner in Barnfield's largest CPA firm. Paul wondered if she had to work or wanted to work. but he had never asked her. It just didn't seem like something you could ask a woman who might spread rumors of your curiosity at the next Women's League extravaganza.

"Good morning," said Paul. He leaned against the door to pull his shoe back on and tie it. "Coffee smells good."

"I thought you'd need some today for sure, Pastor," Ellie said with a smile. "It **is** paperwork day, isn't it?"

"I'm such a pathetic creature of habit. I wonder who else knows what I do every Monday."

"Oh, I haven't told anyone, but a lot of the people have figured it out. Haven't you ever wondered why Mondays are light telephone days for you?"

"I just figured it was the Lord's way of giving me a break since I don't get off on the seventh day, like everyone else does," Paul said. He selected the BOSS mug. It was either that or the one with the Lord's Prayer on it.

"You're such a kidder, Pastor." Ellie giggled and adjusted her dress primly down over her knees.

Not really, thought Paul. And he really wished he could get her to call him by his name instead of his title. He suggested it periodically but she would get flustered and giggle, do it for a day or two blushing all the while, then revert to form. He decided not to suggest it again this week. Maybe when he was in a better mood.

"I've made an appointment for 3:00 o'clock today. Jody Ellwanger is coming by so I'll just use the morning to do some paperwork and a little research for next Sunday's message. I'll be in my office."

"Praise God from whom all blessings flow.

Now leave your message and please talk slow."

Paul grinned at Jim Fuller's voice mail message. He had thought by calling early on a Monday, he'd be sure to reach his friend. He hung up so he could think about a message before he called back to leave it.

He stared out his church office window at the fir trees that hid the baseball diamond from view. He should've gone there this morning. It would have been a good way to start the week. A call to Jim was too, if he had been there. Now the choice was what kind of message to leave—cryptic, comic, or to-the-point. He dialed again.

"Reverend Fuller, it's Reverend Paul Lombard needing a moment of your time to discuss baseball, mid-life crises, and other subjects pertinent to 21st century life. Call me here or on my cell. I'll be here until 6 o'clock or so."

Paul shuffled the in-basket. A note with yesterday's collection amount. Disappointing. A request for a couple to transfer to the trendy Blessed Shepherd Lutheran Church downtown. Also disappointing. A few notices about conferences. He could look at those later. Ah. A letter asking him to present a seminar on pastoral counseling techniques at the Fall Convocation in Syracuse, New York, in October. It wasn't a form letter. A senior church planning official had really written and signed it. Something different. An opportunity to see and be seen, to shine. He savored the moment. He was quickly shuffling through the rest of his mail when he found his Updike book at the bottom of the wooden mail tray.

Paul had first read the book when he was in seminary more than 20 years earlier, because everyone on campus was talking about it. The story about a pastor fallen from grace via burn out and the temptation of several women had seemed ludicrous to Paul and his friends. After all, they were preparing in their studies and readying their spiritual lives to follow His word and His example. That the main character ended up in pastoral rehabilitation with the assignment to write about his fall they found hilarious and certainly to be fiction in the truest sense. After he and his housemates all had finally finished reading it, they had agreed to meet and discuss it.

"Without philosophical debate, how'd you like the book? Scale of 1 to 10." Hal had pulled a chair up to their customary corner table in the student union and grabbed several of Paul's French fries. "Ich. Vinegar. Why do you put this stuff all over perfectly good potatoes?"

"So you won't eat 'em," Paul pulled his tray closer. "And could I just answer one question at a time please? Jeez."

"'Jeez' **is** short for Jesus, you know." Jim sauntered up and slammed his books on the table, sloshing his coffee all over it. "Another quarter for another broken commandment." He grabbed a chair from another table, whirled it around and sat down leaning his elbows on the back of the chair. His bony shoulder blades stuck out as he extended an accusing finger at Paul. "The Lord's name, remember?" He took a rubber band out of his pocket and pulled his thick brown hair back into a ponytail.

"You guys are enough to break the most pious seminarian," Paul said, laughing. "Both spiritually and economically." He threw a quarter on the table.

Hal leaned back in his chair, puffed out his chest and sucked in his generous mid-section. He rubbed his barely visible blond mustache and pretended to twirl it up at the edges, then stroked an imaginary goatee. "Myself, I give it a 2. I found the book entertaining but unbelievable. The main character was completely lacking in the type of moral fortitude St. James Seminary tries to instill in prospective representatives of our Creator."

"Thank you, Professor Terwilliger, astute critic of pulp fiction," said Jim.

"Updike does not do pulp," Paul interrupted. "He is a thinking man's novelist and chronicler of the middle class human condition.

He just happens to have chosen an unfortunate topic this time. One he obviously knows nothing about. He should have interviewed one of us."

Jim faked choking on his coffee. "Seriously. Can you imagine Dean Hansen with the church organist? Late night soirees after practicing the "Toccata in F minor"? Chasing each other around the sanctuary to the light of the eternal flame donated by the church bazaar group? Or, better yet, with the president of the young mothers' group as they share the ultimately sensual task of wallpapering a border in the nursery room? I give it a 7 for humor."

"That's why it's called fiction," Hal explained. "Look at all the good imagination you just used making amusing illustrations of things that happen only in someone's mind. Actually maybe I'll give it a 4."

"I wonder if we might be a little naive," Paul said thoughtfully. "I think if you believe in yourself and in your mission, the story is ridiculous. If you lose sight of yourself and your goals, maybe there is some credence to the behavior of a reverend like Updike's character. I'll say a 9."
"Could you lighten up?" Hal put his face directly in front of Paul. "It's fiction for God's sake. Remember Updike made this up. You've got to agree it is way out there from what we know and have experienced."

"There is such a thing as fiction based on fact." Jim got up to refill his cup. "Where's your quarter?"

Paul absently flipped the pages of a textbook with his thumb. "If taking the Lord's name in vain is the only commandment we ever break, we'll be truly blessed."

Hal watched Jim's back as he tossed a coin on the table. "This quarter business isn't working. Maybe we should up the ante."

––––––––––––

"I'm sorry, Pastor. What did you say? Up the what?" Ellie stood in his office door with the coffeepot. "More coffee, Pastor? Pastor?

Paul blinked several times and held out his cup.

"I didn't hear all of what you said. You said something about 'up'?"

"Sorry, Ellie. I was just daydreaming. By the way, I put a call in to Jim Fuller. He's going to call back on my cell but may forget and call my private line in the office, so if the phone in here rings and I'm gone, please answer it, OK?"

"I always do."

"I know. Thanks for the refill." Paul returned to his paperwork leaving her no option but to return to the outer office.

When he couldn't read another word or offer one more signature, he stood up, stretched and looked out the window. Paul felt the need to escape.

"Ellie, who needs visiting today or at least this week?"

"You have a few shut-ins that need communion, Ed Rice and Aggie Jorgenson. Amazingly, no one's in the hospital right now. Of course that could change the next time the phone rings."

"Okay. Could you give Mrs. J. a call and see if I could come over early this afternoon?"

"Sure enough."

Paul heard her talking loudly to Mrs. Jorgenson.

"She says it's fine and she'll put the coffee on," Ellie popped in the door. "Maybe you should suggest she put on her hearing aid as well."

"That's beyond my scope. I only do spiritual, remember? Doctors take care of the physical."

"Well, be sure to speak up when you get there."

Paul was alone at church when Jim finally called back. Jody Ellwanger had come and gone, wanting in part to talk about the fall Christian education planning, in part to talk more about her loneliness and need for companionship. It had been an exhausting hour and Paul had once again suggested individual professional counseling while he attempted to stay across the room from her as she tried to get more and more in his space.

The sun was setting and the spring sky over the fir trees was that pale pink that signaled another nice day tomorrow. He knew if he would only open his window he could hear the sounds of Little League practice, coaches yelling instructions, kids encouraging each other, goaded on by coaches working to build some team spirit and player cohesion.

"So Rev, what's on your troubled mind?" Jim's deep voice lifted Paul's spirits immediately.

"Hey, there. There's so much, it's hard to know where to start."

"Okay. How about 'How's the family'?"

"All good. Baseball season's here and you know how intense that is."

"No, tell me."

"At a time when everything is already hectic, add three practices and two games for each boy and weekly managers meetings for Susan. Thank God I only have to heal the spiritually bereft and comfort the physically ill."

"Yeah, you got the easy job. Susan must be coaching."

"Yep, I couldn't fit it in again. All the parents are so busy that only one guy stepped forward and Susan, in typical Susan fashion, sat back and waited to be asked. And ask they did." Paul paused for a minute. "Don't get me wrong. She is experienced what with softball and all, and she does a great job."

"Isn't jealousy one of the seven deadlies?" Jim said slowly.

"I'm not jealous. I'm excited for Susan that she's able to do something she loves that she can share with the boys. She's great. If she wants something, she just goes for it and makes it work out." Paul hesitated for a moment. "It's just that there's something going on with Joe and I think it has to do with her coaching."

"I'm sure glad you're not jealous."

55

"I get your point. Really, that part of life is all right. Now on the other hand..."

"Great," Jim interrupted him and then said softly. "Could be better here."

"Now what could be happening in the booming metropolis of Williamsport, Pennsylvania that Super Rev can't handle?"

"Paul. I'm serious."

Paul experienced the increased heart rate he had long ago associated with fear of the unknown and, always worse, the unexpected. A jab of selfishness caused further palpitations. After all, he had reached out to Jim, not vice versa. He was the one who needed an ear, and possibly a shoulder. It took all his self-control not to make a preemptive strike, to blurt out his troubles, real and imagined, take the initiative and aggressively assert his needs. However, not knowing the true extent of those needs, he cautiously said "What's the matter?"

"Nothing I can talk about right now. What do you say we get together? I can check out the gray in your hair and you can see it yourself in the gleam of my receding hairline."

"All right. How about sometime next week?" Paul scrolled through his calendar. Just a bunch of committee meetings and a council meeting scheduled that week. Luckily Easter and the Congregational meeting were behind him. "Like Thursday?"

"That just might do it. I've got ya down. I'll probably leave early so should be there about two. I'll tell everyone here I'm on a pastoral enrichment gig."

"It'll be a gig all right. I'll look forward to it. And I'll let Susan know you're staying with us." They said good-bye and Paul turned once more to the window.

In Jim's casual remarks, Paul had heard trouble. He had always been able to key into Jim, read him like a book all through college. Jim was adept at making light of serious issues. He would wish them away and they'd seem to actually vanish. Paul was always the one who would buckle down and make something happen, just like Susan did. One of the many things he and Susan had had in common. This symbiotic relationship with Jim had worked well in seminary. Paul hoped it would work 20 years later.

"Jim's coming? Great!" Susan had kept dinner warm in the oven on the special plate she'd found in a catalog. It kept heated food at the required temperature and allowed Paul to have a piping hot dinner when he worked late, and allowed her to have a cup of coffee with him like they always did while he wolfed his supper down. She watched him mix the chicken and potatoes the way he liked them. She couldn't let Paul see her relief that he had taken the hard-to-take male step to ask for help. That had to be the reason for Jim's visit.

"He can use the couch in your study, right?" She poured herself some coffee as she visualized Jim's arrival. She and Paul would be all smiles, hugging him, delighted at the intervention of a third party in their problems. And it's not like Jim wouldn't know something was up. Susan knew Joanie Fuller like a sister. Through the years she and Joanie had occasionally sequestered themselves for weekends at what they called a "safe house," really a cheap cabin in the Catskills where they poured out the increasing frustrations and decreasing joys of being a pastor's helpmate. Susan was sure that Jim and Paul did the same at Synod conventions and whatever, but they didn't call it support groups or any so female-oriented a name. They would probably call baring their souls and sharing psychic energy "talking business."

That the spiritual lives of the congregants, the guidance of the Holy Spirit, faith in the Creator, the awesome power evident in the very existence of the world, of earth, of man, of anything, could be reduced to "talking business" made the women giggle as they drank more and more wine. They then would progress to telling their innermost most secrets to each other, sealing their pseudo-sisterhood.

Susan looked out the picture window onto the deck and stared into the darkening back yard. She knew these visits kept them sane, all four of them.

And at their last visit, just around Good Friday, Joanie had asked Susan what was the matter and it had all come pouring out. Why can't people just accept that a minister sometimes wants to be nobody special? Why can't Paul keep faith with his chosen career? Why does he have to be thinking there is something better? What does she have to intuit this? Why can't he share it with her? Why does it have to come between them? And Joanie had held her and cried with her and wailed the same questions, only she was holding back, Susan could feel it.

And Susan had gone back home to Paul and over a late dinner without the kids but with wine and candlelight, she had shared some but not all of what she and Joanie had talked about, all the while making it sound like these were Joanie's and Jim's problems. Susan felt cleansed by the exchange of this information and felt a strange euphoria and a desire for Paul and in the privacy of their room after a night of closeness, pity for Paul and for all men who couldn't be satisfied with who and what they were and what they had.

Knowing Jim was coming gave her some hope that this time it might be resolved, that something would become so clear, like a religious epiphany. And that that something would renew the two of them, Susan and Paul, so that they could help each other.

Paul finished eating quickly and headed for his study as Susan cleaned up. She opened the sliding door and went to sit on the deck in the cool night air that sometimes could clarify her thinking, but tonight, after 15 minutes of star gazing, all was still muddled and instead of Cassiopeia, she saw herself and instead of Taurus, she saw Paul. The kids' faces were twinkling stars around them and beyond all this light she was sure, was the big void. "It's drawing us in," she whispered. "It's creeping closer. How do we keep away?" She folded her hands and closed her eyes.

Chapter 8

Meeting Nicolette

It had been a long several days since his call to Jim Fuller, days full of challenges beyond the normal pastoral duties. Paul was looking forward to Jim's visit more than ever because the Sunday before, at the early service, Nicolette Stone had been in attendance, sitting in the front pew on the right. Of course, the Sundstroms were bent out of shape because now they either had to share their pew or sit elsewhere, neither of which fit in with their preferred location and method of worship. But Nicolette had walked with purpose to the front row, tossing her hair behind her as she sat down. It was a carefree gesture, one that signaled confidence. Men really had no gesture like this to use. They had to use words or actions to let others know they were confident and in control.

Luckily the Sunday school children were doing the service today. That way Paul could break with tradition by sitting in the pew with the kids. He usually sat in the choir loft or otherwise out of the way. He just didn't feel like sitting in the command position today. He felt like being one of the congregation. And in the appearance of that, he could watch and speculate and let his mind wander and think all those things he enjoyed. Besides, from his location, he could see Nicolette.

While talking with Mrs. Culpepper about her sister after the church service, he was amazed that he could concentrate on what she was saying and still keep track of Nicolette at the same time. He felt strangely energized by this rediscovered ability to do two things at once and do them quite well.

Another strange thing was, under normal circumstances, during a newcomer's first visit to St. Luke's, he'd always gravitate toward that person, extend his hand and, at the same time, the congregation's welcome. After they had been two more times, he'd try to schedule a visit to that person, a visit, usually over coffee that would point out the advantages of the church, its spirit, its mission and its social events. That was usually not the time to ask for the person to join the flock; he'd learned that from experience. But Paul could not bring himself to gravitate toward this newcomer. He couldn't walk over and extend his personal welcome. Someone might get the wrong idea. But then, they might get the wrong idea if he didn't seek out this mystery woman. So again he was damned either way. The easiest thing to do was concentrate on Mrs. Culpepper. The other thing might go away.

No, now Ellie was leading Nicolette toward him. He helped Mrs. Culpepper to a bench along the wall and sat next to her, seemingly glued to her every word and complaint. Mrs. C.'s sister was improving, thank God, she'd had such a rough time of it.

"Pastor," Ellie barged in, "I'd like to have you meet Hunter's mother. Nicolette Stone, this is Pastor Paul Lombard."

Paul patted Mrs. Culpepper on the shoulder and turned to face Nicolette.

"Oh God, you're the one from second base," Nicolette burst out, then turned scarlet with embarrassment. "I'm sorry that slipped out like that. I didn't mean to take the Lord's name in vain especially since this is our first formal meeting." She smiled.

Now Paul's normal routine kicked in. He smiled and extended his hand. When she didn't reach back, he took her hand in both of his, exerted just a tiny bit of welcoming pressure and laughed softly. "Suppose we start again. Hello, I'm Paul Lombard. It's nice to meet you, Mrs. Stone. Welcome to St. Luke's"

Ellie left the two of them and moved onto other Sunday morning duties. She saw Pam struggling with her choir robe over by the closet. "I just took that new woman over to meet Pastor. He introduced himself as Paul Lombard. How come he didn't introduce himself to her as **Pastor**

Paul Lombard?"

"I nun no," Pam said. Her words were muffled and she gasped for air as she pulled the green robe over her head. "This zipper's stuck. Whew, I thought I was a goner.

"What did you say?"

"I said the zipper was stuck."

"No, I mean about why Pastor didn't introduce himself as Pastor this time."

"I said I didn't know. Besides, he was dressed like a pastor so why should he have to?"

"It just makes it more official somehow. What if she thought she could call him Paul now because of that or Mr. Lombard? He wouldn't get the respect he deserves. Besides, if I were Mrs. Lombard, I wouldn't like anyone getting too familiar with my husband, you know."

"I wouldn't lose any sleep over it," Pam said, moving toward the church hall and the smell of coffee and coffee cake awaiting those departing from early service and arriving for the late one. "We should be concentrating on having some of Mrs. Culpepper's cardamom coffee cake."

"I still think it's not right. A certain amount of decorum is a good thing, you know."

"Ellie," Pam said. She put her hand on Ellie's purple knit shoulder. "This is not a big deal, you know. Let's get some of those goodies." She hustled Ellie into the church hall, hoping that the coffee cake would help obscure the chink Ellie had noticed in Paul's armor.

Paul deftly steered Nicolette toward the Sundstroms, hoping for a Christian act of charity to take place, that is, once they knew her, they would forgive her for taking their seat. As he helped himself to some coffee cake, he couldn't wait for Jim's upcoming visit.

61

Chapter 9

Jim's Treat

"God, I love pasta. They don't call it angel hair for nothing. I'm having that with clam sauce and let's have a bottle of Chianti to start. My treat." Jim flipped a quarter on the restaurant table, meeting Paul's eyes with a wink. "I haven't forgotten about our deal. Between Hal and myself haven't you saved enough quarters for Joe's first semester in college?" He looked first at Paul to his left, then at the miniature Vatican City surrounding them, one of the big attractions for this Italian restaurant.

Paul smiled and shook his head. "Joe's not going to need money for college. He's determined he's going on a baseball scholarship."

"Aren't they all?" Jim said, shrugging his shoulders. He looked toward the grapevine-laden archway. "Isn't Susan coming?"

"She's going to be a little late. She has to get Willie settled and find out where Joe is. You know the drill mothers feel they have to follow before they can actually have fun."

"I sure do," Jim said. "I sure do." He took a deep breath. "So how're things?"

"Good. For the most part."

"When you called you said they were great."

"You know how things go—up and down—like a rookie's batting average."

"Yeah," Jim said. "But then, without warning they can be more down than up. Here's how it starts." He leaned back in his chair and smoothed his thinning hair back into the rubber band that held his long ponytail. The gray streaks in his dark hair and the black of his turtleneck made the ever-present circles under his deep brown eyes look even darker. He crossed his legs, smoothed the khaki of the pants, and pulled up his socks. Then he leaned closer and spoke quickly and softly. "Incidental little things grab your attention. For example, first you might find yourself staring at the tiny tip of some woman's earlobe. Then there's the mole just above her collarbone, visible only if she wears a button blouse without buttoning the top buttons. She laughs at your dry humor, the humor your wife only gives you 'the look' for anymore, and you find yourself trying to be funnier and funnier just so that you can hear her laugh."

The wine arrived. Jim sniffed the bouquet and took the taster's sip. He nodded at the waiter. The waiter poured and hovered nearby. Paul shifted uncomfortably in his chair and looked around for Susan as Jim continued. "Then those little things begin to consume you. Before you know it, you're arranging it so you can be close to her, then you touch her, at first innocently in friendship, then it gets serious. And then, if she responds the way you hope she will, you eat it up for a while and then end up at the very least in counseling. At best you get shipped off to one of the many pastoral rehab centers that should be springing up around the nation to treat this disorder rampant at least among middle-aged Protestant clergy. Who knows what's going on with the Catholics?" Jim gestured lightly at the surrounding Vatican but neither of them laughed.

Paul sat up straighter, attempted to make eye contact and opened his mouth to speak but Jim continued.

"She's this petite little thing," he said, his eyes looking far away. "So fragile, with dark curly hair. When we danced at the youth dance at church she fit like a new baseball glove that you're going to have the pleasure of breaking in. By comparison," he added, "Joanie is soft and comfortable like the glove I've had since we played in college."

Paul shook his head and thought, what kind of glove is Susan to me? Maybe one that has become irritatingly stiff. One that needs to be oiled so continuously that I feel I'm wasting my time because it just keeps needing it and needing it and soaking it up and needing it again.

"When did all this happen?" Paul said quietly because of the waiter clearing a table nearby.

"It happened several months ago."

"When were you going to tell me?"

"I didn't know if I was going to tell anyone. But your call got me to thinking about why I felt so tense all the time and I decided to take a chance that you could help me lighten this load."

"Well, I can certainly understand 'tense'" Paul said. "That's why I called you. Lately, nothing seems to be relaxing or working and my thoughts are all consumed with—"

"Hi, Jimmy." Susan came up behind Jim and threw her arms around his neck, hugging tight. He stood up to welcome her and they hugged and kissed several times before he pulled back a chair for her.

"Still a looker," Jim said. "And still hanging out with you. How'd you get so lucky?" He looked at Paul who smiled weakly. Paul felt lucky that she had not heard what he was about to say.

Susan blushed and said, "I should get more comments like that. Makes me all tingly." Then she looked at Paul's face and said, "Don't look so serious. A dinner out with a good friend who admires my beauty? I'm looking forward to some fun. Doesn't the woman get any wine?" She slid her glass next to Paul's.

"The woman always gets wine, and as much as she wants," Jim told her in a stage whisper, filling her goblet.

"Thank you," she whispered loudly back. "So what have you men of the cloth found to discuss in my absence? Let me guess. The good old days. The bond of baseball you shared at the seminary. The infield fly rule. The deterioration of your baseball physiques with age. Stop me anytime."

Neither of them answered her right away. They each took long sips of their wine, and then sipped again.

Paul thought Susan looked as though she had walked into something

64

and was regretting it. He had asked her to join them as had Jim. After all, they were all friends, good friends, and had relied on each other for different reasons throughout the 25 plus years they had known each other. He saw her looking around for something non-threatening to talk about.

"Look at those people over there. They're so busy talking and touching each other that they're eating congealed pasta and they don't even seem to mind." She sighed. "They can't be married or they wouldn't be talking to each other." She looked at Paul. He wondered if she would be flattered if she had a clue that he had just compared her to a baseball glove.

"Ain't that the truth, Susan," Jim said.

She waited, but when he said nothing more she stood up and said, "Excuse me a minute, will you? I forgot I have to call Nicolette Stone, you know, Hunter's mom, back tonight. Something about practice tomorrow. She left a message on the machine." She grabbed her purse and headed toward the ladies' room.

"Susan is going to know something's up," Paul said. "We've got to get the chatter going." He swirled his wine in the glass. "Does Joanie know she's the comfortable glove?"

Jim sighed. "I think she wonders if I've tried out a new one."

"How does she feel about it?"

"I'm not sure. We haven't discussed it. Actually that's why I wanted to spend some time with you. You always have a way of making me see things more clearly. I suppose it's the way you probe deeply into my psyche with those succinct questions you don't ask out loud. You always did get high marks for the visual disapproval factor. It's that face you put on, that pastoral face. The one that defines the h in 'holier than thou.'" Jim slapped Paul on the back.

"Knock it off," Paul said, finally smiling. "I'm just thinking and wondering how you got to this point….Bill Wilhelm wouldn't approve.

"I didn't step across any line to take this risk you know." Jim leaned across the table again and spoke softly and earnestly. "I was standing in my usual safe spot and something pushed me over the edge. There I was, wondering idly where I was going next, in my life, in my career, in my family, in my relationship with Christ and all of a sudden those idle thoughts became ambitious. They drove me to look at everything as a possibility, not as some kind of forbidden fruit. My energy level increased. My stress level diminished. Things that I hadn't done out of fear suddenly seemed doable. One of was accepting the notion that I was having doubts about a marriage relationship that was stifling me with comfort.

"Just think for a minute about risk," Jim continued thoughtfully. "You know, aren't the times of your life you most remember the ones where you took risks?"

"You sound like many of my parishioners," Paul said. "They parade in and out of my office needing more counseling than I feel comfortable giving. Here's my standard line to the men: Jeez, fill-the-name-in-here, couldn't you take a risk that won't hurt anyone but you?"

"I wonder what you say to the females."

Susan arrived back at the table as their pasta came steaming via the waiter, a young man who looked to be a college student with blond hair hanging over one eye. His billowy white shirt and stylishly baggy black slacks did not hide the physique of an athlete. Susan noticed that he seemed peremptory with Paul's and Jim's pasta delivery and almost overly solicitous with hers. She knew she looked good; the extra time with her makeup, her hair in a new style, shining and falling over her face was paying off. She had deliberately chosen her white silk blouse and black crepe skirt, an outfit she always felt attractive and competent wearing. She thought the waiter appreciated her look for once they were all served, he hovered close to her side, made eye contact with every offer, of more wine, of water, of bread. She wondered if her dinner companions had noticed this extra effort.

She looked at them over the steaming plates of pasta. This felt different. There was little of the quick repartee that characterized their long time friendship. She shouldn't have come. She should have insisted that Paul have a quiet dinner with Jim alone.

"What did you guys do to him while I was gone?" Susan asked after the waiter moved on with the water carafe. When they shrugged their shoulders, she chuckled then and said, "Well, whatever happened, I'm enjoying this. Getting attention from men isn't easy these days."

"That shouldn't be," Jim said, feigning indignation and watching Paul's face for any reaction. "You got plenty of attention in college from lots of guys without even trying. And you look exactly the same."

"Thanks, Honey. That's why we invite you to town," Susan said, patting Jim's hand. "But that was then. This is now." She wound the pasta on her fork, neatly snapping the last strand inside the clump of perfectly placed spaghetti and popped it in her mouth. Not even the tiniest bit of sauce remained outside her mouth, and none splattered onto her white silk blouse. The men watched in fascination as she prepared another forkful.

"I had forgotten just how good you are at that," Jim said. "Man, remember those spaghetti dinners we cooked at the old apartment?" He turned to Paul.

"Yeah. The most guests we ever had was probably 30. And that would have been the night we debated the divinity of Christ with Susan's heretic phys ed major friends," Paul said, tossing his joking comment at Susan.

"God, that went on forever, didn't it?" she said. "I didn't even think that gang knew anything about the Bible. As far as I knew, growing up they'd spent most of their Sunday mornings at soccer practice or warming up for a cross country meet."

"That's the first time I noticed your unbelievable spaghetti wrapping skill," Jim said, looking at Susan. "I couldn't take my eyes off you. And I couldn't believe how lucky you were," he pointed his fork at Paul, "to find yourself a smart, attractive woman to cancel out your seminary-induced dourness."

"Oh, come on," Paul leaned forward to defend himself and allowed a wry smile. "You know that wasn't a good time in my life, with my folks splitting up and all. Plus we were into some very heavy readings and had some basic decisions to make about our pastoral and spiritual beliefs and direction. Didn't seem there was anything to be bubbly about."

"Unless you were about to graduate with your degree in phys ed and start your first job teaching, actually making money, you know." Susan said. "Things didn't look bleak to me. After all, I had a man I loved, a career I loved, a job to look forward to and a wedding coming up."

She punctuated that sentence by extending her empty wineglass toward Paul. He and the waiter, who appeared from out of nowhere, both reached for the bottle simultaneously. Paul's attempt to be first tipped the bottle over. The red liquid spilled on the white linen. "Sorry," Paul muttered as he grabbed the bottle and stood it upright, then reached for his napkin to sop up the mess. The waiter calmly took the bottle. "More for you, sirs?" he asked. Jim held his glass forward and the waiter efficiently poured.

"And another bottle of the same," said Jim as the last of the liquid dribbled into his glass. Paul noticed Jim was entertained by the waiter's antics. Paul was not. He felt strangely inadequate and agitated and did not appreciate it when Jim mouthed the words, 'lighten up' and turned his attention back to Susan.

Paul saw Susan looking at him in amazement. He decided she was probably wondering what the big deal was about pouring the wine. After all, what did it matter who poured? It was the waiter's job, after all. The silence was awkward.

"As I was about to say," she looked directly at Paul, "little did I know the challenges of being a pastor's wife. You know they should have a class on that. In fact these days it could be a co-ed class on expectations for pastors' wives-to-be and husbands-to-be. I mean, not that you would mind all those expectations if you really loved the person, but it would give you a clue to how much of that person you have to share." She broke a chunk of bread from the loaf in the middle of the table and rubbed it in the sauce on her plate. "That reminds me. How's Joanie doing?"

"More bread, Madam?" the waiter asked, appearing immediately at her right elbow. "Please," she said, giving him a smile.

"She's doing okay." For the first time, Jim appeared hesitant and Susan didn't let it go by.

"What's up?" she asked.

"We've got a lot going on, you know, between her church work and with the kids and all," Jim said. Paul recognized this as hedging and he was pretty sure Susan did too.

"I'll call her," Susan said sympathetically. "I'll give her my pep talk. I keep trying to convince her she should be more like me. I continue to maintain the less I have to do with congregational business, the better. Right?" Paul nodded. "You know what happens, at least here at St. Luke's," she continued." Once you do one thing, then the next happens. First you're attending the Ladies' Guild meetings, then you're organizing them. Then pretty soon you realize when you walk into the room, people stop talking and you don't know if it's about you or your husband, the minister. Then you start to think how un-Christian it is for people to behave that way, then how wrong it is for you to judge them, and everything gets all upset and it's just not worth it. Is that what you mean about Joanie?"

Just then the waiter reappeared and presented a basket containing a deep red cloth napkin covering steaming baked goods. He lifted one corner to show Susan a crusty roll flecked with green spices. "Something new we're trying," he said. "Warm and very lightly seasoned. You're enjoying the food so much, I thought I would try it out on you."

Paul could tell Susan was impressed, her thank you almost a purring. He was surprised at what a little attention could do. He'd have to remember. No, more than remember, he'd have to act, to do something, to find the strength to add energy back into their lives together. I thought I'd try it out on you. A line that contained a mention of risk, but not the real thing. An easy thing to say, and for the waiter to do. Having set up Susan's expectation of excellence, he'd played the trump card with that line.

"He's very good," Susan whispered, reaching for a roll. She took a bite, closed her eyes and said, "Mmm." Paul noticed the waiter watched her intently. "These are truly delicious," she exclaimed looking around to tell the waiter. He smiled, satisfied. "I'll tell the chef you like them." He smiled and bowed slightly as though she were a princess giving a command, and he the manservant gladly fulfilling her every whim. Paul stared at the waiter's back wondering why for him it all seemed so easy.

Her dinner partners were both seeing her in a new light. Her hair seemed more vibrant, her eyes brighter, her skin more glowing. "What?" she asked, staring back. "Do I have sauce on me somewhere?"

"Far from it," Jim said.

"About Joanie." Susan said. "If I can't get a straight answer out of you, I'm really calling her."

"Call her," Jim said, after a small hesitation. "She'd like to talk to you, I'm sure."

"I'll do it tomorrow then," Susan promised. She tried to share her puzzled glance with Paul but he wasn't sharing.

Paul looked away. He knew she knew it wasn't like Jim to avoid talking about his family. She was probably feeling uneasy and off center about it and they would talk later and it would be up to him to explain just enough and not too much about Jim's comments.

"You never did answer my question about what you guys were talking about so seriously when I got here," she said thoughtfully. "You know, I told Nicolette Stone when I called earlier that you two were deep in conversation when I arrived. She laughed and said that whenever two men get together and talk, really talk, they are probably talking about a woman."

Jim gave her a bit of a crooked smile. "Actually, Susan, we were discussing baseball gloves."

Chapter 10

Jim's Advice

Paul usually saved early Saturday morning for running alone; head time before his big workday of the week. Today he would have to run with Jim and he was approaching and avoiding it after last night at the restaurant. Jim had done most of the talking but he wasn't the type of fisherman to let anyone off the hook, and he knew Paul had need for his counsel.

They jogged toward the park and off to the left. At the man-made pond, a heron was barely visible beneath puffs of early morning fog. Jim pointed it out and Paul nodded. "He's nearly always there. Some days you can see him better than others."

They had gone as far as the Little League fields before Jim spoke.

"Is this how you stay in shape?" he panted, trying to keep up.

"This—and worrying," Paul responded, barely winded.

"Ah, now we get to it. What do you mean 'worrying?'"

"You can probably guess I have a few things on my mind."

Jim took a deep breath and sprinted ahead. He turned to run backward looking at Paul. "So?"

Paul hesitated. Would it really do any good for another person to know that his leadership energy was sapped, his spiritual cocoon torn, his Christian charity spent? It could be a relief to share it, but it could do harm. The word would be out. Jim might try to get feedback from others in this situation by using his many connections. He would use no names of course, but small as this pastoral community was, someone could surmise. But if he couldn't tell his darkest secrets to Jim, his anchor through seminary and ever since, the man who until last night Paul had admired as the one with

The Focus, who could he tell?

"So?" Jim repeated. He stopped and bent over, hands on his knees, and took deep breaths. "Have mercy. You do this every day? I run once every two weeks if I'm lucky."

"Sorry," Paul said, leading the way to the bleachers. "Come on."

They climbed to the top and Jim sat down, leaning his elbows on the bench behind him and stretching his long legs out on the bench in front. Paul sat with his back straight, hands on his knees, body tensed as though he were waiting to be called away by one more interruption.

Paul stared across the baseball diamond at the pond and the bird. "How do you do it?" he asked.

"Do what?"

"All of it. Balance on the pedestal your congregation constructs. Coax them into following your lead. Stay in the good graces of the bishop. Maintain your sense of humor." Paul turned and looked directly at him. "Fight the temptation to try out new equipment."

"Ah," Jim said again. "Let's let the last become first. It's Joanie and Susan you want to talk about, isn't it."

Paul stared straight ahead, shoulders slumped, eyes on second base. "You have to let me start where it's meaningful to me."

"Tell me what's going on," Jim said.

Paul's words began slowly talking about the constant interruptions in his life. The lack of time for contemplation. The inability to sermonize. The lack of responsiveness of the flock. The daily effort leadership required. The words picked up steam when they got to the family. The boys and his lack of time for them. The feeling of missing their youth. The difficulties with Joe. The admiration for Susan being able to keep it all together.

And then about him, the choices he'd made early on. His passion for baseball. How much easier it looked, better it looked now than what he had chosen. The words grew softer when they offered doubt about his current path, his fantasies about other women, and their seeming attraction for him.

"So you see," Paul concluded. He stood and threw an imaginary baseball as hard as he could toward the horizon. "It's not easy anymore." He sat down and leaned back against the bench himself. "I should've been a ball player."

Now Jim was staring out over the diamond.

"It was never easy," Jim said turning toward his friend. "And it's not going to be. But you knew that when you chose this way and so did I. And sometimes, it's torment—"

"But as a ball player I could control my torment," Paul interrupted. "If my batting average fell, I'd get a batting coach. If my slider wouldn't slide, I'd grab the pitching coach. If my fielding were off, I'd practice until I got it back. The possibilities were so endless then, and I didn't see it. I didn't choose it. They seem so limited now. Out of reach."

"Man, Paul. I don't know if I'm the one to talk to about this. I may be only slightly less tormented than you. But I am at a different place. I'm not on that pedestal anymore. I got off." Jim's voice grew more excited. "One morning, after I"d gotten breakfast and sent the kids off to school, made love to Joanie, prepared a sermon on brotherhood, organized a youth event, and Lord only knows what else, I just remember I was very busy, I went out to sit on the back porch with my coffee. In that calm moment, I got a strange feeling. I was comfortable, you know in that way that accomplishing a lot in a little time can make you feel. I also felt very uncomfortable because I had done a lot of it by habit because other people needed or wanted me to do it. At that moment, I realized with the clarity of the vision presented to Moses by the burning bush that there should be no pedestal.

"I think people create the pedestal to keep some things, for whatever reason, at arm's length. That when you accept the call, you climb on it,

74

much like we climbed up here, willingly, breathlessly, so that you can see it all, everything clearly and evaluate and judge and pick and choose. When you're on it, people look up to you and for a while that's a kick. But then, they start not looking at the whole you—just at parts, your feet, your knees, the lower parts where they can touch you and cause you to teeter, or stumble and lose your balance." Jim stopped to breathe.

Paul visualized himself teetering, leaning first toward Susan and the kids, then stumbling toward Nicolette, dodging parishioners grabbing at his ankles. He covered his face with his hands as Jim continued. "And I realized if they could do that, then I could choose to get off so that they could look me in the eye, person to person, and see we are not so different."

Jim paused for breath and Paul's reaction. They both watched the heron fly out of the pond, go past the bleachers, change its mind and make an airborne U-turn back to the safety of the protected water.

"So here I am, being less hard on myself." Jim continued. "I'm more able to forgive myself an occasional floundering. That's because I am focused, you know, on the guiding, not the leading, if that makes sense. I take my parishioners as far as the Way, the Truth and the Light. Then they are on their own. It's an easier life for everyone."

"What about the woman?" Paul asked.

Jim laughed softly. "Well, I've given up that equipment. She was exciting, new, different. She was not a parishioner; she was a part-time youth leader and organizer of the bowling teams. I told you last night about how it all crept up on me. Oh, I had thoughts, and if I truly believed that Satan could horn his way into my life, he was there. The temptation was so great after that and the opportunity so available, with all our meetings and all, that I could've done a really evil thing to Joanie and to myself, not to mention that girl, that young girl I might add. But, I didn't. I did go a ways toward that evil thing, all the while using the times we live in as an excuse.

"Things are different now, I told myself. You've got to take what you want; it's not just going to be there waiting. Then I realized that I was using the same cop-out lingo that I hated in magazines and editorials, the same stuff that my parishioners threw at me to justify anything and everything. So I prayed about it."

Jim's words pouring over him were only confusing him more. Paul closed his eyes and saw himself still teetering on a marble pedestal, stumbling in a howling desert, with no direction in sight. Jim sounded far away now but he was still talking.

"Then I actually did what I urge everyone to do but what I had let slide myself. I was deeply into rote praying. You know, pulling up things we've memorized through overuse, adding a little inflection here and there to make it feel different. This time I really prayed—my own words, thoughts, troubles, and I prayed for guidance and His will to be done and you know what? God, I'm getting goosebumps here. You know what? It worked. It was like the miracle you always look for."

Jim stopped and touched Paul's arm. Paul's goosebumps were still there.

"It was like all I had to do was ask, just like we try to teach everyone but when you believe it, oh Paul, when you yourself truly believe it, it is something so right."

Jim paused, out of breath.

A minute later, he continued more slowly. "And I got my focus back. And it was Joanie and the kids and you and Susan and my other friends and family and my congregation that I had an obligation to and I wanted to honor it. Don't you see? I didn't **have** to honor that, I wanted to. It was like I'd had a treasure and lost it and found the treasure once again." Jim stopped and stood up, his arms open wide, his hands extended upward. "Can you understand what I mean?"

Paul opened his eyes and stared over the ballfield, letting Jim's words wash over him.

"You know, in talking to you, here, now, on this field," Jim said, "I feel I've triumphed over something really difficult. I haven't ever felt that to this extent before. I like it. I should've talked to you sooner."

Paul saw Jim's face relax, relieved by sharing this burden, a ballfield confession, without even stepping on second base.

"Why **didn't** you talk to me?" Paul asked. Jim looked at him and shook his head.

Paul's questions gained momentum. "Why did you let me believe that you were perfect? The one I could go to, the one with The Focus? Why didn't you call me when you were thinking about this other woman? When you and Joanie were in trouble? I'm always there to help you, you know that. And I expect the same from you. I call on you to help me and all you can talk about is you. I can't learn from your example, Jim. We are different. We are all so different." Jim started to speak but Paul held up his hand and hurried on.

"Take me, for example. Let's spend a little time on **my** problems. You know about the congregational aspects. Now here are the personal ones. I had some fantasies, just idle thoughts, about a woman with red hair, someone I saw once briefly somewhere, but her image stayed with me. She invaded my thoughts in moments when I should have been praying, or deep in contemplation, or focused on my family. Then, I meet her. I meet her, for God's sake. She's real and she comes to me when I am on my safe territory, on second base, and asks a simple question. And in that moment, I feel that life will never be the same. Now that gives **me** goosebumps."

Jim was speechless now; his relaxed smile gone.

"And I let her in," Paul exclaimed. "I gave her the opening before I even knew she existed. What does this mean?"

Jim stared at him. Paul stared back.

"And what's more she's coming to my church," Paul shook his head in disbelief. "To my church. Somehow she found me. This is a test, isn't it? It's my 40 days in the desert. And I don't have any confidence that I'm ever going to make it out of there."

"Paul," said Jim. "Paul." His voice was hushed. "Think of what you have, all you have, to help you through this. You can find your way. I did. Others do. It's the choices, the choices that are so important now. You must choose wisely. I can tell you what to do but you know, you said yourself, that we are all different. I'm sorry if I was self-centered, but maybe sometimes that's where the focus needs to be, just briefly, just to get something worked out. You need to find your place right now. It's clear that it's faith you don't have right now. Faith in yourself or the ability to forgive..."

"Don't give me the pastoral bullshit. Crises of faith are a dime a dozen. Every other book on the best seller list has some crisis or other," Paul said tersely.

"Doesn't a lot of what we say sound like bullshit? It's what you truly believe that matters. Just remember, these crises are real. There are answers." Jim put his hand on Paul's shoulder. "You have to remember where to look."

The great blue heron had taken flight once again and was looping down closer and closer to their position high in the bleachers. The pterodactyl wings of the huge bird fanned the tips of the oak trees lining the third base side of the ballfield. This silent breeze was relaxing to Paul. He strained to feel its cool air, enjoy its renewing strength.

He visualized himself with wings rising from the pedestal, soaring between the oaks. He felt the moist leaves brush his face and the branches grab him lightly, holding him down, keeping him closer to earth than to heaven. He was aware of something lacking. There was not enough of anything, not enough words, not enough feeling, not enough patience, not enough tolerance, not enough joy. He closed his eyes, waiting for a touch, any sign of something that might reconnect his mind, body, and spirit. He opened his eyes and watched the heron's flapping wings, a slow motion angel with a pointed beak.

Suddenly, the heron dove, a steep dive back toward the pond and Paul stood abruptly to follow his descent. The bird landed out of sight. Leaving Jim behind, Paul stumbled down the bleachers and took off at a dead run in the direction of where he had last seen wings. His breath came quickly, forced by his desire to see this creature close up, on land for the first time, standing with his stick legs on the earth, grounded for a moment in Paul's world. Paul sprinted through fir trees, fronds scratching face and arms, beating him rhythmically as he ran.

When he could run no more, he bent over, gasping for air and looked up to see he was at the edge of the pond. The bird was in front of him; not 12 feet away. Paul saw it as he'd never seen it before, alert but unafraid, confident of its next step, a silent splash of its huge foot in the water toward a meal of fish, its ability to escape assured by its God-given wings.

Chapter 11

Bad Weather

Jim left, with apologies, before church the following morning. He had a youth retreat scheduled for that afternoon, he said, but Paul wondered if being in the Lombard family chaos was too overwhelming for him. Paul was just as glad since he had an ill-prepared sermon to offer, but he wasn't too worried because people had already begun to listen with customary summer disinterest. Their thoughts were perhaps focused on lawn-mowing, sailing, baseball or maybe even the storm that was brewing. After the service and most of the hand shaking, he caught Susan's eye.

"When's the game?" Paul mouthed over the heads of parishioners.

"Two o'clock," Susan called over as she rushed toward the door. "We'll get fast food and go right there. See you at home later."

"Wait! Joe's team or Willie's?" he called after her.

"Joe's," she called back. "Don't kill yourself to come. Joe would probably like it better if you could make the game Tuesday instead."

Just then three parishioners cornered him to ask about starting a Bible study group and all he could do was wave at Susan as she hustled the boys out to the car.

Susan sped to the ball field thinking that things weren't going well. Her coffee date alone with Jim yesterday had done little toward increasing her understanding of Paul's problems. She had used Jim before as a willing sounding board and her hope had been to try to gain another minister's point of view on this situation as well. If not that, then even just a man's perspective on what Paul's troubles were would be some help. Instead, Jim had hedged about almost everything she had tried to talk about. There was no good news about Joanie, the kids, his work, or anything else either. This was not like him. Something was up. She would call Joanie as soon as she got the chance.

It looked like rain and she had called Greg about cancelling, but he hoped to get the game in anyway. Joe, riding shotgun, was rubbing the baseball in the pocket of his glove, working the leather to make it softer, more grabbing. Willie was in the back seat whining that he was old enough to stay home alone until Paul got there. It was interesting to Susan that Paul should ask about this game specifically. Like it mattered. He had only made it to two out of five so far. And on those occasions, he'd had some coaching suggestion that neither she nor Greg appreciated.

Greg was a good guy, she thought idly. He was a physical guy, one who touched the boys often with a friendly punch on the arm for a job well done, a light pinch of their neck with his thumb and forefinger to make a point, a grab on the shoulder while he told them what to do better next time. Over the many times they had stood shoulder to shoulder watching the kids pitch, bat, and scramble for the ball, a friendship had developed. A kind of camaraderie in the dugout was normal. She knew that from years of being the mascot for the Little League teams her dad had coached and from her own college softball coaching experience as well. The camaraderie came of shared success when a player did the right thing, when everyone was really into the game, when a win was in sight.

She really did think Greg was a good man. She was enjoying this coaching relationship and this baseball season. This rush of good feeling prompted a sudden decision to have a picnic at home after the game next weekend, on Memorial Day, and invite Hunter and Greg.

"Hey guys," she said, struggling to get out of the Jeep with the giant canvas equipment bag. Greg rushed to help her and easily shouldered the bag. "I was thinking on the way over," she continued, "how about a picnic next weekend, our house, after the game?"

"Yeah, that would be great," Greg said. "You're on."

He looked and sounded so grateful that Susan immediately felt glad she had extended the invitation. It must be hard to be a man alone, she thought and with a teenage son no less.

Trying to beat the storm, the umpire began the game right away. After the rush of organization, the team hurried to the field. The boys were in sync and things went well. Pitching, catching, fielding, batting all came together and coaches, kids, spectators all could feel it. The team was on a high. It was in that kind of camaraderie that Greg, for the first time, put his arm around her shoulders and hugged her lightly, and also for the first time, she felt less like Joe's mom and more like a true member of the team. She watched Greg do his physical thing with the boys, patting, rubbing, pinching their necks, but then after she whispered a suggested substitution in the lineup, he put his hand on her neck and squeezed gently. For a moment, his finger and thumb lingered. Susan was surprised, then told herself this touch was no more than a gesture of the respect that she'd finally earned from Greg after his initial problem with having a female co-coach.

Then, just as the game was ending, a freak and violent thunderstorm blew in. A lightning bolt cracked in the sky, the umpire ended the game and the coaches sent the kids and parents to the cars. Joe and Hunter lobbied for sodas and ran laughing and cavorting in the downpour to the protection of the snack bar overhang. Susan and Greg stayed in the dugout, planning strategy for the Memorial Day game the following weekend.

"Who shall we start?" Susan had the clipboard and the pencil, ready to write. "If they all show up, that is. It's getting down to the time when the tenth graders have exam reviews."

Greg looked thoughtful for a minute, then said, "Go with your gut. You've done well with the lineup so far."

'Thanks, but you know the team we're playing is the toughest we'll have this year. Wouldn't it be great if the kids could cream 'em? Changing the line up might be the key to this win." She looked up and saw him smiling, at her enthusiasm, she thought. The wind shifted to blow rain into the dugout and he moved closer to her.

Oh, don't reach for the clipboard with that look on your face, she thought as he took the clipboard from her. Don't put it on the bench and move toward me, she thought as he put down the clipboard and moved toward her. Don't back me into the corner with that look, she thought as she moved backward into the semi-darkness. She stumbled and sat down abruptly on the bench. Greg reached out and helped her up, pulling her into his arms.

"Forget the win," he said, his voice shaky. "Just this once." She wondered at the emotion there and his hug, and at the way he lightly kissed her neck, just once. Surprised, she pulled back to look at him and his next kiss was for her mouth and it wasn't light. She closed her eyes. For a moment, it was Paul. But then there was a difference. It wasn't an obligatory or an I'll-see-you-later kiss. A demand was in this kiss, a wanting of more. This is not good, she thought. I need to get out of here really fast.

She turned and grabbed the clipboard and the duffel bag with the lightest equipment in it and stepped out into the rain. "You take the rest. The kids, too!" she hollered to Greg. She ran for the Jeep and tossed the bag into the back seat. As she slid into the driver's seat, she was breathing heavily.

She closed her eyes for a moment and started the engine. Her face grew warm with the thought of what had happened. This type of wanting was new. Paul wanted, but it was familiar and acceptable. With Greg's brief touch, she was back to all the other boys and men she'd known and of their first touches, all of which she remembered like yesterday, the rush of adrenaline, the pleasure at the wanting. That was missing with Paul, gone at some level and she had thought that was fine. There was some value in comfort after all, but she had forgotten about the excitement and lure of the unknown. Greg had taught her more than how to organize the lineup today.

The rain began to pelt the windshield even harder, so hard that when she'd opened her eyes she could see nothing clearly.

———————

A week later, on Memorial Day, clouds were already gathering as they pulled into the parking lot next to Greg's minivan.

"t better not storm today," she said out loud.

"Why not?" Joe asked.

"It just better not, that's all."

.

Chapter 12

Memorial Day

The Barnfield Recreation Center parking lot was a traffic jam. Parents and ballplayers all were trying to get home to their individual Memorial Day celebrations after a long and unseasonably cool afternoon at the ballpark. Flushed with victory, Hunter, Joe and Willie piled in the back seat of Susan's Jeep.

"Nice rip on that triple," Hunter said.

Joe's eyes briefly glazed over with the memory of the game-winning stand up triple that had driven in the winning run. I woulda had an infield home run if your dad hadn't stopped me at third," he said.

"We didn't need it," Hunter pointed out. "We'd won already."

"Yeah," said Joe, "But how often do you get a chance for an infield homer?"

"If Jason Parrini hadn't overthrown first by a mile, you wouldn't have had a chance anyway."

"Yeah, right," said Joe. His voice grew more animated. "Hey. Did you see Valerie and her friends watching me? She said she was coming to see my game today."

"How do you know they came to see you? She's my friend too."

"She told me she was coming to see me."

"So, she was only watching you?"

"Give it up, Hunt."

Willie began complaining about being sandwiched in the middle and about the cleat that was sticking him in the foot. Paul was about to intervene by beginning his post-game analysis when Susan interrupted. "You'll live," she said. All their heads jerked backward as she saw an opening and peeled out of the lot.

"Hey watch it," Paul said, grabbing the door handle. "We won the game, remember? There's no reason to be upset."

"Sorry," she said, "but we're in a hurry. Hunter's mom and dad are coming for a picnic and we have things to do."

"First of all, I can't believe you invited them both for dinner," Paul said. "And then I can't believe you didn't tell me." He handed Susan the large can of pork and beans he'd just opened. She had just come from upstairs where she had combed her hair out of the ponytail and tonight had chosen to let it fall freely to her shoulders. She had put on earrings and changed into a clean pair of khaki slacks and a black knit top.

"I asked Greg last week. I told you that at dinner last Sunday night, at least I thought I did. Anyway, I did it for Hunter," Susan replied as she scraped the beans into a baking dish. "And then he asked me today if I would invite his mother. I like her. She seems interesting. Besides, it's only for a few hours. Everything will be fine. Put some brown sugar in those, will you? Either that or welcome our guest. I hear a car."

Paul knew that Greg was playing catch with Willie outside so Susan was referring to Nicolette's arrival. "The beans," he said. "I'll do the beans. Then I'll cook the burgers so we can get this over with." Susan shot him a look as she headed toward the back door.

Paul's a good sport though, Susan thought, hurrying down the back stairs. God, now I've got to deal with Greg being here. After last week, this is just too awkward. It seemed like a good idea to invite Nicolette too, for distraction, but now I'm not so sure. She sighed. This whole setup was not a relaxing way to spend this holiday.

"Great game," Nicolette called to no one in particular as she struggled to climb out of her car with several grocery bags. Greg smiled and made a move to help her, but her glare stopped him in his tracks. He turned abruptly and ran into Susan coming out the door. She bounced into the doorjamb and Greg put his hands on her waist.

"Sorry. Are you all right?"

"Fine." Susan grimaced and rubbed her shoulder. "But my pitching may never be the same." She felt her face getting hot.

Greg had a strange look on his face. What is it? Susan wondered. Fear? Desire? Relief? What? She usually didn't have such a hard time reading people. He turned quickly and hurried away as Nicolette made it to the door.

"I picked up some ratatouille at the deli," she said. "And here's some nacho chips for the kids. Thanks so much for inviting me. Brrr. I should've worn jeans instead of shorts. You'd think Memorial Day would be much warmer than this." She was chattering amiably, one of the things Susan found intriguing about her. Nicolette seemed to play no games. Whatever she thought, she said. It was refreshing.

"It's such a bummer to have a game scheduled on the holiday that I figured the least we could do is have some fun after." Susan took the bags. "Hope you don't mind that I invited you at the last minute," she whispered. "I hope this is okay, you know, you and Greg?"

"Oh, there are always awkward moments, but don't worry. I've learned to make the best of it."

"Great. I'll put the ratatouille in the fridge until dinner. Help yourself to a drink and go join Paul on the deck. I think Greg's in Paul's study playing video games with the boys."

Paul had put the frozen hamburger patties on the grill. They lay on the grate for a long time before they began to sizzle. Like the beginning of any relationship, Paul thought. A little tentative. The burgers began to cook and the fat fell on the coals causing small sparks. Then things heat up, he thought. An occasional flame appeared and soon the patties were enveloped in flames so hot that Paul couldn't use the kitchen spatula to turn them.

"Could someone bring out the turner with the long handle?" he bellowed as Nicolette opened the sliding glass door and walked out onto the deck twirling the utensil like a baton. Paul sucked the finger he'd already singed.

"Susan wants to know why you aren't using this to keep the flames down." Nicolette pulled a plastic spray bottle from behind her back and dangled it in front of him. "How come she just didn't say to use this? How come she wants to know **why** you aren't using it? Sounds like a control thing to me. It was one of Greg's less lovable qualities. Maybe they're spending too much time together in the dugout." A wisp of hair blew across her face like a red veil and her well-manicured fingers pushed it aside.

Paul wasn't sure how to respond to that comment, so he decided to try to devote his undivided attention to the burgers.

She sat carefully on the chaise lounge, then raised her knees to her chest and put her arms around them. She reminded Paul so much of a young child that any minute he expected her to start rocking back and forth. He didn't expect that her white shorts would ride up, showing a lean and muscled thigh. He didn't expect that her black jersey would gape to show the straps of something black and lacy. He didn't expect her dangling hoop earrings would reflect the setting sun so brilliantly. He didn't expect to feel this expectant.

What would it be like to sit on the chaise next to her? As they talked about her troubles and he only thought about his, he'd touch her hand in a sincere effort to establish a connection. Heat from her palm would shoot sparks up his arm into his neck where tension always gathered. He'd roll his head from side to side, eyes closed as he always did when he was tense, and she would have seen this before, perhaps with other men, perhaps even with Greg. Being the giving person he thought she would be, she'd ask him if he wanted a neck rub and being the needy person he was, he'd say yes. She'd kneel behind him, beginning to knead his neck with capable thumbs. He wouldn't relax because her knees were touching him and her cool hands were touching his neck in the secret spot known only to one other woman on this earth. He'd close his eyes and lean back just as she leaned forward. The back of his head might bump her forehead and, surprised, he'd turn around to say he was sorry. Don't be, her eyes would say. It's all right. What's all right? His body would scream. How far is all right? Pressing your wrist to my lips? Pulling you to me so that we embrace in the shadows here on the deck?

"Do you need this?" Nicolette said. She was next to him now; close enough so that her arm rubbed against his as they watched the flames surround their dinner.

"Damn," Paul croaked and grabbed the bottle from the small serving area attached to the grill and sprayed. The fire crackled and Paul flipped patties madly from side to side. He closed the top and the smoke stopped. When it was clear, they surveyed the damage. The burgers situated directly over the grill's hot spot were charred, those on the edge of the heat were normal and the two way on the periphery were still too rare. Never perfect.

"Paul, what are you doing? The kitchen's full of smoke," Susan yelled out the window. She looked out, wondering at Paul's disorganization. He was usually so meticulous about the cooking. Ah, distraction, she nodded to herself, seeing Nicolette next to Paul, seemingly giving advice. Susan couldn't tell by the look on Paul's face whether he was upset or grateful for her advice, but then they were both obscured somewhat by the smoke.

"The grill seems to be heating unevenly," he called back. "We'll have to have it looked at. We have charred, well-done, medium and rare burgers. Send out a platter, will you?" He turned to Nicolette. "I know the kids won't eat any unless they're perfectly cooked so I'll take one of these rare ones."

"I'll get the platter." Nicolette opened the sliding glass door. "And I'd love a rare one. Rare is perfect."

Chapter 13

On The Deck

"Boys, could you finish setting the table?" Susan called. "Not you, Greg," she added when he breezed in with the kids.

"You said 'boys,'" he defended himself. "Besides, I've gotten really good in the kitchen. Ask Hunter."

"Yeah," said Hunter, "that's why I always have to reset the table to get the silverware right the way Mom taught me."

"That's dining room stuff," Greg tugged at Hunter's shoulder-length blond hair. "I'm not as good at that. Give me something to do, Susan."

Susan knew she didn't want to be alone with him in the kitchen or anywhere else. She looked quickly around for something to get him out of there.

"I'm pretty much done in here. Just take some cheese out to Paul to lay on those pieces of charred cow he's apologizing for, will you?"

Greg accepted the package of cheese slices reluctantly. For a moment she thought he might drop them onto the floor to avoid the inevitable face-to-face with his ex-wife but instead he stood up straighter and made sure his shirt was tucked in. He opened the sliding glass door but didn't close it. "The cheese, Reverend," he said, tossing the package on the serving tray side of the grill. Then he ducked back into the kitchen.

Susan stopped her preparations, folded her arms and leaned against the counter on the other side of the room. "Greg, I'm really sorry I invited her. From everything you've said, I thought you were in a better place with this."

Greg leaned against the counter next to her and spoke softly. "Now that she's back I've got to get used to it all over again. When she left and we didn't know where she'd gone, it was one thing. When I still thought she was the good Nicolette, it was easy to be the concerned husband. Then I saw her picture in the paper with that Stan fellow. She's such a piece of work. People don't know the other side." He stopped to look out the sliding door at Nicolette and Paul. "I swear, Susan, sometimes I'd rather she was a missing person than a...."

"I know. It's hard. It'll take time." Susan instinctively moved to touch his arm as she might normally do to offer comfort. She thought better of it and turned to get the salads from the refrigerator.

"You just said the three things people always tell me these days. I know they're trying to help but if I hear those words once more I won't be responsible."

"What don't you want to be responsible for now?" Nicolette stuck her head in the door. "Oh never mind. Burgers are ready. Can I do anything else?" Before anyone could answer she was back out the door.

"Typical..." Greg muttered.

Susan pulled dishes of potato salad and watermelon slices from the refrigerator. She handed Greg pot-holders and pointed at the oven. "The beans."

The sun was just beginning to set as they all moved out onto the deck. Paul's folding lawn chair had been waiting for him at one end of the table. His place there made it easier to lead the gathering in prayer, but now Greg had taken that chair. Paul was about to comment when Susan asked him to help her, grabbed his arm and pulled him inside.

"Let Greg sit there, OK?" she said when they were in the kitchen.

"But I always sit there."

"Didn't you see them circling the table trying to guess where the other is sitting? Greg probably sat there so he wouldn't have to end up next to her and be more embarrassed."

"I thought you said having both of them here was going to be OK."

"It's not looking OK. I think the best we can do is get through it, and that means letting Greg have your seat." Susan suddenly put her arm around his waist and handed him the pickles. "Think of it as Christian charity."" She looked up at him and smiled.

"My week's allotment is used up." He grinned down at her.

"Borrow some of mine."

"You owe me then. One good deed."

"You got it."

Susan was still smiling. It felt good, the teasing. Like old times. It was always a sign of their connectedness. She looked at Paul. He was intent on carrying food outside, but he was still grinning.

Now the boys were all seated on one of the benches. Nicolette had seated herself in the middle of the other and Paul realized that he'd have to sit next to her. He sat down and immediately felt heat. It was a heat generated by something enticing, by something he barely remembered. He turned to Nicolette, thinking she would be in some way glowing. He saw her scoop potato salad onto her plate and find some left on her thumb. As she handed him the dish and licked her thumb, her leg pressed against his. His leg pressed back as the creamy salad dish slipped from his hand and thudded onto the table.

"Whoa," said Greg and picked up the dish. "Try again, Reverend."

Paul helped himself and passed it to Willie, who said, "Yuck," and refused to touch the bowl. "Hey, we forgot to pray," Willie said.

"Nice catch," said Paul. "Let's hold hands and thank the Great Coach for this delicious dinner." Holding hands to pray was something the Lombards had done at meals since the kids were tiny. Joey's had always been the hottest little hand. It was remarkable how much hotter Nicolette's hand was than Joe's, Paul thought as he grasped her hand and reached across to hold his son's. The prayer was brief and dinner continued.

"You baby," said Hunter to Willie. "Touching potato salad won't kill

92

you." He quickly passed it on to Joe.

"You guys aren't manly," Joe said, helping himself to a generous share. "Potato salad is one of the rights of passage, whatever they are. I heard that on TV."

"I'll show you what manly is," Greg said. He snickered and gave himself a generous portion plus. Susan took a tad and said quickly, "How about that ump? Wasn't he the shortest guy you ever saw?"

"He made some lousy calls," Greg said, his mouth full of potato salad. "Great burgers, Reverend."

"I used to ump, you know," Nicolette volunteered.

There was total silence at the table.

The temptation was too great for Greg. "Ump what?"

"Ump fights between my mom and dad," she said. She went back to her burger which was so rare that the red juices had colored the potato salad next to them. "This is delicious, Paul, just right."

"You're awfully quiet," Susan peered around Nicolette to say to Paul.

"I'm eating. And it's good too." Paul hurried to help himself to more of whatever was close by. It didn't matter what it was really. He couldn't taste anything but heat.

"It's getting really chilly," Nicolette said, hugging herself and shivering. She turned to Paul. "Look at the goose pimples on my legs." Paul looked down. Their legs were still touching under the checkered tablecloth. Paul found himself looking at her earlobe with wonder. As a siren went off in his head reminding him of Jim's comments, he observed that Nicolette's earlobe was pink and soft-looking with a tiny coating of finer-than-baby-fine fuzz. The thin wire of the golden hoop pierced it, appearing to make a continuous circle, no beginning and no end.

I've been at this minister thing way too long, Paul thought. I can't even admire a woman without thinking in biblical imagery. If I were a baseball player noticing these bodily offerings, it would be acceptable, even expected. As it is, I feel the need to confess.

"Let's huddle together for warmth," Nicolette said enthusiastically scooting toward Susan and pulling Paul with her. She hooked her arm with theirs and trapped them both close to her. Paul felt light-headed.

"You are resourceful, Nicolette, I'll give you that. But I've got a better idea," Susan said, laughing uncomfortably and pulling away. "I'll get some sweatshirts. Paul, where are all your extra sweats anyway?"

"Hey Dad. Let's make s'mores for dessert," Willie interrupted. "I know Mom bought all the s'more stuff 'cause I was with her. Won't that be a great dessert? And you guys won't have to do any of the work. We can do it all." He gestured at the older boys.

"Oh yes, let's make some," Nicolette said. "All that delicious warm marshmallow dribbling over the chocolate. S'mores always take me back to Girl Scout camp. Come on, the grill will keep us warm too. It'll feel like camp—only co-ed of course." She giggled and nudged Paul.

"Um, could we wait until we're **all** finished with dinner?" Susan asked.

"Who all's done?" Nicolette called out in a little girl voice as the boys all raise their hands.

Susan held up her hand. "Dinner first," she said firmly.

The kids groaned and sat down to pick at unwanted food.

"I'll get the stuff so we'll be ready," Nicolette offered. She crawled over the bench, holding Paul's shoulder to steady herself. She went into the kitchen then leaned back out the sliding door. "Where do you keep the graham crackers?"

Paul could sense Susan's annoyance as she continued to chew the last of her hamburger. "Worse than the kids," she said tightly. "Paul, help her out, will you please?"

Like one of the kids. Impatient. Exuberant. Immediate. Expectant. Paul found her zealously opening and slamming cupboard doors.

"Because we are such big s'more fans," he announced, walking to the louvered cabinet door, "all the ingredients are in one spot. Right here. Close to the deck." He handed her the graham crackers and marshmallows. "I always carry the chocolate," he added.

"That's cute." Nicolette declared. "You should've been smiling when you said that. Don't you ever smile?"

"Only when provoked." Paul smiled.

"Much better." She took his arm and led him out onto the deck.

"I'll need to start the firepit," Paul nodded in its direction. "We'll use that. It works better on marshmallows."

Willie begged to start the pit and Paul showed him how.

"Ta da." Willie bowed as the flames appeared and everyone clapped.

"I've never had one of these," Nicolette said. "We only ever had a hibachi and we always had to eat in shifts, the cooking surface was so small." She moved closer to the grate.

"Hibachis always made great marshmallows though, you have to admit," Greg said.

"I don't have to admit anything" Nicolette fired that comment his way, punctuating it by waving a table fork. "Can I cook the first marshmallow?"

Willie frowned. The first one was usually his.

"Sure," said Paul quickly. "Stick one on this long fork. It's safer."

"I need two." Nicolette reached impatiently across the firepit in front of Paul to grab another piece of white fluff. As she bent forward her hair brushed against the firepit grate and in a split second her long red hair was in flames.

She screamed. Greg and Susan leaped from their seats. The boys froze. Paul grabbed an oven mitt and beat at the fire. "Water," he yelled. Hunter jumped over the deck rail and grabbed the hose. He held it at ready but nothing happened. "Turn it on!" Paul screamed. He was now beating

95

on the remaining flames with the oven mitt and his unprotected left hand. "Willie, do it!" he shouted. Willie was already scrambling down the steps and turned the faucet handle as though his life depended on it. Hunter aimed the hose at his mother. The water found the flames and everyone and everything else around the pit. The smell of burning hair and propane covered the area. Greg quickly made sure the fire was out as Susan helped Nicolette to a chair.

"Oh God, are you all right?" Susan cried.

"I think so," Nicolette sobbed. She was shaking and grabbing at the ends of her hair. "Is my hair all gone? Oh God, I could've died. Burned right here. Paul, God, you saved my life." She moaned and reached for his hand.

Paul yelped at her touch. His hand burned wildly. "Get me some cold water. Shit, this hurts. Goddamnit, this really burns. Hurry up."

"I'll call 911," Susan croaked, running into the house.

Greg examined Paul's hand. "Joe, get a bucket of water," he barked. "Willie, tell your mother we need an old sheet. Hunter, comfort your mother for God's sake. She's hysterical."

Nicolette was shivering and ranting about escaping death and Paul saving her life. She pulled at the singed ends of her hair, considerably shorter now and uneven.

Paul was alternately cursing and moaning and gratefully sank his hand into the bucket Joe pushed under it.

"Dad, are you OK?" he asked.

"No. I'm not OK. I've burned the shit out of my hand and it hurts like hell." Paul groaned.

Susan appeared with a clean white sheet as pale as she was. "The ambulance is coming."

"I don't need an ambulance," Paul protested but closed his eyes and groaned more loudly. Greg tore the sheet in pieces and soaked several of them. He gently lifted Paul's hand and covered it with the dripping wet rags.

"It's my fault. It's my fault. It's all my fault," Nicolette wailed. Hunter's arms awkwardly wrapped around her offered little apparent comfort.

"It's OK Mom, it's OK," he repeated over and over again.

Out of habit, Susan put her hand on Paul's forehead prompting him to yell, "This isn't the goddamned flu for God's sake. The only temperature I have is on my goddamned hand." He pulled the piece of sheet off to show her and screamed as the air surrounded the red and already blistering skin.

Greg firmly applied new wet rags and said, "I hear the siren." He turned to Willie who was barely holding back tears. "Go hail them down, will you, son?" he said gently. Willie gulped and tore down the steps toward the driveway.

Hurrying around the corner of the house, the emergency medical technicians quickly spied a female with singed red hair mumbling incoherently about heroes and marshmallows and a man with dark hair with rags wrapped around his left hand. "What a madhouse they must think this is," Paul thought as they kicked quickly into gear. Inside half an hour they had everyone calmed down and bandaged.

"You folks should get dry clothes on," said the largest of the technicians. "It'd be a shame to get you all fixed up and have someone get pneumonia. Now Reverend, remember what I told you to do with that hand. And tomorrow, you call your doc, OK?"

"Thanks," Paul said. "I will."

"And you, little lady," he said to Nicolette, "you should get some rest. Worry about your hair tomorrow." Nicolette gave him a brave smile and grabbed at her raggedy hair.

"You guys are great," Susan said. "Now I'm going to get these people inside for some coffee and dry clothes."

"Don't bother, Susan," Greg said. "I'll just take Nicolette to my house and Hunter and I will watch her tonight."

"No bother, Greg. It's the least I can do."

"Really. We gotta go. Paul needs to rest too."

"Yeah. S'mores some other time, I guess." Susan, out of impulse and relief, gave Greg a hug.

"Definitely," Greg said, hugging her back. "A rain check."

Nicolette smiled weakly as she let Hunter and Greg help her to their car.

The boys helped Paul inside and set him in the leather recliner in his study. It was obvious they were worried and Paul felt enough better to say, "I'm OK guys. Look. I'm sorry I swore so much. I didn't mean to frighten you."

The kids relaxed. "No problem," Joe said. Willie said "Now that you've taught us how to curse really well, we'll be able to do it ourselves."

Paul reached for a dog toy and flung it feebly at their retreating backs.

Susan stood at the door. "Are you really OK? Do you need anything?"

"No. I'd just like to relax here for a while. Join me?" He reached out with his good hand.

Susan pulled a chair close and Paul reached for her hand. It was a comfort he had missed. She'd held so many hands since the kids came that she'd had little time for his and he'd wondered how it would feel now, the comfort of her touch. Warmth, not heat, spread through him and he squeezed her fingers. He closed his eyes for a moment.

"Nice Memorial Day," he said, laughing a little, opening his eyes. "And I was really up for dessert too. Greg was great, wasn't he? He really took charge."

"I have only one thing to say," Susan replied. She leaned back in the chair and closed her eyes. "Boy, is she a piece of work. You'd better be careful." She squeezed his hand tighter.

Chapter 14

Pieces of Work

The following week was a blur activity for Paul, events and situations to deal with and decisions to make. It was a slow motion sequence for Susan. She watched him come and go with a different eye; especially on the two evenings he went to Nicolette's apartment. She knew she shouldn't be feeling this way. And if Nicolette were still staying with Greg, she might not. Or if they were meeting at the church she might not. And now on Thursday at 7:32 p.m., she had a headache.

She didn't think she could cope with any more of these thoughts she was having. She trusted Paul. She did. My God, through all their years together and all the women, and men, he had helped, she had never felt this way before. She didn't like it. Even two weeks later, Susan could hear Nicolette's little voice saying, "Who wants s mores?" and snuggling up to Paul. Shameless flirting, her mother would say. Just shameless.

Maybe caffeine will help, she thought as she finished wiping the counter. She grabbed the bag of Copenhagen blend she usually saved for company and measured it out for two cups. As she snapped on the switch, a little pang along with a jolt of warmth coursed through Susan as she remembered Greg's kiss. Would her mother call that shameless? She wasn't flirting. It had been Greg. All Greg. What a piece of work those two were. But somehow, she couldn't stop thinking about it. Just like when Paul first kissed her in the literature section of the college library, how for days afterward she'd savored that kiss. A kiss like that meant something. Just as Paul's kiss had had promise, even though the volume of Shakespeare sticking into her back should have given her a true example of the pleasure and the pain of love, but she hadn't paid enough attention.

That kiss. That was the problem. If Greg hadn't kissed her, if she hadn't at least a little enjoyed it or been flattered by it, she probably wouldn't be feeling this way about Paul. She had strayed from their marriage path, just a little, of course, but then might Paul not do that too? Was he capable of that? She'd never considered it. There had never been doubt. Trust was the issue.

She fixed her coffee just right and curled up with her book. He should be home soon. Maybe they could talk. She'd have to tell him. About what? The Stones? Pieces of work. The Lombards?

Chapter 15

Pam's Revelation

Another Thursday, another meeting. Paul sighed. At least after the budget discussion, he might get a chance to talk with Pam. He hadn't seen her all week and he needed to talk.

When the meeting let out a little after 9 o'clock, he spied Pam hurrying out of the sanctuary toward the choir robe closet.

"Hey, friend. Missed you Sunday," he called.

"Sunday after church is not a good time to try to talk," she said.

"I know. I just wanted to tell you that I was really moved by that Sergeant Pepper variation you played for practice. I don't know why, it just got to me. I don't get as moved by many of the other blatantly religious preludes you select."

"Life is a mystery, isn't it?" Pam turned to straighten the robes.

A retort like that given in a teasing way would have been typical Pam. But this one had an edge. Paul sensed something was the matter.

"It is when there are people like you helping the plot along," he continued. "I'll bet you played that on purpose."

"Is that an accusation, Inspector?" Pam asked, trying for humor but again not quite making it.

"Actually, it's a revelation. Lately I'm afraid I'm more affected by your choice of music than the congregation is by my preaching."

"If I can cheer someone up or make the same old words we always sing mean something new, I'm doing my job," she said.

"What happened to just supplying music to the glory of God each Sunday?" Paul said. He smiled expectantly, hoping for a witty comeback.

"You think by doing things my way, I'm not?" she said. Her response was clipped.

"Oh, so now you have divine inspiration?" Paul shot back.

"Someone needs some"

Paul stared. This remark wasn't like her. Pam's normally friendly and open face was serious and concerned. The smile that dimpled her plump cheeks, the warmth of the sparkle in her blue eyes, both gone.

"All right. We are better friends than this," he said softly. "What's up?"

She turned to the closet and continued to silently rearrange the already perfectly aligned choir robes.

When she still didn't respond after a minute or so, Paul turned away and made his way, more calmly than he felt, into the office to take refuge behind his desk. He heard the heavy door to the church proper open. He heard it close. He waited a few minutes. She must have gone inside, he thought. Why hadn't she followed him to his office like she normally would have?

The inside of the church was bathed in the dim red light of the Eternal Flame donated by the Women's League. He searched the shadows for Pam and found her in the back pew of the choir area. He walked toward her but she didn't look at him. He sat down in the pew ahead of her and put his head in his bandaged hand. He hoped she'd know what he needed and blurt out the things she'd observed, overheard, been told—all the things he'd done that had in some way allowed the people he served to feel less cared for, doubtful of his commitment, cheated and spiritually unguided. He could try to fix those things with the same holy glue he'd been using for years. Sermons would be written and given, confessions would be heard, communion would continue and congregational life would proceed uninterrupted, as it should.

Then through the quiet, he heard her sniffle. He turned around in surprise and she covered her face with her hands. When he moved up beside her and sat close, she wouldn't look at him.

"Pam." He willed her to look at him. His heart was thumping so hard he was afraid he wouldn"t hear her if she did speak.

She pulled a wad of tissue from her sleeve. "It's so sad," she whispered. "Everything's so wrong."

"What's wrong?" Paul asked but he was already framing his response. He knew what he would say. He'd resolve not to look at Nicolette in church, not to attend practices where she was, not to visit her at home any more like a solicitous clergyman. He would pray for strength if thoughts of her intruded into family moments, or Bible study time, or sermon preparation or any activity except confession. He would call his mentor Bill Wilhelm in the morning and make an appointment.

As he watched Pam wipe her tears, he would never have guessed that this was all about Susan and Greg and a kiss in the dugout spotted by Pam's 11-year-old son in the middle of a thunderstorm and innocently relayed over a dinner of cold pizza.

"You don't deserve this," she said softly. "People just don't know how thoughtful you are, and how much you care about them. How much time you spend trying to keep their lives together. How warm and loving you can be. It's just not fair."

Paul felt if she didn't say something concrete soon, his chest would burst and the ethereal red "A" he had imagined would be all that was left. "Pam, tell me," was all he could say.

She looked at him. "I'm sorry. Right now it's all just rumor. Something I heard. I need to make sure before I tell you. I don't want you to be upset too."

"Why would I be upset?" he said, putting his hand on his chest. His heart was pounding.

"No, I've got to be sure," she said, putting her hand on his. "Give me some time. A week."

"Don't know if I can." His throat was dry and his ears were buzzing.

"I'm so sorry I let you see me like this. I wanted to have all my information before I came to you. I was actually avoiding you because I knew this would happen. You asked me to keep my ear to the ground and I did. Now I have to make sure of what I heard." She patted his hand. "Don't worry."

Now Paul wished she would shut up. The hairs on his arms and the back of his neck stood at attention. A cold prickling sensation traveled from the top of his head to his stomach. He closed his eyes and clenched his fist, took a deep breath. It was dark in the church now. Paul felt the definitive calm before the storm.

Paul had been kneeling at the altar rail where he had nearly collapsed after Pam left. He turned around, leaning his back on the rail with his arms spread out, elbows hooked on the smooth wood. He gazed at the dim glow of Jesus carrying the lamb on the stained glass window at the rear of the church and began to pray out loud.

"We try to love and live in the ways you've guided us to do. I know things have gotten in the way these days but I've always known to go back to You. I know You give grace freely. I know You forgive. I used to be able to do that too. Teach me to be more like You. Lately I'm questioning all the time. And remember that Sunday, with the treasure chest? There was nothing in my treasure chest. Nothing at all. Why?"

Paul covered his face with his hands. "I'd settle for joy," he whispered. "Just some joy again."

After a while, he looked up. He'd been sitting there long enough for the automatic heater to have shut down, leaving it cool and drafty up by the altar. Poor Pam. It was a difficult charge he'd given her. She had hugged him and rubbed his hand and reassured him that she'd do whatever it took. She loved him. A kiss on the cheek. Good-bye.

He kicked pebbles in the parking lot as he walked to the car. Maybe he was making too much of this without knowing the whole story. He drove home in a fine drizzle that was turning into fog.

"Hi," Susan said. She was curled up in Paul's leather chair holding her favorite pulp fiction. "Hope you didn't cruise over to the field. Too rainy and foggy for practice. We'll just have to hope we're good enough to make the Padres eat our dust tomorrow." She said all this without looking up from the book.

"No. I didn't."

"Oh. Where were you then?"

"I just stayed at church for a while."

"You were gone so long I thought you might be out there on second base again," she said, smiling a little.

"Why?"

"You just seem very thoughtful and when you get that way, your tendency is to head for the canvas bag."

"I have a tendency?"

She dropped the book, surprised at his offended tone. "You know you do."

"So do you."

"I guess I probably do. Let's start over." She sighed and stood up, dropping the book. "I'm sorry for being bitchy. Something's been bothering me and I was waiting to talk to you about it. When you didn't come right home, I got upset."

105

She went to him and rubbed his back. "This has nothing to do with tendencies, but something really odd happened at practice last weekend. I've been trying but I can't sort it out in my head. I guess I need you to help me."

"Can I get a beer first?" Paul asked, heading for the kitchen. "Want one?" She nodded.

While he rummaged behind some leftovers for the beers, Paul tried to put himself in the non-critical listening mode that pastors are supposed to be so good at. But he could never go there if he was vested in the outcome. He figured it was probably purely a husband-wife-family thing that was about to occur and he wondered what now. The best he could hope for was to listen and not overreact. He hoped Susan could do the same.

He grabbed two mugs from the freezer where Susan always kept them at the ready and walked slowly back in to the family room. Through the archway he saw her standing at the sliding door, staring up into the darkness out past the deck. He wondered if she was wishing upon an available star.

Susan turned to look at him. "I can tell you anything, right?"

"You have to ask?" said Paul.

She took the mug and bottle he extended and sat on the couch, making room for him but Paul took the rocker telling himself he could see her face better that way. They poured their beers in silence.

"It was the oddest thing," she began. "You know last weekend when it rained so hard and the thunder and lightning caused us to cut practice short..."

"Sunday, right?" Paul asked, sounding calmer than he felt.

"Yeah. God. This is hard. I'm taking a huge risk here but ... I guess I can trust you to understand." She turned and looked at him for support.

He nodded.

"Well, the boys just had to have some sodas so they ran to the snack bar and Greg and I were alone in the dugout. And well," she took a deep breath, "Greg kissed me." She looked right at Paul with a kind of wonder.

Paul blinked. "He what?"

"He kissed me." She threw her arm over the back of the couch and shifted her weight so she was facing him directly.

Paul tightened grip on the arms of the rocker. "Did anyone see this?"

Susan looked perturbed. "Now why would that be your first question?" She turned away shaking her head. "I just told you an attractive man kissed me, your wife, and you want to know if anyone saw it." The upset in her voice escalated with the next sentence. "I don't know if anyone saw it." Her nails scratched on the upholstery.

Paul felt himself beginning to seethe. A pastor's wife, kissing in the dugout. Appearances must remain the same, unchanging and above all else positive. This Susan herself had told him a million times. Then the seething turned to a cold chill. If it had been me and Nicolette, would I be confessing this so trustingly?

"What kind of kiss?" Paul could not conceal the tension in his voice. He leaned forward and looked at her face.

"More than the peck you'd expect after, well, like celebrating something. You know how those sports things go. Well, we hadn't won anything; in fact, it was only practice and it was canceled, you'll recall."

She stopped for a moment and leaned forward. "Are you okay?" she said. Paul nodded slowly.

She continued. "I just wanted to make sure because this is hard enough for me to think about and I know exactly what happened. You have to rely on my perceptions."

"Go ahead."

"Okay. Well, the kids went to get sodas as I said, and he looked at me this funny way and then kissed me, kind of tenderly actually."

"Mouth?"

Susan leaned forward even more. "Mouth, and it was very confusing. I know he's lonely and we're friends now but ..."

"So what did you do?"

"I bolted. Told him to take the kids and left right away. For once, I didn't know what to say, so I didn't say anything. It wasn't like I willed him to do it or anything. It was a total surprise. And shocking. I've tried not to be embarrassed the few times I've seen him since, but it's hard." She sat back. "Really hard. It's something unresolved between us now. Then I had already invited him to join us for a cook-out on Memorial Day and couldn't renege because of Hunter..." She continued to talk about the picnic they had had, how difficult it was, how he kept trying to talk to her and she tried to avoid it. All this unnoticed by Paul who was thinking about Nicolette, before her hair went up in flames.

As Susan talked, Paul could feel her relief in the air. He heard it in the way she breathed out, her lower lip forcing air up to her bangs which puffed out briefly, then laid back on her forehead. "Between Greg and Nicolette, a shrink could be kept busy full-time," she sighed.

Now Paul sat forward. "Why do you say that?"

"Oh come on. It's so obvious she's flirting with you. God, at our house that night, before her hair caught on fire. At the games. It's so obvious. You ought to do something to discourage that." Susan looked right at him.

"So should you," Paul offered back with a level gaze.

"Oh, you can't possibly be jealous about this onetime kiss," she said with a nervous laugh. "It's so ridiculous. It meant nothing to me."

"What about to him? And, I don't call having another man kiss your wife ridiculous. There are other words I'd use but that's not one of them."

"Paul. Really, it meant nothing. No more than Nicolette's flirting does, that's for sure."

Paul could see Greg's face at the Jensen's party. He remembered his sad face in counseling sessions after Nicolette had left town. He could hear Greg talk about women. Too many images, none of them good, were coming back to Paul.

"It happened. One of those things," Susan said. "We have to move on. But you know, we're stuck with them at least through the rest of the season. And they go to our church. We have to see these people."

She thought for a moment. "Let's at least make a Beware-of-the-Stones pact for the rest of the summer. You know, just be careful, be a little aloof and not overly involved." Susan took Paul's hand. "I thought you would freak what with everything that's been happening. You do understand, don't you, that I never wanted this, that I really am upset by it and at a loss as to what to do? I just feel better having told you."

"I know," Paul said. He stroked her hand. By now he was struggling for a way to end this conversation. He managed a smile. "For starters, you've got to promise you won't invite them to dinner again."

"That's a given," said Susan. She picked up the bottles and mugs and was on her way toward the kitchen when Paul said, "Then I forgive you."

Susan stopped and turned.

"Forgive me? For what?" she asked, her cheeks flushed.

"You know."

"No. Tell me."

"You know."

"I don't feel I did anything wrong. There's nothing to forgive." She paused for a moment.

"All right." Paul sounded unconvinced.

She watched him closely. "Is there?"

Paul said nothing.

"I knew this was too easy," she said as she wiped away a tear. "Do you honestly think there is anything to forgive?"

"I guess not."

"There isn't. I did nothing to make it happen."

"Fine," said Paul, hands extended in the way he would use to perform a blessing, seal a sacrament, pronounce forgiveness.

Susan, in her anger, didn't make the connection. She didn't know it but she was forgiven for unknown transgressions and for sins yet to come. He gave it freely so it would be given that way to him, if need be.

Chapter 16

More Weather

Saturday late afternoon was unseasonably chilly. Susan sat in the dugout watching the Yankees warm up for their game, waiting for Willie to return from the concession stand with her cup of hot coffee. The sky was overcast and the wind was picking up. A windbreaker would be nice right now, she thought, trying to think about anything and everything other than men.

"Lousy day for baseball," Greg said briskly, slamming the oversized equipment bag on the mud floor of the dugout.

"There's never a lousy day for baseball. There's only lousy weather." Susan scooted sideways on the bench out of his way.

"What's the difference? Whatever it is, this isn't gonna be comfortable and it isn't gonna be fun. The kids are shivering already and what with practice being rained out last weekend, it's a bad start." Greg pulled the collar of his jacket up around his ears. "Can you believe this is the eighth of June?"

"Got the lineup from Henry?" Susan nodded toward the enemy dugout.

"I'll go in a minute."

"Hunter," Greg called to his son as he began the pre-game paperwork. "Here's the car keys. Get the windbreaker in the trunk, will you? Looks like Mrs. Lombard could use another layer."

"I'm fine," Susan started to protest, but Greg held up his hands. "The coach needs to be comfortable so she can focus on the game, not the blueness of her fingernails."

Susan shivered. She knew that when two caretakers meet, galaxies collide. Their wanting to do for each other exceeds all else. They stumble over each other's good deeds and thoughtfulness like a blind person in the dark, not seeing what is there and imagining furiously what is not.

About that kiss. Paul's talk of forgiveness had had her tossing and turning every night for a week. Had Greg been anticipating a need she had unwittingly telegraphed? She figured he would want to talk about it or do something about it and she knew she didn't want to do either. She grasped for the first topic that came to mind.

"How's Nicolette doing?" she asked.

Greg leaned against the dugout wall with his arms folded.

"Okay, I guess. She stayed with us two days after the fire before she went back to her apartment. She had a hell of a nightmare the first night. Must've been the sedative the doctor prescribed over the phone. Kept moaning Paul's name and sitting up straight in bed. Then the next day she got on this thing about being so ugly. She had her hair cut somewhat to even out the damage." He smiled. "Actually, she did look a little scary. You know, like you'd envision Mr. Rochester's crazy wife to look if you ever got a peek in the attic." He chuckled at Susan's surprise. Saw 'Jane Eyre' on the late show the night I sat up with her."

"I'm just glad she was only singed," Susan said.

"Nicolette feels so lucky that Paul was right there. I'll bet she wonders if I'd have done the same for her."

"You would've."

"I'd like to think I would."

Hunter returned with the jacket, red-faced and out of breath.

"That was fast." Susan accepted the jacket with a smile. Hunter grinned, making her wistful once again for a similar reaction from Joe sometime, for any reason.

Hunter was going to look just like Greg. His hair beneath the Yankee;s cap was blond and his eyes, under the visor, were steel blue. When and if he got a growth spurt for height, he'd be a tall, lean good-looking young man with straight teeth and a charming smile and if he didn't, he'd be all those things only medium height and a bit stocky, like Greg. Stocky though didn't mean fat, mostly muscular and tight from what Susan could see. She watched Joe take his place at the chain link backdrop starting his own intense warm up pattern. Joe had Paul's tall, trim physique and athletic build. Broadening shoulders and a narrow waist. Wanting to pump iron but unwilling to commit the time away from his friends, especially girls, especially Valerie. Things were intense when Joe was around. Even more so when Paul was there, too. Whatever happened to happy-go-lucky. Susan sighed.

She watched Greg hit balls to the fielders and the umpire brush grit off home plate. Their opponents were good and were focused, if that meant they dropped very few balls and knew where to throw them. What a great thing baseball was. It made you appreciate skill and dexterity and strategy and patience—and the value of luck.

"Three solid days of rain," Paul said to himself as he sped toward the ball field. Then his thoughts turned to the game. "Can't miss the game today. Too much at stake. I really should take Mondays off. Sunday is so stressful, too much of a performance. I wonder what God had in mind for a day of rest for the clergy. Oh, I forgot. We selfless men of God don't need regeneration. We'll just make up our own spiritual reference passages like this: blessed are the harried for they shall know rest and recreation when they see it. Be nicer to thyself and all else good will follow. Pay attention to thine own house or cheating, lying, betrayal, dishonesty and discomfort will prevail.

He pulled carefully into a parking space, delicately helping to turn the steering wheel with his bandaged hand. Which ball field, he wondered. There were three choices. He figured calling Susan would be the safest way to find out. As he turned around to reach for his phone and the umbrella that would probably be useless in the wind, Nicolette pulled up next to him. She hopped quickly out of her car and opened his passenger door. As she slid in, he noticed once again the difference in her hair. With almost six inches burned off and the resultant new hairstyle, she looked younger to him and innocent.

"Glamorous, huh?" She smiled ruefully as she pulled at her shaggy hair.

Paul grinned and held up his bandaged hand. "So's this. At least you can wash your own hair. I have to have someone help me."

"I'd do it," she retorted, looking him straight in the eye. "It'd be the least I could do for you saving my life after the stupid fool I made of myself. I still can't believe I did that. Strange things are always happening to me. If it hadn't been for you and for Hunter, I just don't know. And then Greg taking me in for a few days and Susan being so concerned. And you coming to see me twice so far, even though Pam had to give you a ride the first time because you couldn't drive yet." She stopped, breathless. "I should just say thank you and shut up." Nicolette leaned forward and kissed his cheek.

"I take it you're feeling better now," Paul said. The thought of her helping him wash his hair made him unable to think of anything else to say. His cheek suddenly burned and he was tempted to touch his cheek to see if it was really hot.

"One hundred percent. Even Greg wasn't his usual bastard self while I was staying with him. Sorry. I didn't mean to say that. I guess I need practice being charitable." She punctuated her sentence by touching his knee and giggling.

"Let's find the Yankees," Paul said.

———————

'There they are. Hi, guys!' Nicolette hollered, waving in the general direction of the Yankees' dugout. Joe waved back. Hunter nodded in her

114

general direction. Susan waved and cupped her hands around her large paper cup of coffee as she leaned over to say something to Greg, causing him first to smile, then to leap up yelping in pain as she spilled the steaming liquid on his thigh.

"Damn that's hot," he cried, then immediately apologized. "Sorry. It's so cold out here I should have enjoyed being scalded for a moment."

Susan dabbed at his jeans with the spare tissues she always carried in her jeans pocket for just such emergencies. "I'm so sorry. I'm usually not that clumsy."

"I should be used to it. Nicolette was always spilling things or dropping things on me. Actually," Greg said with a sly smile, "between Paul saving Nicolette and you scalding me, you could say that the Stone and Lombard family relationships are pretty hot." He grinned and reached for her cup from which he took a long swig of the hot liquid. "Now you could say they are pretty hot inside and out."

Susan blushed. "I guess you could say that," she replied.

"It's freezing out here," Nicolette said shivering from their seat on the bleachers. "If I'm staying for the whole game, I'll need coffee." She stood up and went to get some. She didn't ask if Paul wanted any, but then he didn't expect her to. Her disorganized way of thinking didn't include other people. You just wouldn't expect her to anticipate anyone else's needs. She would take what she wanted, do what she wanted without inhibition or guilt.

On her way back from the concession stand, Paul watched her dump some of the coffee out of the paper cup and lick the drip on the side, holding the cup a little higher than her mouth, moving the cup slowly down across her tongue.

He would have to call Jim again. Not that Jim would be able to sort this out for him, but at least it might get him to start actually talking about his emotional disarray and the Susan-Greg thing. And he had to talk about it. Not to anyone who would judge him, but to someone who would listen sympathetically. He knew some of his congregation saw their pastor as the first line of defense against the temptations of marital discord. But he didn't have the benefit of a first line. Bill Wilhelm was a logical choice for a call but the idea of having Bill know his foibles gave Paul a queasy feeling. Jim would be the better choice, knowing Susan and all. Paul hoped this would work. He didn't have a fallback plan.

He moved over to make room for Nicolette on the rapidly filling bleachers.

"Maybe I should get the blanket I have in the car," he said.

"I won't make you say that twice," she said. "Go!"

To unlock the trunk, Paul had to fumble with the car keys in his bandaged hand. Probably he should offer this blanket to Susan. No, she had some windbreaker on and anyhow coaches aren't supposed to sit wrapped in a blanket during a game. It would be a sign of weakness Susan would not want to show. He grabbed the stadium blanket and hurried back to the field.

"Nice," Nicolette grabbed the bunched up cloth, shook it out and wrapped it around them both before Paul even had a chance to think. They were wrapped shoulder to shoulder and knee to knee. She had her end of the blanket pulled up over her head while Paul scrunched his end around his shoulders, his head protected by a baseball hat.

"Now isn't this much better," she said into the wind. Paul told himself her words were only audible if he watched her lips carefully. In watching them, he saw their perfection as just another temptation sent his way to result in confession and forgiveness or eternal damnation.

Watch the game, he reminded himself. Your kid is playing.

"Want a sip?" Nicolette held out her cup.

Paul took it and swirled the cooling coffee around a few times. He took a big swallow before he realized that she had a little cream and a lot of sugar in it. He tried not to make a face. Susan and he had shared many a cup of black coffee, coffee the way they both liked it.

"Thanks," he said.

"You can have the rest." She pushed the cup at him. "I've had enough."

"No, really. I'll get some later. The game's starting."

Paul smiled. He thought Joe looked great out there. Confident, focused, muscles poised, ready for disaster or glory. Unaware of anything but his second base responsibilities. Second base where you were alone until the ball came to you, then everyone depended on you to make the right decision, choose the right play, and then make it happen. You were alone and you liked it that way.

Now the wind was wailing and dust was everywhere. The kids in the infield had their turtlenecks rolled up over their mouths and noses, leaving only their eyes vulnerable under the brim of their hats. To show that they were cold would be a sign of weakness that might reflect on their skill at the game. The coaches had drilled into them to do nothing that could give the opponent the edge. These were boys on the periphery of manhood. What tipped them over the edge was always a mystery.

"Look at those guys," Paul muttered, huddling down deeper in the protection of the blanket, and therefore closer to Nicolette. "They act like they don't even notice the wind and dust, never mind the cold. God, I used to be able to do that. Now look at me, I'm even shivering under this blanket."

"Look," said Nicolette, turning abruptly to face him. "If we're going to spend 12 more games together on these bleachers and who knows how many Sundays in church, we need some ground rules. First, is it OK to say 'God' or isn't it? You know, like you just did. Second, will Susan mind if we're huddling under this blanket together? Or any other blankets in future, I mean at future games? I don't care if Greg cares, and why should he, but even if he does, it doesn't bother me because he has no claim anymore. But Susan, that's different. I don't want her to think anything bad about me."

Paul didn't know these answers. He stood up abruptly. "I'll think I'll get that coffee now. Want some more?"

Her eyes got bigger. "No thanks," she said. "What about my questions?"

"When I come back, okay?"

"Okay."

Paul helped himself down the bleachers with his good hand and hurried toward the concession stand. This is nuts, he thought. Just when I was convinced she didn't care about anyone other than herself, she's worrying about Susan. Or maybe she's not. Wait, yes. Maybe she's worrying about what Susan will think of her. She's too hard to read. I need an interpreter.

He waved hello to several parishioners and was trapped in conversation with several others while the teenager in the hut poured his coffee.

"Need a top, Rev?" The boy grinned, nodding at Paul's bandaged hand.

"Good idea, Justin. Thanks." Paul waited while Justin pushed the plastic top down tight. "Wrapped only for a few more days, hopefully." Paul gestured with his hand.

He pulled his jacket sleeve down to make a barrier between his hand and the flimsy paper cup and walked by the dugout to wish Susan luck. He peeked his head around the corner and saw Susan and Greg knee to knee, deep in conversation. Greg looked up and jumped to his feet, yelling at the pitcher to take his time before the throw. Susan leaned back against the dugout wall with her arms folded in that most stubborn of postures Paul had come to know so well.

"Good luck, Susan." He yelled into the wind, but she must not have heard him because she didn't look his way.

Paul struggled back up the bleachers with the cup and into the blanket Nicolette had open and waiting.

"About your questions, Nicolette," Paul began.

"Niki," she said.

"Niki. When I'm at the ball game, just forget I'm a minister. Here I'm just the second baseman's father," Paul said.

"I'll remember you said that," she said.

"And what was your second question? Oh yes, the huddling. Susan doesn't mind." He said this reassuringly and hoped it was still true.

"I'll remember you said that too." She laughed and moved yet closer.

Chapter 17

Under The Bleachers

"What a week." Susan sighed, flopping on the couch in the family room. She threw her arm over her face and kicked off her sneakers. Her tucked-in hair stuck out of the sides of her baseball cap. Her jeans shorts were covered with grime, her knees too. "TGIF."

"You!" Paul sank into the easy chair across the room and kicked his feet up on the footstool. He briefly remembered a time when he would have sat next to her and stroked her arm the way he learned in childbirth classes, to help her relax. Instead he added, "I need a vacation."

"You!" She shot back, laughing and peeking out from under her arm. "I'm whipped. Our game was rough today with all this wind. In fact, this is five straight days of wind now. Is this one of the plagues or something? It's impossible to play ball when you have to cover your face all the time. One of the kids was protecting his eyes and got conked in the nose by a bad hop today. Talk about bloody."

"Okay, so we all need a vacation," Paul chuckled.

"Yeah, what a mess," Joe said, walking tiredly into the room and tossing his mitt at Paul. "We had to call the ambulance because blood was gushing out of Dan's nose and no one wanted to touch him. You oughta keep rubber gloves in the dugout."

"Great idea. I'll mention it to the coach. He'll take care of it." Susan closed her eyes, stretched luxuriously and said, "I'm getting in the tub before dinner. Can you guys start the spaghetti water?"

"What about the sauce?" Paul asked.

"Oh, yeah. Start that too. Use the blue pan so it won't splatter all over. Throw some lettuce in the salad bowls, while you're at it. Have Willie set the table and cut the bread. It's his specialty. Be down in half an hour."

"Notice how we went from spaghetti water to full meal preparation?" Paul said in a stage whisper, loud enough for Susan to hear. He grinned. She turned around and winked before starting up the stairs. "Can't you take care of it?" she asked.

"Yep." Joe's voice interrupted, muffled by the baseball jersey he was pulling over his head. "If I tell Valerie I made spaghetti for dinner tonight, she'll think that's cool."

"That wouldn't actually be the truth," Paul said. "Don't you have any other ways to impress this young lady?"

"My manly muscles." Joe grinned and extended his hand to help Paul out of the chair.

"That ought to do it. When you get some, that is." Paul took his hand but Joe let go at the last minute, sending Paul deep back into the chair.

Playful Joe is here, thought Paul. I should capitalize on this since Moody Joe is always lurking just around the corner. He laughed. "Just for that, you go get started. I'm going to sit here and think another minute."

Paul heard the water running, cupboard doors opening and pots slamming in the kitchen. He relocated to the couch and put his feet on the coffee table and arms under his head in true relaxation mode.

What had Susan said? Greg would take care of it. What she had probably intended as a throw-away line didn't quite make it. She said it with confidence as though she had a history of relying on Greg Stone to "take care of it." And here Paul had been taking care of everything all week. Three hospital visits each day to people who were critically ill and time spent with their families for prayer and support. Two Bible study sessions about the prophets. Music and Worship Committee and Christian Education Committee meetings Tuesday and Wednesday evenings. A Church Council meeting last night that caused him aggravation in three ways: first just because they were frustrating in and of themselves, second because it was supposed to be his day off and third because it had caused him to miss Joe's game. Three counseling sessions down and one session left to go this evening with Nicolette. Energy sapped and spirit faltering, he still had the biggest challenge of the week to go.

"Hey, come on and help," Joe called. "I have to hurry. Hunter and I are meeting some kids tonight. Willie, get in here and do your jobs!"

"Sure, Joe, gotta rush out to kiss your girlfriend," Willie teased in a whining voice. "Dad, you oughta see Joe and his girlfriend. Joe and Valerie sittin' in a...." Willie's tune grew muffled. Paul suspected Joe had slammed a heel from the loaf of Italian bread into his mouth.

Joe kissing. He'd have to ask Susan if she knew what Joe had learned in school about sex and relationships. Joe wouldn't tell him, he was sure. Joking was acceptable but serious things Joe and Paul could not share. Paul's father and he had been unable to connect in that way as well and Paul had sworn for him and his sons, it would be different. Whatever it took to make it different, Paul had not yet found.

"Coming." Paul rose slowly from the couch and strolled into the chaos in the kitchen.

The food was on the table and the Lombard men were in their seats when Susan came down. Clean and refreshed, damp hair pulled back with a ribbon, she looked completely rejuvenated.

"Great job on the dinner, guys. Thanks. Just for that, I'll do dishes." she said. "Let's dig in." She began reaching for the pasta, then quickly remembered the prayer and bowed her head.

Paul began the prayer they had said since the kids were small. "Come Lord Jesus, be our guest and let your gifts to us be blessed." Now they each had to add some gift they were thankful for, an embellishment added by Paul when the prayer had begun to proceed too much by rote.

"Thank you for my goldfish," said Willie. He always used that when he couldn't think of anything.

"Thank you for my double play today," Joe offered.

"Thank you for letting us win today and for Coach Stone for his

122

good advice," Susan said.

"Thanks for letting me make it through this week. Amen," Paul prayed.

"That bad?" Susan looked at him.

"You know it. Please pass the bread."

"Great supper, Mom," Willie said, mouth full.

"Great supper, Joe, you mean." Joe was picking at his pasta and half-heartedly dunking his bread in sauce.

"Joe, you should be starving" Susan said. "Eat."

"I ate a lot of bread while I was fixing it," he said. "Can I go now? I hear the kids in the driveway."

"Where are you guys going?" Paul asked.

"Just down to the ballpark to hang out. There's a senior league game tonight under the lights."

"Great," said Susan. "Dad has a meeting tonight so maybe I'll go. It'll give me something to do."

"Mom, don't."

"Why not?" Susan asked feigning innocence.

"Come on." Moody Joe was emerging.

"I want to go."

"Why can't my parents have lives?" Joe grumbled.

"What time shall I pick you up?" Paul asked. "I'll probably be coming home a little after nine.

"I'll walk." Joe got up, put his dishes in the dishwasher, grabbed his baseball cap and escaped.

"They're gonna be kissing, you know," Willie said.

"Who's going to be kissing?" Susan asked.

"Joey and Valerie and Hunter and some girl. They don't know but

Sammy and I spy on them sometimes. We're really good at finding 'em. They always got their arms around each other and it's disgusting." Willie stood up, cleared his place and went to the study to play video games.

"Have you seen any of this 'disgusting' stuff happening?" Susan asked.

Paul held up his hands and shrugged his shoulders. "No."

"Have you made sure Joe knows what he should know?"

"No. I'm sure there is something about that in school."

"It's your job."

"I know. It just hasn't come up in general conversation."

"Well, it's not going to. You're going to have to make a point to talk to him. I know the school has all these programs for teens, but we want him to know how we feel, right?"

"Right. I'll do it."

"What did your father tell you?"

"Not much. It wasn't something we could talk about easily. Actually we couldn't talk about anything easily."

"I remember. But you shouldn't let that get in the way of your talking to Joe."

I know. I know. I know.

———————

"I should've worn my denim jacket," Valerie said, snuggling closer to Joe. "It's still so windy." Joe looked down at her. Her jeans and T-shirt were cute but not warm enough at all. Her long wavy hair blew wildly around her head and into her face and his. He pulled a handful away from his mouth and said "Let's huddle down behind Hunter and Ashley. They'll be our shields."

Valerie giggled and made Joe hunker down to her size. "Great idea."

"Hey, we're freezing up here," Ashley complained. "Get ahead of us."

"No. Let's go under the bleachers where it's calmer," Valerie suggested.

"What if we want to see the game?" Joe asked.

"Oh, stop worrying. You'll still be able to see," Valerie said, grabbing his hat and laughing as his hair flew all over. She broke away from him and ran toward the field, Joe in hot pursuit.

He caught her near the snack bar, under the big oak tree and pinned her arm back to get his hat. She yelped and broke free again, heading into the shadows beneath the bleachers on the visitors' side. There weren't many spectators and less than half of the seats were taken and then only at one end. She headed for the other end. Her mind was racing, remembering her favorite television show and how the women lure their men, teasing and flirting until that passionate kiss, the one that lasts five minutes and leads to whatever happens next just as there is a commercial break. She hid behind the pole way at the back and watched as Joe stumbled into the darkness. She could see his hands, strong with long fingers, imagined the veins popping up like they did when he grasped the bat, sinews stretching, waiting for the release that came with the swing, imagined his strong arms around her yet one more time.

Joe saw her behind the pole and walked slowly toward her. Sneaking a kiss in school was one thing, feeling her with him as they danced another. But some other connection was developing now, something that might be beyond his control. He couldn't wait to see her, to smell her hair, and to feel her against him as they walked, arms around each other. Sometimes she did things or said things that sent both shivers and heat through his body.

Joe heard the crowd cheer. He shuffled over to the seats and stood level to one of the bleacher openings. The first and second base runners were jogging toward their dugout. A double play and he'd missed it. He swore under his breath. Then he felt slender arms wrap around his waist. He turned around to Valerie's upturned face, glowing softly, lit by the reflection of the ballpark lights through the seats. He leaned forward to kiss her as he had before but this time she was breathless and shaking and he felt it would be good to hold her close. He reached for her in the darkness and felt her breasts through the T-shirt, her nipples hard like the ones pictured in the magazines under his bed. He pulled at her shirt and she helped him until he could touch her flesh with his hands, her nipples with his palms. Joe pushed on her breasts, stuck his tongue as deeply as he could into her mouth, and pressed his body as close to her as he could get. She began making noises that he was afraid someone would hear. He covered her mouth with his and was grateful that somewhere out there, some ball player had done an excellent thing bringing the crowd to its feet in a roar. When the crowd quieted down, he stepped back, fingers still lightly stroking her.

"Come on." Valerie pulled him behind the pole. "I'll take this off." She crossed her arms in front of her and grabbed the bottom of her shirt.

"Hey. Joe. Valerie." Hunter called, running under the stands with Ashley in hand. He squinted. "Where are you guys? My dad and your mom will buy us ice cream, they said. They're up there." Hunter pointed straight up.

Behind the pole, Joe and Valerie didn't move and didn't breathe.

"Ash, maybe they're not here." Hunter pulled Ashley to him and hugged her lightly. "Hey, this is a great place to make out." They grabbed each other and kissed, making loud slurping sounds.

"Gross," Valerie hissed. She straightened her shirt and stepped out from behind the pole. "We're over here. We were playing tag. You're it." She touched Ashley's shoulder and tore out from under the seats into the artificial light.

Joe ran after her, confused by everything, everywhere on this night.

Susan had found a seat up high on the bleachers in the semi-darkness, out of the reach of the screaming floodlights that lit up the field and Greg had joined her there after he had looked all over to find her. She knew that because she had watched him from her perch. She had asked him about the rubber gloves and he was so agreeable. He had immediately agreed to get some for their team equipment bag when she'd mentioned it. No argument, no questions. "Great idea. I'll get them tomorrow," he'd said. He'd offered to buy her coffee first then he'd held her hand to help her climb a few more steep bleacher steps way to the top. He'd asked her if she needed a jacket, then didn't try to convince her she did when she'd said no. There was no bickering, Susan realized. All the pleasures of a male companion with no bickering.

———————

Paul knew he should have told Nicolette to meet him at church. Going to her house was a bad idea. He knew it in his gut but went anyway with a certain anticipation. He had the vision of the longhaired redhead on the baseball diamond firmly in mind when he rang the doorbell.

Nicolette had just finished cleaning up the kitchen when the bell rang. She had been enjoying the satisfaction of finally doing the dishes that had been calling from the sink for several days. She could never have let those sit if Greg had still been around. It's the bickering that isn't there, Nicolette thought as she ran toward the door wiping her hands on the dishtowel. The pleasure of the company of a man with no bickering.

Chapter 18

Ivy

"I'm glad you're here," Nicolette said. "This is always my loneliest time of the day. I've just put the coffee on." She locked the door to the apartment behind him and led him to the kitchen, their customary place for his visits.

The room was ivy everything. White wallpaper was covered with vines wrapping up toward the ceiling, leading over to the white moldings around the windows curtained with ivy-covered valances. Salt and pepper shakers were small ceramic ivy leaves, one with one hole, one with three holes. Coffee mugs were white with green handles curling into vines for the drinker to grip. Dark green mini blinds lent a certain sophistication to the room that might otherwise have crossed the line into the comical.

Paul couldn't stop staring at the ivy on the dishtowel that perfectly matched the ivy on the apron she was hastily removing. When he finally tore his gaze away, he saw a large overstuffed green recliner in the living room casually draped with a green and white afghan. He sat down at the table.

"I'd hoped to be all done with this cleaning up before you got here. Let me just put this away." She turned to the pantry door and hung the apron on an ivy shaped brass hook. The apron had helped her white jeans remain pristine and Paul knew before she even turned around that her dark green top would match her eyes.

He was just wishing he'd worn his collar like he usually did on home visits when Nicolette said, "How come you aren't wearing your collar? Just curious because I thought ministers had to wear that as a uniform all the time, especially when they are on official church business." Her eyes sparkled like emeralds as she reached for the coffeepot. "Want some?"

He held his cup out and as the hot liquid filled it, he had the strange notion that the vine on the mug was creeping up his wrist.

"Sometimes by the end of the day, that collar just feels really tight." He made the gesture men make to loosen their shirt collars a little after they've pulled their ties too tight. "On Friday nights I usually shoot for comfort."

"Me, too." She filled her own cup and flounced down in the chair closest to him. "Don't the weeks seem to be getting longer?"

"Actually they seem shorter to me, but maybe it's because of baseball practices and games. Seems like Susan's constantly hustling the kids into the van and heading off for the baseball diamond. Then she comes home, goes to bed and does it again the next day."

"She must be exhausted. I know I would be, even if I liked baseball a lot like she does."

"Love." Paul corrected her. "This time of year, it's really our lives, well, her life. She has a great strategic mind for the game. And she's really good at it. I'm proud of her."

"Don't you miss her?"

"It's a sacrifice we agreed to make this year."

"I guess we all make it in some way, don't we?"

"I guess we do." Paul shifted in his seat. "Why don't you tell me what you needed to talk about?"

Nicolette got up, poured more coffee and put the coffeepot back. She puttered around the room, neatening this and adjusting that.

"I want to talk about sadness." She sat down again, folded her arms in front of her and slumped in her chair, the very picture of tired sadness, the kind Paul himself knew was hard to make disappear.

Paul looked at the wallpaper and waited. And waited. He looked at his coffee mug and waited. This was going to be too hard. On this Friday night, he was too tired to use pastoral counseling techniques to extract just what was bothering Nicolette.

"You've got to give me more than that," he finally said looking up to see her eyes riveted on him. The vine was tightening around his wrist, squeezing so hard that he could feel his pulse pounding.

She put her elbows on the table and pressed her manicured fingers to her forehead, just above her perfectly made up eyes. "You might think this sadness is related to my hair and the fire still, but it's not really. It's different sadness. You know, I go to church every Sunday. I sit in the front row so I won't be distracted. I watch the other people. I watch their kids. And I watch you. I listen to what you say, to the gospels you read, and to the messages you give. And, you know, no matter what you say, it all makes me sad." She leaned toward him now, hands folded on the table in front of her.

"It's like I'm missing something that everyone has and I'm jealous. I feel alone. And I shouldn't, you know. When you're part of a church family, you should care about people and they should care about you and it's not happening." She leaned back and waited a few seconds, then said, "It's like I don't fit in somehow."

Paul hadn't expected a troublesome congregation might be the topic of conversation tonight. Before he could regroup and come up with a comforting word or two, she continued. "And I'm not alone only at church. I feel alone everywhere, everywhere except at the baseball games when you're there. Then there is comfort, and friendship and sharing. And even so, you touch me in some way that makes me sad and I have to tell you that."

"Nicolette," Paul began.

"Niki," she interrupted.

"Niki, after all, you've only been here about 6 weeks. The flock is a little leery of people new to the fold. It didn't used to be this way. It's gotten worse and quite frankly, even I'm wondering what to do."

He'd noticed his congregants seemed to be friendly to families where the mother, the father, and the children all joined the congregation. They seemed to be friendly to single men who showed an interest in worship, but toward single women who wanted to join this Christian community, it was another story.

"Well, it's not very Christian. The reason for joining a church is to have some kind of community, isn't it? I don't want to feel on the outside."

"You know," Paul placed his hand on his forehead and leaned forward on the table. "There is also the Greg situation to consider."

"Oh." This wasn't a questioning remark, more an accepting remark—like she'd heard this one before.

'He's been part of us now for about two years and he's an active participant on council, in Sunday school, and in the singles group. People know him and they like him and some of them know the pain he had in your leaving. Perhaps you should give them time. Put yourself in their place."

"Oh, come on. I haven't done anything to any one of them except be friendly and interested." She stood abruptly and strode to the counter. "More coffee?"

He pushed his mug toward her. "Why did you choose this church anyway? Didn't you think it might be embarrassing for Greg and Hunter to have you show up here, a year or so after you suddenly left your husband for another man and broke off all contact with your son? Why did you even choose to come back?"

She turned and, still holding the coffee carafe, began in a measured voice. "While I was gone, all I thought about was being with Hunter again and if Greg told you I skipped out on Hunter, he's a lying bastard. I love Hunter and I missed him. It was Greg who drove me away from that marriage." She put the carafe back and turned to look out the window over the sink. "He wanted me to be his fantasy object, the beautiful wife with the porcelain skin and red hair, who had perfectly mixed cocktail ready when he got home and the perfectly planned meal ready and waiting in the oven.

He wanted to make perfect conversation about perfectly uncontroversial topics and make perfect love right at the end of a perfect evening at home with the family. God, I was suffocating." She collapsed into her chair.

"Besides. Even if it had been my fault, what about forgiveness?" she said."What about all those parables you use, all the prodigal sons and servants who disobey their masters and are still forgiven? Doesn't anyone listen to what you say except me?"

"People hear what they want to hear and—" Paul began but she interrupted.

"So try harder. Talk stronger. I don't care. Just get the message across that there is a sister here who needs their acceptance. A sister who is sad."

Paul felt all the anger, helplessness, whatever he had been fighting for months now, converge. Her words seemed to pull something all together for him.

"Let me tell you about sad," Paul said. He leaned forward. "I've used everything I've learned and know, and even resorted to trickery and manipulation to bring this Christian family together. Right now, I'm used up. I think there are others who feel like you do. I think sometimes they transfer to other churches but do they ever tell me why they are leaving? No, they add insult to injury and lie. They say it's closer or more convenient, and the powers that be at the church home office in Boston smile beneficently and fax me memos about beefing up the evangelism committee to get more communicants. No one gets how hard it is to try to make a team out of all these people. You think you're sad? You think you're tired? I've got news for you."

Nicolette stood up.

Paul leaned back in the chair and pushed the cup and its vines away. "Sorry. I'm supposed to be helping you with your sadness, not unleashing my own. I think I should leave." He made no move to get up.

"Forget my problems, Reverend. You need to relax." Nicolette said quietly. She put their cups in the sink and wiped off the table. Tossing the dishrag into the sink, she dried her hands and leaned up against the counter. She slid her hands into her pockets and asked, "How can I help you?"

That's it, thought Paul. I have to go. But in the long silence that followed her question, he saw himself at bat, poorly prepared, elbow low and weak, unable to focus on the pitch. The coach was hollering directions, his teammates yelling encouragement. "You can do it. Just hang in there." But he didn't want to any more. He wanted just to swing and see what would happen. At some point you had to swing and take the consequences. None of his history or training was any good now. As a pastoral counselor, he'd failed. As a minister, he'd given up. As a husband, he'd betrayed the trust. Now, he was the ball player he might have been, on the road, traveling town to town, finding the comfort of the moment with the woman of his fantasies.

"How can you help me?" he repeated. He stood up and went toward her, drawn by an invisible chord super-charged with heat. "This will help" he said. He kissed her deeply. When they could breathe, he murmured, "And this." Their kiss deepened even more.

"You know I've been waiting…" she started.

"Don't talk," Paul whispered.

They moved quickly, connected by their kiss and some shared rhythm, into the living room. She gently pushed him into the oversized recliner and crawled onto his lap. Their connection continued while she undid the buttons on his shirt and he unzipped her jeans.

He looked up at her, her hair hanging in her face, eyes closed. "Yes, and this," he said. And when they settled back into the soft upholstery, she gave a deep throaty laugh that ended when he covered her mouth with his. With his hands on her hips he guided her toward their mutual comfort, and closing his eyes he silently prayed. I just need this one moment. Then I— then everything—will be all right.

A prayer? A command? A promise? Paul didn't care.

Her knees fit perfectly on either side of him and he lifted her the small distance it took to make them both catch their breath with awe. "I want to be closer to you," she whispered huskily, rubbing against him.

"Not possible," he breathed.

"The bed," she moaned. He opened his eyes to see hers were still closed. Her head was back, hair tousled and her hands gripped the chair on either side of his shoulders. She began to slowly rock forward and slide backward, moving with increasing intensity, rocking both him and the chair. The chair heaved and rocked, moving across the floor until it lodged against the wall, banging and scraping with a desperate rhythm. The more noise it made, the louder she moaned.

And then for a moment, forgetting all others, they shared no more words, other than to cry out the name of the Heavenly Father again and again.

Paul lay in the chair trembling with his arms draped over the sides, his shirt open down the front. Nicolette, curled up on his lap, grabbed a green and white afghan to cover them.

"My God," she said as she stroked his chest. "Unbelievable." Nicolette snuggled closer.

"Um." She stood up and pulled the afghan around herself. "I'll be right back." She went into the bathroom and shut the door. Paul stood up and felt slightly dizzy. He used the chair for balance as he pulled on his slacks and buttoned his shirt.

The grandfather clock in the hallway sounded. Paul looked at his watch. Nine-thirty. It had only taken one half hour to unravel what it had taken him 20 years to construct. If he could turn back time to 8:55, put the coffee cup in the sink and say good-bye, he'd be pulling into the driveway now and Willie might be waiting to play his new video game with him. Susan might be waiting to cuddle up and watch a video, maybe even her favorite—"The Way We Were" with Barbra Streisand and Robert Redford. She might cry in anger and sadness when Redford's character left Streisand's for another woman with much less depth of character. She'd wipe her eyes and they'd go to bed. They would kiss goodnight. Perhaps some heat would develop and in the darkness of their room, lit only by the TV with the volume on high, they might please each other gently, nothing supercharged, no chord between them, but a feeling nevertheless that they had connected. Satisfied that they had, they'd fall asleep tangled together, not wrapped around each other in an overstuffed chair covered with a green and white afghan, one yawning, one guilty, one wondering how he would handle this one lapse, another possibly dreaming about the next. But it was 9:30 and passion spent, it was empty. For all his wondering and fantasizing, approaching and denying, desire had flared briefly—and for what.

He sat back down. He should go. He wanted the peace and quiet of his car, headed anywhere away from here. When he heard the toilet flush, he got up and went to the front door. The bathroom door opened and Nicolette came out in a dark green robe. She looked at the chair and not finding him, glanced around the room.

"I'm here," he said. He steeled himself against her look of confusion, against her sleepy tousled look, and against the softness of the robe, and held out one hand, keeping her away, protecting himself as he turned the doorknob.

"I've got to go," he said. He opened the door and stepped out into the hallway.

Chapter 19
Guilt

Paul sped away from the apartment complex. With thoughts racing, Paul assumed his automatic pilot would lead him to the church, his safe haven. The gnash of tires on the grit of the ballfield parking lot told him otherwise.

He looked at his watch as he got out of the car. It was 10:02. Just an hour later and all joy gone except possibly the joy of second base, where everything was easier. He walked in the darkness toward the baseball diamond.

The moon was obliging. Its soft light allowed the canvas bases to glow, three light squares in the dark field. Paul felt the cool night air all around him and smelled the spicy fragrance of the newly mowed grass. The infield track crunched under his feet. He moved toward second base—the prism through which all else usually became one stream of clear problem-solving thought; where he was in control and would know what to do. He put his foot on the bag. Then he crouched forward, ducking down in the dark for the imaginary ball, bobbing and weaving, dodging the sliding runner. He leaped for the overhead hop, tagged the base and mimicked an inning-winning throw to first base.

Paul sat on the bag, panting, cheers echoing in his head from that wonderful baseball year—that pivotal year of decision, a decision only slightly less momentous than the one he'd made an hour ago. He bowed his head.

Where was Your arm around my shoulder when I needed You? Where's Your warmth and comfort now? Help me please to know what to do. Free my mind. Forgive me. And let me know You do.

A teenage giggle and a low adolescent voice in the dark startled him out of his prayer.

"No one will see us. It's so dark out here," said the giggling voice.

"I can't see anything," the low voice agreed. "Where are you?"

"Over here." More giggling. Footsteps padding on the grass and shadows from the moonlight told Paul there were teenagers at play in the outfield. He didn't dare breathe. He quietly moved to a prone position, the canvas serving as a pillow for his head. The flatter the better, he thought. They'd have to go soon. He would just wait.

Except for rustling now, no sound. Paul rolled on his side toward the outfield, curious as to who would be creative enough to use his personal playground. He could see two shapes on their knees in a clinch, probably a passionate one, probably as Joe so glamorously put it, sucking face. He lay so still he could hear their breathing, heavy, heavier, and they fell to the ground, rolling over and over, farther away, closer to the center field wall, the farthest spot where a long homerun would disappear over the fading wood slats.

"Let's," breathed the giggly voice.

"Umm," groaned the other, "Do that again." More groaning, giggling, then "Ummm, Joey, you kiss real good."

The hair on Paul's neck stood straight up. It was all he could do to breathe.

No laughing now, no sound at all. Barely breathing, Paul heard Valerie say, "Here I have this. Do you know how to use it?"

The sound of tearing plastic.

"Where did you get that?" Joe said.

The snapping of latex. "Who cares? I have it. Do you?"

"Sure, but..."

And suddenly wings were flapping near Paul's head, faster and stronger than a bird. A bat. Swooping again. Paul leaped up, strangling a scream, and ran toward the dugout. He tripped on third base and went sprawling in the grit. Pieces of stone ground into his left elbow. The word "Damn" rolled off his tongue, resounding in the quiet as he crawled down the dugout stairs.

"Hey. Someone's here," Joe said.

"Come on," Valerie hissed, "let's go somewhere else."

Their shadows ran under the bleachers toward the street.

Paul sat on the bench in the dugout. He started to pick the stones out of his arm but it took too much energy. He put his head in his hands and wept.

Just a tiny display of life-energizing passion, that's all he'd wanted. The rush of joy that accompanies it. But you pay for passion, you always do. To feel alive you must owe someone. Comfort isn't passion. Comfort is not energizing or focused. It is stifling. Passion is what comes to you serendipitously at first, and then insidiously lets you know you've been missing it. That you have once had it and could have it again is a potent thought. But at a cost. You will owe.

He had to talk to Joe about danger, risk, right and wrong but mostly about the treachery of passion. A father and son should share these things, should help each other. He'd talk to Joe. He'd find a way to really talk to Joe. If he didn't, there was no hope for either of them.

The strength of his sobs frightened him. He wiped his eyes and tried to breathe deeply but his shoulders quivered still. He stood. The grass smelled nasty now and the field shone harsh in the moon's glare. His arm hurt. How could he tell Susan what he'd seen tonight?

He heard the flapping of wings, wings much smaller than an angel would have. The bat was back.

"Joe, it's after eleven. I thought you said you'd be home at ten or so." Susan looked up from her copy of "Vanity Fair."

"We were hanging around the ballpark."

"Who's we?" asked Susan.

"Just some of the gang."

"You look pale. Do you feel all right?"

"Just tired." He headed upstairs.

"I'll wait up for your father."

Where was Paul anyhow, Susan wondered. He couldn't be still at Nicolette's. She could call but that wouldn't look good. She would just wait a while longer.

Susan leafed absently through a few more pages. She thought how much fun it had been with Greg tonight, watching the older boys play baseball. She knew he had wonderful instincts for the game, great anticipation, and just the right touch to be coach. He was firm but fun, business-like in a playful way. The team loved him and she did like the way he paid attention to her, to her comfort, to her way of dressing, to her femininity, and admired her knowledge of the game. He recognized her need to be noticed and played to it. He genuinely liked her, and she him. No passion needed or intended. That kiss was just one kiss.

She wondered again what had gone wrong between Greg and Nicolette. Maybe just the passage of time. It could erode even the best of matches. Being a pastor's wife, she certainly had heard that often enough, from friends in the congregation and from Paul at the dinner table when the kids had left to play.

Look at her. Nearly 20 years ago a physical education teacher and the wife of a bright, energetic young pastor. Their union was strong and nurtured by common goals and enjoyments. Their shared agonizing over

Paul's choice of careers had come much earlier on—her choice for him would have been baseball and it had taken a while but she had understood his need to commit to a life where God was coach. On a sunny afternoon in their antique bed, they'd even laid out a baseball schematic for the church—coach, manager, front office, team, players, fans—and saw with delight that it worked, the one downside being that Paul couldn't play second base.

So why was he trying to now? Why was he hopping around the canvas bag trying to cover all the territory out there? That long ball to center field, the one he had always caught with confidence during his college ball days, wasn't fielded so accurately now that the fielders were church council members who didn't exactly have the arms to make that throw. They constantly threw short and Paul used to be able to compensate. But no more. He lacked the will and struggled for the energy. She could see it but was helpless to put in a substitute player. This was his game. The players, the front office, the fans were all too demanding. His family was left in the cheap seats to fend for themselves until the season was over. He definitely needed some new blood on his team. What about Greg? Under the circumstances maybe it was unrealistic to think that Greg could boost Paul's enthusiasm by sharing some of his. Maybe she should just pay more attention to Paul. She drifted off to sleep, propped on the couch, "Vanity Fair" falling to the floor near her feet.

Susan woke abruptly with the feeling that someone else was in the room. She looked at her watch. Midnight.

"Paul?" she called. No answer. She heard rustling in the kitchen and padded barefoot to see who was doing what.

"Joe, honey, what in heaven's name are you doing?"

"I'm hungry."

"You've got to get to bed. You have an early game tomorrow. You know what I've told you about getting overtired. Then there's the point at which you can't..."

"I was just hungry, okay? Besides, Dad woke me up just as I was drifting off."

"Dad's upstairs?"

"Yeah."

"Well, turn out the lights when you come up. And that will be soon, right?"

Joe nodded, mouth full.

"You still look pale." Susan left the comment behind as she went up the stairs.

Susan stood in the doorway watching Paul do his nightly routine. Change on the dresser in the ceramic plate shaped like a baseball that the kids had given him many Father's Days ago. Shirt and pants on the chair. Socks under it. Glasses on the nightstand. Fluffing up his pillow and flicking off the lamp. His deep sigh.

"Why didn't you wake me?" she said, turning the light back on.

"Huh?"

"I was sleeping on the couch, waiting up. Why so late?" She dropped her denim cutoffs to the floor and pulled her sweatshirt over her head. She folded both pieces neatly before she tried again.

"Tough night?"

Paul turned over on his back and brought one arm behind his head. "Tough week, all told."

"How'd it go with Nicolette?"

"She had some concerns."

"About what?"

"You know I can't say."

"She must have had a lot to say to keep you there so late."

"Wasn't there the whole time. Went to the ballpark for a while."

"Could've called."

"Sorry."

Susan crawled into bed and leaned over to turn off the light. "What's that on your arm?" She turned the lamp higher. "Paul. There are rocks in your arm and you were bleeding."

Paul propped himself up on his good elbow. "The infield in the dark tripped me up."

Susan called from the bathroom where she was rummaging for the first aid kit. "For the last time, why didn't you wake me up?"

"It's nothing."

Susan examined his arm. "There's all sand and dirt in this. It could get infected." She dabbed at it with a wet cloth. "Looks like you slid home."

"Ouch. What are you doing?"

"Alcohol."

"I'd rather drink it."

"I know," she laughed. "You can do that too. It's a free country." She finished cleaning his wound and turned out the lights.

"I missed you tonight, but I had a lot of time to think," Susan said, snuggling close to him. "Does your arm hurt too much to put it around me?" Paul stiffened. "Why are you so tense?" she said softly.

"Time to think about what?"

"Oh, your situation. Our situation."

"I'd rather not talk about situations right now, okay?"

"Maybe you'd rather not talk at all." Susan kissed his neck and began to play with the hairs on his chest.

In the dark, Paul winced. Wouldn't this just be the ultimate evil? Have sex with a fantasy woman turned real, and then what? Make love to your wife two hours later?

"Susie, I'm beat. Take a rain check?"

"You already owe me."

"I'll make good."

"Yeah, yeah." She moved to her own territory. "I get it, but you owe me big."

Long after Susan's silence turned into regular breathing, Paul lay awake, looking at the one glow-in-the-dark star stuck to their ceiling. Willie had stuck it there at Christmas time jumping on the bed in trampoline fashion, finally getting enough height to stick it on. Willie's reasons for doing that escaped Paul now but he had gotten used to it as a focus, for thought, for prayer, for getting to sleep. But tonight, the harder he tried, the less focused he felt. He got up and went into the bathroom, lit softly by the nightlight.

In the mirror, he saw himself years younger, wearing his college baseball uniform. His hair long and curling down his neck, dark black, not flecked with gray. His arms bulged beneath the tight-fitting sleeves and his hands were strong, his wrists quick. There was no tiny bit of flab underneath his arm. There was no ring on his left hand. There was that grin he hadn't seen in a long time, the grin that had been described by various people as contagious, sexy, rakish (that from Susan), condescending, menacing and deliberately misleading. Best of all, there was no guilt. Only the innocence of a young man on the verge of deciding what to do with the rest of his life.

Now as he continued to look, his shoulders began to slump, the weight of his 49 years and thousands of decisions upon them. The grin faded into the straight line of worried lips. His muscles felt heavy. He couldn't move. Now the image from the mirror became his father's: stern and unforgiving, no joy, only serious business, as serious as in his father's own 49th year when he had found his fantasy female behind the perfume counter.

And then there was Joe. Well, at least he knew about condoms. He was going too fast, growing too fast. It seemed that one day girls were yucky, the next day, fascinating. Information about them was to be shared only in moments of teenage euphoria; when they had articulated something about Joe that was extremely amazing or insightful or pertinent to his hair, eyes, physique. His brain was of no significant interest, way secondary to his smile.

I should do something, Paul thought. Say something. But what, and how? To whom? I should pray. But why should He listen. I'm undeserving and so messed up.

Chapter 20

The Morning After

After a night of no sleep, Paul jogged half-heartedly to the ballfield just before sunrise. The pleasure normally associated with pumping adrenaline was not there. Coffee sloshed in his covered cup. The sweetness of the first sip of the morning was gone. He stopped at the dugout, went down the step and sat down, placing his cup on the bench beside him. Sticking out from under the bench were several condoms, one still in the package. One used.

He thought about his own lack of protection the previous evening. A chill crept up his spine. What a Saturday this was going to be. Joe's game was at 9:30. Nicolette was sure to be there and probably Valerie as well, and Susan and Greg for certain. There were only three more weeks in the season, six more games to live through, then it could all be over unless Joe's team made the county finals. Susan would be around the house more. There would be fewer practices so he would have more time with Joe. He could focus on his family, the Word, the flock, his spirit. He would see less of Nicolette. Yes, things would be much better in three weeks. He could hang in that long. He dumped the dregs of his coffee and started home.

By the time he got there, everyone had left for the ballfield. He showered quickly, lathering with more care than usual, scrubbing harder to feel more clean. He didn't bother to shave. He then threw on khaki shorts and a black sweatshirt, stepped into his sandals and was in his car on the way to the park before he remembered the book he needed at church.

He hung a quick U-turn and cruised to the church. Cursing the parking lot once again for the pebbles, he reached for his key but when he pushed the door, it opened. He quickly glanced back at the side parking lot and saw Pam's car.

Now he heard the organ blaring, not truly holy music but some variation of a hymn infused with a subtle reggae beat. He stopped a moment to listen, spontaneously smiling for the first time in a week. Pam. He crept by the door to the sanctuary and took the stairs to his office two at a time. Where was that Updike book? Last time he had seen it, Pam held it in her hand, probably wondering what it had to do with their church, their conversation, or his congregation. He rooted under the pile of correspondence and ads in his basket, frowning at the quantity of paper he would soon have to push; frowning at the abuse he was going to have to take from Ellie for not pushing it fast enough. He glimpsed the book on the coffee table in his counseling corner and relaxed. He sifted through a few papers, in the back of his mind justifying those few moments, since on the field, it would be warmup time anyway.

Two more transfer requests, both young couples going to large inner city churches. Let 'em go. Another flyer about the October conference. He had to get his proposal ready soon. A note from Ellie asking for his monthly report—baptisms, funerals, weddings, hospital visits—all already known to her except his personal category, the indiscretions report. He needed to talk to Jim. He'd come back later to call.

Paul got up to leave, quietly closing the door and had nearly made it back past the sanctuary when he realized that the organ had stopped. He sprinted toward the door to try to avoid Pam when he heard her say, "Hey, this is for you." He turned around to see her extending a note that he would have been able to smell if he hadn't seen, so heavy was it with perfume.

"Who's it from?"

"Well, you can bet it's not from the church council president. It's not Henry's fragrance."

Paul laughed and thanked her. " You got that right. Sorry, but I'm on my way to..." he started to say, when he stopped, the reason for his inability to continue being Pam's bright red hair. He stuffed the note in the pocket of his shorts and sputtered, "Your hair."

"Something different," she said. She smiled sheepishly, casually puffing it up. She turned around to let him see the equally bright back. "I needed it."

Common decency and friendship dictated a favorable comment but all Paul could muster was, "It's so red."

"Yeah, I figured I might as well go all the way. When you need a change, why not go for a big one? Being dirty blond wasn't all that interesting and after what I've been through with Henry and his true love," she grimaced, "I deserve a treat."

She moved to peer at herself in the window to the outdoors. "Henry will just die when he sees this, I mean, not that it's gonna make him want me back but it just might make him think twice or remember what we had. Just give him a twinge. Besides, men have a thing for red hair." She paused. "Listen to me going on and on like this was a counseling session. I know you have to go." She stopped, her plump cheeks approaching the redness of her hair.

"It's sure interesting looking," Paul said.

"Do you like it?"

"What's not to like?"

"Is it more shocking or more pretty?"

"I'd say more pretty, I guess."

Pam puffed her hair again. "Thanks. It's strange, you know. It gives me a whole new look on things. I even feel like losing a few of these pounds I picked up during the past ugly year and a half."

"Wow," Paul said. "It's amazing that just a hair coloring could do that much."

"You'd be surprised. You guys just don't get what this female thing is all about."

"You don't need to say that twice," Paul replied so sharply that Pam took a step backward and frowned.

"Nice music in there," Paul said to change the subject. "For tomorrow?"

"Do you think the flock is ready for thinly disguised reggae?"

"Probably not. But still, do something different tomorrow, okay? Surprise me."

Pam chuckled. "I did that already."

Paul smiled again, always surprised and thankful at how easy it was with Pam, talking, joking, kidding. No judgment. Just comment.

"Time for some coffee? It's brewing."

"Sorry. I really did just come to grab a book. Baseball game revving up now."

"I'll lock up," Pam offered. "I've got a little more traditional practicing to do."

Paul picked his way across the lot, stopping once or twice to shake the stones from his sandals. Christ had worn sandals all over the Promised Land. How could He have concentrated on healing, teaching and making believers of so many when the pain under his feet must have been constant? Maybe that was it. He had gotten used to the constant pain and it had become a cost of doing business, of saving souls. Something ignored in the grand scheme of things. Or else He'd adapted; His feet calloused in survival adaptation so that the pebbles had no effect on the teaching of the greatest teacher of all.

Paul got in the car and felt the note crunch in his pocket. Actually he'd never not known it was there. It was burning like Willie's forehead in his middle-of-the-night fevers; burning like his wrist in the grasp of the imaginary ivy vine on Nicolette's coffee cups; burning like her lips when he first touched them with his. He took the note out and opened it.

"Great counseling last night. Hope for another session soon. Always, N."

He read it again. Had she been angry when he left? The note didn't show it. Maybe she understood. No, she obviously didn't if she thought this could ever happen again. Once, thought Paul, once was weakness, a temporary insanity. Twice, now that was with intent, inexcusable and betraying. Once Susan might be able to forgive; and he might be able to forgive himself. Twice, not a chance.

Paul heaved a sigh, started the engine, slipped the note in the glove compartment and pulled out of the lot.

Pam watched all this and went straight for the organ to play Beatles' tunes slightly off key.

On his way to the field, Paul wanted desperately to focus, focus on anything; but, Christ's sandals, Nicolette's note, Pam's hair, Susan's soft touch on his wounded arm, all swirled in his head. He closed his eyes for a second, squeezed them tightly closed. When he opened them, they were wet. Allergies, he convinced himself. Got to remember to take those pills.

At the ballpark, the usual Saturday morning madness had begun. Parents of players were at the snack bar, clamoring for coffee, any type, and any size. Their smaller children were hanging on their clothes already begging for bubble gum, the shredded kind in a pouch resembling the container tobacco comes in.

"Pastor," yelled Hunter. "What's up?"

Paul looked at the boy waving and running toward him. "Where's the rest of the team, pal?" Paul called back.

"In that dugout." Hunter whizzed right by him still talking. "Mrs. L. and Dad sent me for coffee, big coffee." He grinned, propping his eyes open with his fingers to show their level of fatigue. "Why is everyone so tired?"

"Someday, you'll understand. Is your mom here?"

"She's coming a little later. Said she had to look extra special good today."

Paul frowned.

"I don't get it either, Pastor. Women freak me out." Hunter grinned and pointed to Ashley, waiting on the bleachers.

So young and so wise. Paul had to smile. Then he saw Valerie next to her and glanced at Joey, certain he wasn't paying attention to the pregame pep talk the coaches usually doled out, but he appeared to be.

Paul sat behind the girls. He took a deep breath and closed his eyes. This is the way it should be. A Saturday morning with the sun shining in all its glory. The smell of coffee brewing in the snack bar awaited by people disheveled by the previous week, their pre-shower hair mussed by sleep, their water-splashed faces un-shaved or un-made up. Just people, fathers, mothers, grandparents watching the earnest and innocent efforts of youth guided by the more experienced efforts of middle age. And the kids might learn much today. It might be something about the team or the individual or fair play or betrayal—something that might influence their future. All the glories of baseball were Paul's at this moment. Every great play or strategic move or extra effort he'd ever made on the diamond rushed by on the backs of his eyelids. His youth, his high school years, college moments, religious epiphanies shot past and he relaxed for a few moments. It was almost like watching a televised ball game, or listening to his transistor radio on a lazy Saturday afternoon, laying on the bench, the breeze blowing the infield dust around him, at peace when the Red Sox had the lead, not so when another team would dare to exhibit better fielding, stronger batting, a better second baseman. He even heard his mother's voice interrupting this Saturday moment to strongly suggest he had chores to do.

"Paul." He opened his eyes. Nicolette was waving and pointing at the snack bar. "Want coffee?"

He shook his head and she proceeded on to the snack bar. He tried to rehearse a casual conversation he hoped they might have; the one he knew they couldn't have. There wasn't one casual thing about last night but he intended to pretend there was. That's what sitting behind the girls would help him do.

Greg was hitting balls to the fielders while Susan was hitting them to the basemen. Susan was great. Her true enjoyment of life shone best at this moment, Greg thought; smiling and hitting the ball to her players, in full control of each shot, ball placement good, her compact form excellent.

"Hey coach," Hunter yelled. "Dad! Quit watching the infield and pay attention out there. You're gonna get beaned."

Greg ripped his gaze from Susan to pay attention to his son. "Just checking Joey's reach off the bag."

"Yeah right," Hunter yelled back. "Here are the coffees for you and Mrs. L."

Paul watched this exchange yearning for a casual relationship with anyone.

"Hi," Nicolette stepped carefully up the bleachers balancing her paper cup of coffee. Paul nodded hello.

"You get my note?" she asked. Her fingers worked the plastic top on the Styrofoam cup.

Paul nodded again.

"I would've told you in person but you left so quickly."

"Nicolette, I..." He stopped, took a deep breath and started again. "We can't discuss this right now."

"There's nothing to discuss. That would mean talk about. Give and take, right?" They both stared intently at their children on the diamond. Then she said, "It was waiting to happen. We were both wondering. And now we know."

Paul turned to stare at her, willing her to be quiet lest the chatter of the teenagers in front of them was only pretend, that they were really listening to what Joey's father the minister was saying. His intention was not to respond and he didn't know where this came from but the words hurled forth. "I don't know anything."

He could see what he thought were recriminations welling up behind her deep green eyes.

"You know a helluva lot you don't let on," she snapped.

The game was beginning. Paul heard Susan calling to the kids. "Be sharp. Think. Breathe, guys. You hear me?" She held up her fingers in an OK sign. All the kids okayed back to her. She crouched down, leaning against the chain links of the fence, arms folded, eyes riveted on the activity to come.

"God, I hope we win this one," she muttered to Greg who had placed himself at her side with the clipboard. "They've worked so hard."

"They're ready, Susan. Now we just have to call the right plays."

"I just wish Hunter would try pitching again. He did so well last year." Susan talked more about strategy but Greg wasn't listening. He was watching Nicolette sitting on the bleachers next to the Reverend, who oddly, seemed to be ignoring her, if that was possible to do. Nicolette had that tense, pinched look Greg knew so well—the one that appeared when she was thwarted and losing hope of turning it around. What now, he wondered. What could have gotten to her now? She thought leaving him would let her have it all. Her freedom all the time, her son when she wanted him, Greg to be there whenever she needed him. It was too far away for Greg to hear anything but the delivery was bound to be terse and probably acrimonious. What would she have with Paul to move into true Nicolette mode? You don't treat your confessor and counselor like a lover who's scorned you unless he is and he has. No. Too many years of this. Too many. You're reading into things, Greg, he told himself. Focus. Focus. The game's the thing. Nicolette shouldn't interest you at all. You are over that. You are getting on with it. Didn't Paul say that letting go was the first step toward forgiveness?

His thoughts were abruptly brought back to the game when Susan poked him with the clipboard. "What do you want to do now?" she said.

"About what?" Greg sputtered.

"Dave's walked the first three batters. Bases are loaded and it's only the first inning. Stay with us here!"

"Let him work out of this." Greg said automatically, but the pitcher's shoulders were tight, hunched over in early defeat.

"Dave's gonna have to dig deep to pull this one out," Susan muttered, digging her hands into the pockets of her shorts.

"He'll do okay, Susan." He said this gently.

Her glance told him she'd heard this one before. "I say yank him."

"Let me talk to him," Greg said. He walked to the edge of the playing field and didn't even have to motion Dave to the field boundary. The boy was there way ahead of him.

"Whaddaya got, David?" Greg stood close to the boy, peering into his face. He wondered what psychology to use. Dave had good skills but they weren't on. How to turn them on. David just looked at Greg and shook his head. He tossed the ball up and it hit the edge of his glove and tumbled into the grass. It rolled to a stop at Greg's feet.

"That your curveball?"

David snickered, then grinned. "Slider," he said.

"No more of those, okay? Throw the heat, Dave. You can do it." He grabbed the boy's shoulder, gave it a little shake and patted his backside, sending him back to the mound. "And breathe," he called. Dave waved his hand and took his place on the mound, still grinning, standing up straighter. He took a deep breath and squared his shoulders.

Greg ambled back to Susan's side and turned to watch. Dave smoked it over the plate leaving the batter looking, then threw two more of the same. Greg gave him a thumbs up. David's imperceptible nod acknowledged Greg.

"What did you say to him?" Susan wanted to know. Greg smiled sheepishly and Susan grabbed his arm and shook it. "Give."

"Nothing special. Just appealed to his sense of humor. Got him to relax. Told him he could do it."

"Nice job. You're so good with the guys. Oooooh, will you look at this?" She jumped up and down hugging his arm and screaming. The other team had hit into a double play. Joe scooped the ball up, tagged second, then fired the ball to first a minisecond before the runner got there. The spectators were on their feet. Cheers from parents on Paul's side of the bleachers rang out, "Atta Boy!" "Great job!" "Now that's baseball."

Susan stood up and peered at the bleachers to catch Paul's eye. She wanted to share her pride but Paul wasn't standing up and cheering with the rest. He was sitting down and, she thought, deep in conversation with Nicolette. He was rubbing his hands through his hair like when he couldn't do the end of the sermon, when the words wouldn't come. Susan willed him to look her way for the wink, their secret sign of success but he didn't. Instead he seemed all of a sudden to realize the shouting around him meant something good and looked up in surprise. But he didn't look at her. He watched the kids run into the dugout, confusion on his face. Nicolette tugged at his arm for attention that he didn't give her. Now he looked at Susan for the sign but the moment was gone.

"What happened?" he asked the girls in front of him.

"Joey made this great double play," Valerie squealed. Pride played across her lightly freckled face. She scooped her hair behind her ears, craning her neck to catch Joey's eye, to be a part of his momentary greatness. But he wasn't looking. His teammates had surrounded him and were pounding him on the back and whooping for joy. Joe was cool in the glow of adulation. Paul thought he hopefully was learning from his previous successes that this one too would be fleeting, and not to take it too seriously as it's soon past. Dave's success at getting out of the inning had been surpassed by the glory of a scoop and a lucky toss. Paul hoped

154

Joe was learning about luck.

"Paul," Nicolette said, "Susan is waving at us." She stood up and waved. Susan waved absently back looking to make eye contact with Paul. He pretended to have something in his eye and rubbed at it, waving in her direction without looking there. He didn't want that intimate look, the one that said isn't-what-we-created-together-grand, right now.

Greg took advantage of the post-inning jubilation and confusion to jog down to the bleachers.

"How about those kids? Looked just like real baseball, didn't it? Too bad it could be a fluke. Just dumb luck on this 13th day of June. Hunter looked great, didn't he, Niki? He stretched out like a real first baseman."

Nicolette nodded and gushed with excitement for what she should have seen but didn't.

"And Joe," Greg continued. "He's making that play more often than not. He's found his niche at second base for sure." He waited exuberantly for Paul's response.

"All the kids looked great," Paul said.

"Yeah." Greg seemed deflated. "They did. Hey, gotta get back. Five innings left to go." He laughed dryly and jogged back.

"Let's go somewhere," Nicolette started to say but Paul shook his head.

"We have nothing to say," he whispered convincingly.

"I do," she said loudly.

"Later then."

"Fine." She turned her attention toward the field.

Chapter 21

The Week After

Jim. Emergency. Call me anywhere, any time. I'll talk.

Paul wondered if he should say more. He wondered until the answering machine beep told him there was no more chance.

Paul returned to the computer to resume pasting parts from previous sermons together, his message for tomorrow. He comforted himself that no one would notice. It was summer, after all. He cursed himself for not sticking to his normal routine of sermon creation.

"The church is a gathering place," he read on the screen, "a place where spirits are nurtured by human interaction coupled with spiritual...." He rubbed his eyes. Give it some distance, he reminded himself. He tried to focus on the words but every word he wrote or did took him right back to Friday night. Damn, where was Jim, anyway?

Maybe his mentor should be the one to call, the older, wiser, not having had these same trials as he and Jim. Had he ever had them? If so, how had he made it through? Too bad spotty Internet access here at church. There might be hundreds, thousands of ministers on line verbally cavorting through electronic media, baring their souls with aliases to protect them. Maybe he should talk to Pam. Or maybe he should just finish this damn sermon.

Susan finished cleaning up the kitchen after dinner and heard the clock in Paul's study chime 11 o'clock but she knew Paul wasn't there. She supposed he was at church, totally out of his sermon-writing routine, doing last-minute message preparation, pulling an all-nighter just like he had for his college deadlines. She thought after all this time he'd settled into a workable routine that took some pressure off this major weekly chore. She could see his anxiety increase as he pondered a subject and she

156

had noticed his displeasure when she asked about his progress. His relief was palpable when he had the idea. Once that came to him, the rest was a snap.

She folded her arms and leaned against the counter. They used to talk about what ailed them. But for the past month Paul had been so busy, much busier than a normal beginning of summer. So many people were sick and needy and out of whack. Baseball had always been a constant during the transition from school to vacation, from mild to hot weather, from harried to relaxed, from mom to coach, from pastor to, to what? Usually to baseball fan, a dad helping on the team when he could, an advisor for team politics, and a person who might offer a team prayer. This year Paul was someone who kept his distance from their games so as not to get too involved, too deeply into the effort and the psyche and all those things he'd once loved about the game. He'd had a passion for it almost the way they'd had a passion for one another. Now it was all controlled, his days by the needs of many others, her days by practices and games, his evenings seemingly avoiding family contact.

If she weren't married to a minister, she might consider going to one for counseling. He'd never go and she wouldn't love it. Maybe she should call someone. Jim or Bill Wilhelm. They might be helpful. They might talk to her.

She dialed Jim's phone number. She sighed as the answering machine kicked in and when it was time left her message. "Jim, this is Susan. Emergency. Call me during the day."

There, an unretractable message, a step in at least some direction.

Chapter 22

Calling All Sinners

"Pam, can you meet me at church this afternoon?" Paul asked.

"Hang on, let me think. Henry has the kids and I was going to exercise but I can come over later. How's 4 o'clock?"

"That would be just fine. And thanks," Paul hung up just as he heard her say "What's up?"

A positive step. Forward progress. Pam would help him out of this. Only four more hours until some relief. Four hours to kill. Or to fill. Writing next week's message to get a sermon ahead would make the hours fly by and he'd have to be focused. Calling Jim wouldn't take long but he'd have much to think about after that contact. Spending time with the boys would be fun. Being at home with Susan wouldn't. It was either the sermon or Jim.

On the fifth ring the answering machine would kick in and Paul was frantically searching his mind for an appropriate message, his second in two days without response from Jim. Then he heard a voice. "Hey. Reverend Jim here."

"It's about time you religious types answered your calls," Paul said. His teasing was forced and he knew it.

"Paul," Jim exclaimed. "Isn't always getting back to everyone the eleventh commandment?"

"Could be."

"So, what's up? I just got in and I usually don't find messages from both the Lombards in one day."

"Susan called you?"

"Yeah and you both used the word emergency. I'm wondering what you both wanted to tell me about individually that we couldn't talk about together over pizza and beer."

"You'd be surprised, Jim," Paul said softly. "You'd really be surprised."

"Now, my friend, you know I try to maintain an element of intellectual flexibility so that not much surprises me. I really don't like the way I look when I'm surprised. You know my eyes get big and the wrinkles in my growing forehead stand out. It's just ugliness unbefitting a pastor." Jim stopped, waiting for Paul to joke back. When he didn't, Jim continued. "I'll shut up now. Tell me what is so surprising."

Paul could see him playing impatiently with his ponytail, twisting the end with the hand that always held the cigarette, always flirting with pyrotechnic disaster.

"Am I on your speaker phone?" Paul dodged for a minute.

"Yeah."

"Take me off."

A click on the line. "Done."

"I've done something I shouldn't have." Paul began.

"Wait," Jim cut in. "Shouldn't have as a regular person or shouldn't have as a pastor?"

"Either."

"Okay." It was a questioning prod to continue.

"Don't interrupt me now," Paul continued impatiently. "This is hard."

It was a moment frozen in time. Paul saw himself as he must look, sitting at his desk, hair rumpled, unshaven, wrinkled and anxious, pale and penitent. He saw Jim, turtle-necked, khaki pants neatly pressed and hair smoothly pulled back, the air around him fragrant with cologne and cigarettes, his forehead furrowed with concern, his mouth already opening for an off-the-cuff retort.

"No off-the-cuff retorts, Jim. I need thoughtful advice."

"Okay." It was still a question.

"I've," Paul hesitated. "I've been with another woman." He rushed on. "It just happened, that's all. I was overwhelmed by the desire to do it and I did. It felt good for those 20 or so minutes. Such fire and want. Great heat. Newness. Release. Energy. And now I feel like shit or hell. I don't know what to do." He ended this breathless, his heart pounding, waiting.

"Wow." Jim breathed a long slow breath.

Paul couldn't say anything more. The ticking of the clock was so loud, the birds"chirping so piercing, the shouts of the children playing so strident. His own breathing so unbearably loud.

"When?" Jim finally said.

"Last Friday."

"Does she mean anything to you?"

"No," Paul said emphatically, then softened his voice. "No. She doesn't. But the package was attractive."

Paul went quickly through it for Jim, his fantasies, Nicolette's magical appearance, Susan's good-natured invitation to the picnic, the fire, the need for pastoral home visits and support, Nicolette's general neediness.

"What about your neediness?" Jim countered. "It does take two."

"I didn't think I needed anything." Paul wondered if he was telling the truth... "I didn't plan anything. It just happened."

"We've had this conversation before. We both know that nothing just happens."

"Why did you ask if she means anything to me?"

"Because that's a crucial first question to answer for yourself before you can begin to forgive." His voice was cool, defining parameters for the following discussion. Jim had moved into pastor mode.

160

"I don't need your counselor persona here," Paul said. "I need a friend, not a critic."

"You didn't call because you need a friend right now. You needed to unload this and decide what to do with the guilt. Then forgiveness."

"Forgiveness," Paul repeated. "I should know the answer to this but for whom?"

He sensed Jim struggling to keep his voice calm.

"If you have to ask that question, you're in more trouble than we both think. Paul, this isn't like you at all. You're OOC."

"OOC?"

"Out of control. You sound like me, not like you."

"That's why I figured you could help me. What would you do? What **did** you do? When you were here last, we had that long conversation about the baseball gloves, remember? You said you thought Joanie knew you were trying a new one."

"Yeah?"

"So, what's happening with you?"

"No. No. We're talking about you now."

"No. NO. Don't you see? Help me out here. Maybe I can learn from your experience. I know I can. You can help me."

"What I would say to a parishioner is just what I said to you. First, figure out the meaning in this. Then decide what to do with the guilt. One bit of advice I can give you from experience is that you can't pray this away. No matter what we've been taught or what we teach about forgiveness, this kind of thing goes too deep."

"That's not comforting."

""Have you tried praying about it? Well, have you?" Jim repeated when Paul didn't answer.

"I can't. I tried but I can't find the words."

"That's because you've got to deal with it first," Jim said. Paul imagined him twirling his ponytail furiously, searching for the right words, frustrated that they didn't seem to be there.

"If you're going to give me the party line on this, I can do without your help," Paul said, his voice measured. "That I already know."

"You obviously don't."

"What?"

"If you did, you'd know I'm right. You have to deal with the guilt. You have to."

"There's just too much for too many reasons. It's easier to keep it in, to myself, and I could until now. This guilt is big. All the little guilts disappear by comparison. They were all to do with me, my lack of involvement or energy or interest. They were not to do with my family, with Susan."

"Ah. There it is."

Paul felt hot, a warm tingle creeping from toe to head, a huge embarrassment. He should feel like saying "sorry." Instead he wanted to joke it away, a simple error in judgment, getting too far off the base, getting picked off. Like no big deal. It could happen to anyone.

"This could happen to anyone," he muttered. "At least five of my parishioners have gone through this type of thing."

"But you're not just anyone," Jim began, then paused. "What did you tell them to do?"

"It depended on the person and what they told me. One guy I told to examine his heart and ask God to show him what was right. One I told to see a shrink. Another I suggested should tell his wife and take it on the chin."

"That's three."

"This gets better. The fourth guy is Greg, the ex-husband of the woman I was with. His situation was different. He was heartsick because

162

she left him. I'm watching him try to cope; especially now that she's back in town." He paused. "Actually, now I think he's coping by making a play for Susan."

"Wow," Jim said. "We'll get back to that. Are either of them parishioners?"

"Both."

"What? A 'B' movie plot unfolding before my eyes." Jim could not hide his incredulity.

"That's helpful," said Paul tightly.

"Sorry. Okay. Let's ask ourselves how you got to this point."

"First, let me tell you what I told him," Paul paused trying to remember exactly how he had put it to Greg. "She had really roughed him up emotionally. I told him if he could forgive her in spite of everything, he would find peace and a new beginning. Sounds like drivel now but it sounded like just the thing then. I believed it." Paul sighed ruefully.

"I guess we have to start at the bottom line. Will this happen again?"

"No."

"You're sure."

"Yes."

"Fine. I believe that the decision to say no helps you find a way to say it and stick with it. It's the first step out of the spiral of despair. I know I sound like Dante but this is something I've been thinking about, for myself as well. You know the next step."

"Help me. I can't think of it. All I can think of is Susan and Joe and Willie and my parents and my friends and supporters and how I've let them, you, all down. Help me." Paul put his head in his hands.

"Paul, for God's sake. Hold it together. You can do this," Jim said softly. "We can do this. The next step is honesty. With yourself and with

Susan. Admittedly it's the hardest step but you can't skip it."

"I don't even know where to start." Paul said, laying his head on the desk, eyes squeezed tightly closed.

"I'm coming down there. Just need to make a few arrangements. I can be there tomorrow afternoon." Paul knew Jim was pacing back and forth, long strides like he was leading disciples to a huge gathering on the hilltop.

"You have responsibilities."

"I'll be there."

"Meet me at the church." Paul breathed, his voice a husky whisper.

"Got it. I'll be there." The line went dead.

Hold it together. You can do this. Just reach over and put the phone in the cradle. Click. Just get up and open the window to let the stifling dead air escape and new breath begin. Just reach for the yellow pad and just begin to make some notes for next weekend's message.

Paul sat up straight, took a deep breath and stood up. He took three steps and ripped open the window. He yanked a yellow pad from under his pile of correspondence and jerked open the desk drawer to get a pen.

"Let he who is without sin cast the first stone," he muttered. "And let him throw it really hard."

The phone rang 4 separate times before Paul put a word to paper. Each time he felt on the verge of starting, the ring would cut through his thoughts and he'd wait until the answering machine kicked in after the third ring. Who would be calling the church on a Saturday afternoon? Susan, he thought, she's probably wondering where the hell I am. Could be Jim having changed his mind. Could be Nicolette, a call best not taken. The fourth ring could have been a wrong number.

The ringing had distracted his thinking. Does confession come before forgiveness? How do you ask someone to forgive? In his career, he'd told hundreds of parishioners hundreds of ways. But did they work?

Were there any outcome measures? He's told parents to forgive children and children parents. He'd told husbands to forgive wives and wives husbands, employees to forgive supervisors, and neighbors to forgive irritating neighbors. He always helped reveal the way and moved on to the next pastoral duty. He used to give brief thanks to God for his successes but even that sharing of credit had been lost in too many committee meetings, too much paperwork, too many demands by the congregation, too much shirking of family duty.

How would you tell someone you loved that, during a blip in time, you lost all sanity and succumbed to your basest urge? And that's truly what had happened. Forget all the lead up, the tantalizing reality, the ongoing harmless fantasy, all the arrows pointing to a neon sign flashing trouble. You really had no control. Do you have to forgive yourself, before you can ask others to forgive you?

Paul realized he was writing furiously, his thoughts covering page after page of yellow lined emptiness; filled now with his reasons for every perceived failure leading up to this biggest failing of all.

He looked up only when he heard the church front door.

"Pam," he called.

"No, me," Susan answered.

He heard her trudge up the three steps, and continue down the narrow corridor to his office. He had only a few seconds to catch his breath, to try to stop his heart from racing, to try to act normal.

"So you **are** here," she said.

"Sermon time," he shrugged his shoulders and held up the scribble covered yellow pad.

"I figured. Got an idea?"

Paul leaned back in the chair. "I've got a bunch. I had to sort them out."

"Don't let me keep you from it." Susan wandered around the office using the tips of her fingers to wipe dust from the bookcase, straightening the books stacked high on top of it.

"I've got to get back home before the kids get out of control. But I need to ask you something," she said.

Paul saw spots before his eyes and felt light-headed. "Shoot," he replied.

"Where were you this morning? I thought you had a personal pact to miss no games."

"I was there."

"There where?"

"Up high on your right opposite first base. Same place I always sit. Sat behind Valerie and Ashley. Talk about chatter." He smiled, he hoped not grimly.

"I know you were physically there, but every time I looked up there, you weren't into the game."

"Nicolette needed to talk."

"Didn't she say everything she had to say Friday night?"

"She has a lot of problems."

"We both noticed you two didn't seem to be paying much attention to the kids."

"We both?"

"Come on, you know." Susan said. Her voice was impatient now. "Greg's worried about her. Said she's been acting strangely the past few days. Did you notice anything?"

"No."

"He think she's troubled." It was a question.

166

"Susan, you know I require people to ask me for help themselves. I just can't pop in on people's lives. We pastors don't intrude unless we're asked to help."

"That doesn't help Greg." Susan stood with her back to him staring out the window.

"Maybe Greg should talk with me himself, without using you as a go-between."

"No one is using me. I just want to help out. Christian charity if you remember what that is."

"You just want to fix it."

"What if I do? If it helps."

"Helps who?"

"Helps them." She paused. "Helps them figure the next step. You know, he says they never went for marital counseling. She just split as you recall. Maybe counseling would help them more clearly see the path ahead for their relationship, for Hunter. Maybe you could get it started."

Paul focused his gaze on his hands, flat on the desk in front of him. "It's not my call."

"It **is** your call. Isn't that what ministers do, minister to the needy? And you've done it before. Why can't you do it for these two? For God's sake, Greg's like a puppy following his owner and occasionally licking a kindly hand that reaches down to pet him before turning and following her around again. And he doesn't deserve that."

"Whose kindly hand?"

"Mine," she blurted out then quickly added, "Everyone's."

"Not mine," Paul said, lifting his gaze to Susa's face, shaded by the brim on her baseball cap. "Certainly not mine"

Susan was pale under her mid-summer tan, he could see it. There was another reason for her being here, saying this.

"Just do me a favor, okay?" Susan said. She sat down in the chair across from his desk. Paul waited.

"Aren't you going to ask me what favor?"

"You'll tell me."

"I want you to be honest with yourself and with me. I think in your own way you're as troubled as Nicolette. Greg and I are at the end of our ropes as to what to do with you two."

"I told you. I've been telling you. I have things to work out.'"

"Not good enough. I can't wait around like this. I need to move ahead. I need for our lives to be like they were. For our story to continue. You need to stay with me. It's taking too much energy to drag you along."

"I'm working it out, I am doing better. I've taken a step. In fact, Jim's on his way here right now."

"He called?"

"No, I called him."

"So did I."

"He told me."

"I want some time with him."

"We'll work something out."

'We'd better."

"We'd better what?" Paul felt his temperature rising.

"Work something out."

"It would help if you'd quit the snide comments. Just come out and say it."

"Unbelievable." Susan made eye contact for the first time. She was on her turf. "You just don't get it. I've been saying it and saying it and you've missed it again and again."

"So tell me," he continued. "You know, your style is going to drive me to something someday."

"Oh really. I wonder if it already hasn't."

The final "t" echoed in his office and found its way along with the rest of their words out into the long hallway and into the narthex where a visitor sat on the pale pine bench.

"Could I get back to my sermon now? We can talk at home."

"Fine." She left his office. He knew she was standing in the outer office. Fuming? Crying? Making plans to fix this too, or deciding to leave him. And he wasn't even sure she knew the worst.

"Will you be home in time for supper?" she asked with the voice she reserved for her very coolest interactions.

"I don't think so."

He heard her start down the three steps. She mumbled something additional as she went out the door. Something like, "Maybe this will help." Or was it "I'm sick of always talking later."

Paul looked at the yellow pad. The last two words he had written were "fair play."

Chapter 23

The Worst That Could Happen

Paul looked at his watch. Three-fifty p.m. Maybe 10 more minutes until Pam arrived. He tried to relax. With Susan's aura and Nicolette's name hanging in the air, relaxing was not possible in his office now. He heard the church doors open.

He got up and crossed the narrow hallway to the larger church lobby and moved toward the church doors. He was sure he'd heard the doors but Pam wasn't inside.

"Anyone here?" he called loudly. "Pam?" Hearing no answer, he went inside, sat down on the altar steps and did not look at the stained glass window where he knew the Good Shepherd was gazing calmly down at him and all that was happening. He put his head in his hands and just waited.

He was still sitting that way a few minutes later when Pam blew in, her usual canvas bag bulging with choir director and maternal paraphernalia. A *Sesame Street* book slipped to the floor and she sighed deeply before bending over with considerable effort to pick it up. Paul didn't even try to help her. He was too busy breathing deeply, joyfully and comfortably for the first time in many hours. He was waiting for Pam's comforting words to make everything all right. She would understand and gently reach out. She would know what to do. All the intellectual bullshit he was throwing at this would be displaced by the logical reactions and decisive solutions that Pam would bring.

"Hey. I'm early so I thought I'd drop this music off in here first. Why are you sitting in here?" she stopped. "Don't we usually talk in your office?"

"Things aren't as usual."

"Oh. Is this a conversation I'm going to want to have? Oh my, you're not quitting, are you?"

Paul put his hands over his face as he shook his head. "I just need your advice. Pretend I'm the penitent and you're the confessor. Just give me a minute."

"We've done this before, haven't we?" she said, anxiously, wondering at his actions. "Only you haven't put it in just those words."

"I guess we have, "Paul said.

"Okay. So why don't you start." It was a get-on-with-it, no-nonsense statement.

Just what he would expect of Pam, to find a way to lead him.

"This is really hard to say. Don't feel badly if you think less of me when I'm done. I don't want to make this your problem. I just need advice."

"Okay," she said quietly. She sat down beside him on the altar steps, smoothed her denim dress, and began fiddling with the top button. "Shoot."

"This isn't easy so I won't pull any punches. It's about Nicolette."

He thought he heard Pam gasp softly so he stopped, waiting for her to say something. But she didn't.

"Something happened that shouldn't have. I mean something dire that is just making me crazy. I don't know why or how but..."

"Oh God," Pam said. She put her head in her hands. "Sex?"

Paul nodded. "How did you know?" he said.

"Your actions. Her actions. So transparent. God, Paul. I don't believe you did this." Pam spat out the words and stood up. She began pacing in front of the altar steps, back and forth, her face flushed.

"Really stupid," she said emphatically. Paul was surprised by the anger in her voice.

"I've saved you from a lot, you know," she said sarcastically. "I've been your friend and protector. I've made excuses for you. I've defended you. I've fixed things with people who had issues with you. But guess what? I can't fix this. I won't." She began to cry.

Paul was looking at the shadow her pacing cast across his feet, listening with increasing alarm.

He stood up and moved toward her. "Pam. It meant nothing. You can believe me or not. I don't know what happened."

"Don't do it. Don't do it." She stepped back and held out her hands, holding him off. "Why did you have to tell me this? Why me? Good old Pam." She hesitated, thinking. "Oh. Oh. Susan doesn't know. You haven't told her. And you wonder if you should, or how you should, don't you?" She wiped the tears with her hands.

Paul looked directly at her. "Yes."

"Oh sure." She laughed bitterly. "Avoiding consequences is your specialty but this time you need help. Well, I don't know what to tell you. I can barely stand to hear this. How do you suppose your **wife**," she hurled the word at him, "your **wife** will take it? And here I was all upset because I thought Susan was looking outside your marriage, going to cheat on you, on you, with Greg. This is so bizarre. You must have known this couple was trouble; even I knew it from the start. Who would be unlucky enough to burn their hair at your house if they didn't intend to? Who would be lucky enough to be so needy after that you had to make home visits, visits encouraged by her ex-husband when all he wanted was to get her so interested in you that he could go after your wife without you knowing. What a team. Oh, poor Greg, so bereft of his fancy wife's love, that he makes moves on yours while he's going to you for counseling. Well, there's only misery here, folks. And none of it is Christian."

She was out of breath from pacing and ranting. She stopped, chest heaving and stared up at the stained glass Christ at the back of the church. Tears of frustration and pain rolled down her face.

Paul sat on the steps to the altar. He followed her gaze, expecting fully to see a frown on the face of the Good Shepherd. The shepherd was

172

still smiling even though He shouldn't be. Paul felt His face should be contorted in sheer contempt for Paul's stepping from the path. But His eyes picking up the late afternoon sun glittered in welcome, His face serene still, His staff still leading the flock of sheep around him, keeping them from danger. Not letting them stray from the safety of His influence. Not even one of them.

"It looks so easy, doesn't it?" Pam said. "The lambs follow him without question and you've got to ask yourself why." She had calmed down considerably, taking deep breaths and focusing on the window. "I know what my answer is. They've had no reason to question. They trust Him to be there and they've seen the gentle way He prods them back into the fold. He lets them know He's forgiven them for leaving the path, and they believe as long as they stay with Him they will be all right."

She picked up her bag. "I've gotta go."

She rooted in her purse for a tissue and wiped her face, then blew her nose.

"I don't know what to tell you." She moved down the aisle toward the double doors.

"I know."

The glass doors closed behind her and all was quiet. So quiet it was grating. Paul longed for some sound—music, conversation, laughter, anything. What had caused Pam, after all the confidences they'd shared, to lay into him like that? He felt physical pain in the back of his neck from her frustration and disgust. And if he could live the last ten minutes over again, what would he have said differently? What could he have done differently?

Paul closed his eyes to help himself think. Maybe he could live with this. If Jim could just help him deal with the guilt and he should be able to, given what he'd been through himself. If Pam could keep quiet, and she would. If Nicolette would be reasonable. This was risky and a true variable. If he could throw himself with renewed vigor into his ministry, that would make up for a lot. It could be done. Paul wondered briefly if he was thinking rationally. No, it could be done.

Then something dark, a shape, moved between his closed eyes and the late afternoon sun in the darkening room. Something, a presence, stopped in front of him. He felt someone was there. He slowly opened his eyes, and it was Joe, face red and damp, eyes glaring, shoulders heaving, breathing shallow, fists clenched.

Paul stood up quickly, reaching for his son. "How long have you ..." Paul started to say.

"Long enough." Joe stepped back. "I gotta get out of here." He turned and with the largest strides Paul had ever seen, was gone before Paul could blurt out the words he'd been trying to find for it seemed like an eternity. "I'm sorry." He whispered the words again and again and when he stopped they echoed still.

Chapter 24

Joe and Valerie

"There's some lasagna in the oven," Susan called from the living room, as Paul straggled exhausted through the kitchen door at around 7:30 p.m.

"Did Jim call?" he asked. His throat felt tight.

"He did. He got delayed. He'll get here tomorrow, but later. I told him he could stay with us as usual."

Paul sighed and went to the cabinet for a plate. "Where are the guys?"

"Willie is in your den playing computer games. Joe didn't come home for dinner, but he called and said he was going to Valerie's. Said he'd be back around 9."

"I'll pick him up." Paul grabbed some silverware.

"Said he'd walk. He was in kind of a strange mood, more so than normal."

"It's a long way through the park."

"Paul, he's a hulking big guy. It's only four blocks. Give him some space."

"It would give me a chance to spend some time with him. At least a little."

Susan peeked her head in the kitchen, "Whatever. By the way, there's wine on the counter. I needed something."

"I'll leave shortly. I'm actually going to try to eat my dinner in a leisurely fashion without interruptions, I hope."

"Want company?" Susan waited with her hand on the cellar

doorknob.

"I'm okay." Paul opened the oven, took out the pan and grabbed a foil-wrapped chunk of garlic bread as well.

"Be that way." Susan clattered down the cellar stairs, to get the laundry or to be alone.

Paul stared at his food, then at the clock, then his food, then the door, then the clock, then his food, and then the bottle of wine. Then at Joe's baseball cap on the doorknob. It was all too much. He got up and poured himself a generous glass.

The lasagna was good. Spicy and moist. It felt sustaining, an energy-giving nutrient. He wondered what made it feel that way? Couldn't be the pasta and tomatoes and cheese separately. Each separate, they were easily bought and stored in closets and refrigerators, waiting for the right moment to be melded together. Then they were prepared and layered carefully, individual items blending together to create a new whole, a oneness that usually tasted something like the previous attempt but could also be unpredictably different based on the quantities of ingredients selected and mixed by the creator. But it always worked out.

Paul finished dinner and sat back, contemplating the wine as he swirled it in the glass. Maybe that magic ingredient was the love, the nurturing brought to it by the cook, the creator. This is what people do for each other. They offer love in so many ways and isn't it too bad that the most seductive way to men is the way of the flesh, not the many other ways, of heart, mind, of stomach. A bite of the bread took Paul's thoughts back to the first communion altar rail where, armed with knowledge of with all its rich history and symbolism, he had first tasted the bread and wine. His eyes had met the eyes of the minister and he'd wanted more. And now he remembered Joe, much younger, kneeling at the rail, meeting Paul's eyes with his, oh so wide, oh so innocent, waiting for his first gift of communion.

Paul chomped down on the crisp bread. There was definitely a sermon in this, a lesson in this. The phone rang, signifying the end of his dinner.

Paul hung up the phone, having learned that the youth group had forgotten to bake bread for tomorrow's communion. One more thing.

It was 8:45 p.m. Paul slid his dishes onto the counter and started toward the door. He glanced back at the white counter, pristine except for his dirty dishes. He wheeled around and grabbed them, opening the dishwasher, holding the door with his foot and sliding the dishes into the appropriate dishwasher slots. He let the door slam while he snatched the dishrag and made a quick swipe of the white surface. Cleaned up and taken care of just like a second baseman should.

He got in the car and headed in the direction of Joe as he had so many nights before. Picking up his son was a time when he would look forward to a few minutes alone with him. Tonight's few moments would be critical. What would he do if this were another man's son and he was the helping pastor? No hope in thinking that way. There was no detachment here. His heart started to pound as he pulled into Valerie's driveway. He honked the horn. A few more honks yielded no Joe. Irritated, Paul pushed open the car door and strode up the stairs. He rang the bell, pacing on the stone stoop.

"Reverend." It was Valerie's mother. "Come on in." She patted her hair. "Sorry about the sweatshirt here. It's just that I'm in relaxation mode." She looked behind him. "What's up?"

"I'm just here to pick up Joe," Paul said.

"The kids aren't here. They said they were going to your house to play video games and that you would bring Valerie home." Her voice rose, questioning.

"The version we got was that Joe was walking home from your house at 9 so I came to get him." He stood helpless at the door, breathing harder and harder, his breaths shorter and shorter.

"Well, I wonder where they are?" she said, her voice not hiding her concern.

"Where do they normally go?" Paul realized he was clueless about Joe's whereabouts if he wasn't at the ballfield.

"Amy's house. The schoolyard. The recreation center. The ballfield."

"I don't think we need to panic," Paul offered, inwardly racing ahead to all those places. "You call around and I'll drive around and check back in about half an hour okay? They probably just went for a walk or got sidetracked by friends."

"That's a plan," she said, smiling weakly. "I wouldn't worry except that Valerie is always good about telling me where she is."

Paul slammed his car in reverse. It was just after dusk, always an eerie time when things could happen. Things that had been on hold all day came clattering out from everywhere. It was always the time when, at home, arguments began, kids got anxious about school, people called with bad news, you remembered you had something important to do tomorrow and you were not prepared. It is darkness that hides what by day is comfortable, and relegates all that you know into shadow and uncertainty and worst of all doubt. Remembering the dugout and its condom collection and the night of the dive-bombing bat, Paul discounted the schoolyard and rec center and headed directly for the ballfield.

To cut the headlights or not to cut the headlights. Not. He wasn't going to lurk this time. He screeched to a halt in the dirt lot, the car sliding a bit on some stones. He flung open the door and approached the field in a dead run, yelling, "Joey. Joe. You out there?" The pounding of his feet and his heart roared in his ears. He stopped to listen, his breathing so heavy he finally had to hold his breath to hear. Nothing but crickets and other sounds of night. "Joe. Valerie. We're worried about you. You here?" Then, "Let's talk." Paul winced having said the minister-father words no teenager would consider responding to. Then, "I know you're here somewhere." Then, "Valerie, your mom's really worried." Nothing still. Could he be wrong? Would Joe not be genetically steered toward the ballfield in times of crisis? Then where would he go? Certainly not the church.

Paul waited a moment longer, panting and pacing, the coolness of the now complete darkness unable to calm him. Okay then, the church. He stumbled toward the car and with his hand on the door, looked over the top of the car one more time. He saw two shadows approaching, arms around each other, glued together as the hip. Emotions played across Paul's face in the dark: relief, anger, then guilt. Words would be critical now; saying the right thing a necessity.

"Thank God you're here." He moved around the car toward them, to greet them with a touch, but they stopped, wanting to touch only each other.

In the darkness lit by a single security light on the field and indirectly by his headlights, Paul could see Joey wrap his arm protectively around Valerie's waist, pulling her closer, uniting them against him.

"We didn't know what to think when you weren't where you said, Joe."

"Why think anything?" came the tough response.

"Valerie's mother's worried. Hop in and I'll drive you home."

"We'll walk," Joe said.

"Come on, get in. It'll be faster."

"You go ahead, Mr. Lombard. We'll meet you there." Valerie said, not looking at him.

Paul didn't move, wondering whether to force the issue. He felt vulnerable and powerless.

"We'll be there," Joe sneered. "We don't sneak around behind people's backs and lie. Like some guys do. We'll be there. Trust me."

Paul got in the car and pulled away, going slowly and weighing Joe's choice of words. Sneak. Lie. Trust. Incongruent and so apropos. The stakes were elevated now.

Valerie's mother was relieved at Paul's call saying that the kids were

179

on their way. Paul could tell she would have preferred it if they would get out of the car when he pulled up; if they had been eight years old and hopping happily out of the back seat, just home from a classmate's birthday party. She had changed into a scooped neck T-shirt and asked if he wanted some coffee or soda.

"No thanks. I'll wait out here," Paul said, unable to bear her concern another minute.

A few minutes in the car alone. He didn't want to be alone anymore. His head was too full, the noise was too great, the effort to cut it out unsuccessful. He flipped the radio to his favorite contemporary jazz station and leaned his head back to try to relax, not daring to close his eyes, afraid he'd miss his son's return.

The two approached the front door, still attached at the hip. By the porch light on the stoop, they turned to face each other, then Joe, looking to make sure Paul was in the car, bent down to kiss her, something he'd never done in front of his father. The kiss was innocent at first. Then Joe pulled Valerie to him, his hands rubbing her back, his mouth hard on hers, taking for a long moment her sweetness and innocence away. They did this expertly, Paul thought sadly, not fumblingly as he had at that same age begun to find his sexual self. His hands squeezed the steering wheel and he felt anger welling up at this flaunting.

They lingered for another moment, then Valerie's mother opened the door, grabbed her by the arm and hauled her inside, Valerie yowling with pain and surprise.

Joe shuffled toward the driver's side of the car. "I'll walk," he said.

"Get in," Paul snapped. When Joe turned away, he barked "Now, Goddamn it!"

The boy turned, not surprised at his father's words, but by their intensity, and got in the car. He didn't look at Paul but his face was set.

"Thanks. Thanks a lot," Paul said.

Joe said nothing.

"I've been worrying about you for hours," Paul said.

Joe looked out the window.

"This isn't easy," Paul began.

Joe shifted his weight and opened the window. "Can we get going?" he asked.

Paul realized he hadn't started the car yet.

"We need to talk." Paul turned back toward the ballfield and Joe moved as far away as he could from his father.

"I'm tired."

"You'll live."

"Mom will be worried."

"She'll live too."

"Yeah. Like you care." Joe threw the words across the front seat.

Paul felt the pressure rising again, the roaring in his ears unbearable.

"I care very much. That's why we've got to talk."

For the first time since that afternoon, Joe looked directly at his father and said, "You just don't want me to tell her."

"I just want you to understand..." Paul said.

"I can't and I won't." Joe bit out the words and hit the car door with all his strength. Then he hit it again.

"You must feel really..." Paul started again.

As they passed by the ballfields again, Joe , his voice cracking, said, " I've got to get out of here. I can't..." he opened the car door even though it was still moving. Paul slammed on the brakes and Joe hopped out and ran. Paul pulled the car over and with more agility than he remembered having in years, leaped out of the car and chased after his son. Joe was fast but not as clever as Paul and he was running more with anger than purpose. Paul

181

quickly gave up the direct chase and tried to appreciate where Joe might be headed. Under the bleachers maybe. No. Behind the concession stand. No. To the outfield where it was the darkest. Where he could hide from what Paul might say and from his own feelings.

Paul looked toward the darkest part of the field, let his eyes acclimate and listened for crying, anger, panting, any clue. If he could only touch Joe and murmur the same words of comfort that once worked so well, that had brought them so close that for many years, a single wink from either of them could comfort the other. But it was too dark to see a wink here. Paul ran the periphery of the field, allowing the warning track to guide him.

He knew he was close when neither of them could conceal their gasping for air.

"Joe, I'm here," Paul wheezed. "Hear me out." He struggled to hold his breath so he could make out Joe's exact whereabouts.

"Just leave me alone," Joe hollered. Paul thought he could hear it throughout the suburb. "Can't," Paul whispered. He fell down on the wet grass as close as he dared. "Have to talk to you."

"I can't breathe the same air as you," Joe spat out. Paul said nothing.

"I don't know what to do or what this means or who to tell," Joe croaked in a low voice. He was close to tears.

Don't do anything. It means nothing. Tell no one, Paul wanted to scream so the whole suburb would hear, so he would believe this would work.

"I know you're confused," he said instead. "I am too. I don't know what to do or who to tell either. Or what this means," he added. "But I do know I'll never do it again. It was just a moment, son, Joe. When I wasn't myself. You know I've been having some moments like that lately. I'm tapped out," he continued. "Everyone just needs too much of me." Paul immediately regretted saying this. "Not you guys. Not you, Willie or Mom. You can never need me too much. I'll always be there. It's all the

182

others who are always needing and I don't have enough left to give." He stopped.

"So what did Hunter's mom need?" came the question meant to shock. Paul said nothing.

"What did you need then?" Joe asked. "Did you need to hurt Mom? What did she do to make you go nuts?"

"You don't understand."

"Tonight, all I could think of was you and Mrs. Stone together." He swallowed back a sob. I was pissed and Valerie suggested we go for a walk and we did and we ended up here and before we knew it we were doing it. It was like I wanted her to make the pain go away, and to belong to me forever was the only way." A few sobs escaped and he swallowed a few times and covered his mouth so Paul would not hear.

This was a confession Paul felt he should be making, not hearing from his son.

Paul felt adrift. Sadness, anger, deceit. Tears streamed down his face.

Dear God, Paul prayed, let me not be inadequate at this moment, so important. Let me find the honest words to comfort my son and help us both out of this huge mess. Please forgive me for where I have taken us all. And let me know You do.

And, on this clear dark night, lightning lit up the field. Paul and Joe's tear-stained faces jerked toward the light and goosebumps began at the top of Paul's head and moved to the tips of his toes. All the things he had known to be true about faith and had discarded and forgotten over the past several months were clear again. This is what it is like, he remembered. This is what it's like.

He moved closer to Joe and put his arm around the boy's shoulders and his son did not move away. "I'm here just like always," Paul whispered. And he wished for a moment that Joe would snuggle in, like when he was younger, fitting himself in Paul's protective arms, safe from all of it. But he knew that wouldn't happen. Just letting his father put his arm there was enough, Paul sensed, as much of a connection as Joe could have right now. For now it was enough.

Chapter 25

The After Sermon

Rain, thunder and lightning ushered in Sunday morning. Paul tossed and turned for a few minutes and then sat straight up in bed, his head filled with the happenings of the previous evening, the rain on the ball field, the lightning and Joe. Sensing an instant headache in the works, Paul turned off the alarm 45 minutes early and stumbled down the stairs for coffee.

"You're up early," Susan murmured quietly. The newspaper rustled a little as she turned the page nonchalantly. "You and Joe came back pretty late." She looked up from the paper. "I thought you were just going to pick him up at Valerie's."

"I did, but then we went to the ballfield to talk. Father-son stuff." Paul tried to capture some of her nonchalance, to keep it surrounding him.

"Oh," Susan said. "Anything I should know about?"

"No. Just father-son stuff."

"Um hum," she replied. "Well, on another topic, your sermon this morning, is it worth going to hear considering the elements I'd have to brave?" She looked out the window at the teeming rain.

"Don't ask."

"That bad?"

"No. It's just that you've heard it before only on several different Sundays."

"Oh, Paul. You're cutting and pasting?"

He said nothing.

"Maybe I'll go anyway. The boys should go. They haven't been since, well, since baseball started and we allowed the powers that be to schedule Sunday morning practices."

"Just let them sleep in today," Paul said.

"This, coming from you?"

"They don't listen to me at home. Why should the pulpit make a difference?"

"That's an over-statement. You know they're good guys. Now Hunter. There's a challenge. Nicolette, and Greg too, really have their hands full."

Paul thought she looked sideways at him when she'd mentioned Nicolette. It occurred to him she might be waiting for a reaction.

"What now?" he said. "Hunter seems okay to me. More good-humored than most teenagers, our own included."

"If you kept your ears to the ground and your hand on the community pulse you'd know that he's been hanging out with Ashley 'til all hours. Nicolette says he's been very sullen and won't talk to her when she talks to him about his late nights. They used to share everything and now nothing. Sound familiar? So now she says she just wants to stand by and be there for him if he needs her."

"I'm not so sure just being there is enough," Paul muttered.

"That's one way to handle it, I guess," Susan said. "What would you do? We may be facing this, you know."

"I guess I would hope and pray all that's gone before, including values and life lessons and parental lectures, weren't somehow overrun by rampaging hormones. Think that will work?"

"Praying is good. Is that what they taught you at Pastor school?

"Isn't the coffee done yet?" Paul asked.

She got up to get the coffee pot and began to pour. "What do they teach about teens?"

"Nothing special. I always thought baseball was good instruction for

186

what kids need at this age. Mental discipline. Physical activity. Camaraderie. Lots of time spent practicing to keep them from other pursuits."

They stood close together at the counter, arms rubbing, the small hairs on their arms touching. Paul felt the softness of her skin. It was a comfortable connection, a companionable action, one borne of familiarity, not of excitement. A creeping sadness filled Paul as she poured the coffee. His right eye began to tear.

"Stop. Stop. Enough." he said too loudly. The coffee stopped at three-quarters full. He wiped the tear away. To Susan's surprised expression, he responded "Allergies. Gotta take a shower. Remember, I'm the one guy here who doesn't have the luxury of being a heathen."

Paul arrived at the ballpark late, after church, and tried to get into the game. With Nicolette nearby, it was as hard as getting started on a sermon. The boys weren't as energetic as they should be. There were a few feeble attempts made but it was near noon and the hot dead calm of the June day and the humidity after the rain sapped the energy of players and onlookers alike. Except for Susan.

"Throw strikes," Susan hollered at the pitcher. The boy looked her way, looked at the runner on first, looked at the batter, wound up and threw the ball in the dirt, a yard or more in front of the plate. The catcher dove to save it.

"Way to go," Paul yelled. The boy had done a great job of keeping the ball in front of him, something every catcher should do. If the ball gets behind you, you don't know where to look.

He looked around the crowd of parents dotting the bleachers. How many of them kept the ball in front of them. Kept their lives in play. How many of them had never made a mistake. Paul fidgeted in his seat, and got up intending to go to the concession stand. Instead he ducked under the bleachers and leaned his forehead against one of the metal supports.

After a time, he turned and leaned his back against the metal and slid to the ground. As the cheers, moans and crowd comments floated above him, he was reminded of the old radio in their garage where he and his father had sat and pretended to fix broken lamps, mixers and other household items whose time had seemingly come. This was all an excuse to listen to the Red Sox games. They'd poke, prod, unscrew and retighten every nut and bolt while the Sox announcers hurled names and feats their way making every player, for a moment, the best first baseman, shortstop or batter in the game.

His father would wax poetic. "That's the life, isn't it, son? To have a job playing the game you love. It must not even feel like going to work. Then to be the best at it...you must anticipate with joy every day rising and going to a field covered with grass and God's good earth where the possibilities are endless for success or failure and it's only your effort that makes the difference."

His dad had fiddled with a lamp socket. "Well," he smiled, "I guess add a little luck to that."

Then there had been the day that Paul had told his father, right there in the garage that he was answering the call. His father had used the tuner a little longer than necessary to lock in the Sox game and taken a deep breath. "I hope you made the right choice, Paul." Then he had smiled. "Choosing between God and baseball can't be easy."

You don' t even know, Dad, Paul remembered thinking. Even now Dad, you don't even know.

The hard edge of the metal supports were gouging into his back. There's something about you, Paul thought. You are everything I can't have. I don't want comfort but I have it. I want joy and it eludes me. I want passion but it's obscured by the everyday. I live for its brief moments and now they pass so quickly I might miss them. Nothing wells up in me. The adrenalin of a double play always sustained me. The chance that the ball might come to me and I might make the tag and wing the ball to the first baseman who waits with faith in the skill of my well-honed abilities. Who has faith in me now? The boys. My mother. Maybe Niki. Perhaps Greg.

188

I can count them on one hand and I'm not one of them. Would they have faith if I were on second base? He stayed there until the game was over, sitting on the dirt, his back against the support, half the time eyes closed, the other half looking up at the calves of people seated on the wooden slats above him.

"Good game, Joe." Paul heard Susan's voice outside the bleachers. "Where's your father? He was here, wasn't he?"

"He was here, but I don't know where he went."

"Just can't keep track of that guy, can we?" Susan said. Paul heard the irritation.

"You don't have to say that twice," Joe said, kicking dirt ahead of him as he walked.

"What's with you today?" Susan asked.

When Joe didn't answer, she said "Well, let's get going. He's got his own car. He's a big boy." She called for Willie.

"Drop me at Valerie's after I take a shower," Joe said. It was a command.

"What are you guys going to do?"

"Just trust us to hang out at her pool.

"Will her parents be home?

"Yes," Joe answered sarcastically. "They always are."

"Just checking. Let's go, Willie," she called one more time.

"Coming, Jeez." Willie flipped Joe's hat off and ran zigzagging toward the car.

Through the bleacher slats, Paul saw them head home. His family.

It was quiet on the field, just stragglers left over from the game. Indecision pinned Paul to the pole. He raised his head and straight ahead and through the bleached slats he saw Nicolette, her arm around Hunter chatting as though she had no concern other than his performance in the game. What had she gotten from that night? Paul wondered. What had she wanted? What did she want now? She'd tempted him for nearly a month, being in his face at every opportunity, needing him after her accident. And hadn't he been there before with members of his congregation who had done just that. But he'd risen above it, said no to it and felt stronger because of it. Temptations were a part of life, he told his flock , an everyday presence that gave life meaning as you triumphed over them. What was so different here? She'd seemed like a gift. He'd thought about her and there she was peering down at him, awakening him from his second base snooze and from his complacent acceptance of life as he knew it.

He stood up and again leaned his head on the pole, both hands balled into fists. He softly grazed the steel with his right hand. It was warm, even hot from the noon sun. He struck it again, intentionally this time. It made a quiet clang. Not quite a churchbell. He whacked it again; harder this time. A jab of pain shot through his wrist. His pounding became rhythmical, the pain constant, the clanging louder, he closed his eyes against it all. He added his left hand and tried to see only the void—not the faces of Susan and the kids, not Nicolette's long slender neck, not the friendly face of Jim, nor the stern countenance of Bill Wilhelm, not the face of the Son of God. Finally it hurt too much. His fists stung and his knuckles were raw. He stopped, breathing heavily, and tightened his eyes. For a moment all was green like the softest grass on the infield, then bright when the sun comes in your eyes when you're in the infield waiting for the play to happen. Then gray like you would see shading your eyes with your glove against the brightness. Then red like Pam's new hair color.

He went to church instead of home where Susan would be waiting for some explanation.

He heard the organ before he got in the building, an unusually loud rendition of a popular Beatles' tune from the past. "Speaking words of wisdom, let it be."

Instead of going to the office, he slipped in the church doors and sat in the back pew. Pam was lost in the tune. She was hitting the keys heavily and stomping on the pedals. She stopped for a minute, started over and started singing and continued on until she saw Paul. She stopped playing and singing.

"Did you like it?" she called out to him. Her words echoed in the empty room.

"Yes. That song says everything. Is that practicing for Sunday?"

"No. I just felt like hearing it, so I played it. It's always pertinent, it seems. Let it go. Give it up to God. You know. Those things you say to people."

Paul closed his eyes and shook his head. "Easier to say than do."

"I hope you'll get there. I still have some faith in you. You need to find a way to let all this go so you and Susan can carry on."

This hopelessness is overwhelming, Paul thought. I have to find a way to regain hope enough for us.

Chapter 26

Susan Works On It

When he finally got home, Susan was swinging in the hammock on the deck, looking at the dark sky, searching for any twinkle of starlight. There was none. Paul slid the door to one side, stepped out and closed it tight, even though the house could use the cool evening ventilation. He sat on the deck steps, leaning against the wooden slats, pressing a cool beer bottle to his forehead. "Want one?" he asked, remembering too late. The tiny light by the sliding door let him see Susan shake her head.

"Where's Joey?" she said.

"His room."

"He'll be down for food soon enough."

"Maybe."

"Willie still in the study?"

"No. He's in his room too."

"Ah." Susan made a little sound, the satisfied sound she made when everything was as it should be, everyone was in his appropriate place for the night. "And here we are," she said. "I think we're waiting to talk."

"We're talking."

"Not about the real topic. Not about what's bothering you. And maybe once again we won't even talk about that," Susan said. She sighed and looked over at Paul. "Okay. Go," she said.

Paul still had the beer on his forehead, had not yet taken even one sip. He felt so tired, fatigue settling in his rounded shoulders, in the tightness of his neck, even in the dryness of his throat.

"There's something I have to tell you," he said. "It's not easy to say and it's not easy to hear. But you have to know."

"Do I have to know? Or do you have to tell me?"

"No games tonight, Susan. I can't handle it."

"Tell me. Do you just want me to know something or do you have to tell me personally?"

"Stop it."

"No." She sat up, swirled around and dangled her legs over the side of the hammock. "Because I already know what you're going to tell me."

Paul thought he was staying incredibly calm. His heart was not racing, he was not short of breath. Just tired.

"What am I going to say then?"

"You're going to tell me about Nicolette."

"What about her?" he said cautiously.

"Oh come on." Susan snapped. She stood up and began to pace, shoving deck furniture here and there to create a path for her pacing. "Pam told me."

Paul felt some undeniable energy surge. His shoulders straightened and the knots in his neck disappeared. Pam. Making it easy for him. The telling would have been the worst, now he could focus on the explanation. He wanted to be both penitent and apologetic. He'd use the explanation he would create on the spot, the way his best sermons often happened. He'd use the shared blame theory of marital infidelity, the one he'd heard so often from parishioners that he'd come to believe in it himself. He almost would have done it if he hadn't, in the tiny light from the deck, when she turned around to pace by him, seen the tears on her cheeks. She was hugging herself tightly and pacing with vigorous strides, aggressively and wanting to seem in control.

"Did Pam also tell you it meant nothing?" He waited.

"You know," Susan said starting slowly, "I've had some time to think. I remember there's something that happened the year my father coached my brothers' Little League team. It's part of our family story, but part of just Mom's and Dad's too. He always wanted my brothers to do their best and sometimes he didn't think they were. He'd get really mad and yell and it would get worse. He would blame them for the whole team's mistakes and even though I was 10, I swore I'd never do that." She stopped for a minute, then continued. "I started to take that kind of reaction for granted. We all knew he loved us but it was hard to remember when he was ranting and raving about the missed play at second or the poor pitching performance of my brother Tad. Then one day, as he was yelling, he stopped suddenly. God, I still remember that day. It was an evening game, we'd skipped dinner because it was too soon after his work. He still had his suit pants on and his team hat, although my mom was holding his jacket and tie. We were walking to the car and he didn't even wait until we were in it to start his harangue. Tad and Billy's eyes had already glazed over. I wanted desperately to cover my ears but I knew that would make things worse. Then I saw him look at Mom and I looked too. She had this helpless look on her face and she was crying. I think only Dad and I saw. I ran and grabbed her hand. My Dad followed me and gently took his clothes from her arm. He had the softest expression I'd ever seen on his face, so relaxed, like she'd given him permission to back off and he was thanking her. Then her face got determined, like it did when she wanted us to do something and would not hear a 'no' and she said the most spiritual or whatever thing I'd ever heard her say or have heard her say to this day. She said 'We should breathe forgiveness with every breath.' And she didn't say it in a nasty way or a criticizing way, rather a comforting way. And even my brothers stopped walking and looked at her and then at Dad like they'd heard something they should understand but didn't. And at age 10 I was awed by the power in those words. And I think my father was too, because I never again heard him rant and rave at my brothers or at anyone else, at least over baseball. And he coached for many years after that. He just took a breath and eased into the next situation. We could see him do it. And I think he always thanked her for that." Her voice broke and she stopped right in front of Paul and bent forward, like she was reacting to a punch in the stomach.

And Paul saw her tears, and he saw himself walking beside her, gently taking her burden away. Making it his, as it should be. And straining to hear her whisper the words about forgiveness that had made her family stronger.

"I've tried breathing those breaths a lot lately as I watched you turn inside yourself and shut me out and only hint at the problems you carry alone. I've used every bit of hope I've had that things would turn around … that we could turn things around. I've forgiven you for a lot but about this, I don't know."

"About you and Greg. Pam seems to think…" Paul said slowly.

Susan had started pacing again but at this, she whirled around in anger. "I don't care what Pam thinks, and No. No. I can't believe you would bring that up. There is no parallel. One kiss vs. sex is not even worth comparing. And I've already told you about that and about the nothing that it meant. I wouldn't go there. I really wouldn't.

What made me madder than anything was that I warned you about her and you just weren't hearing it from me, the person most likely to tell you the truth.

She continued, "You know, you use religious words to comfort and explain to your flock. Those words of comfort are there for everyone else. Why not for me? Find some for me. You must have the words to fix this. Just say the right thing." She gulped back a sob. "You know that sermon you gave at the start of the season, the one with the chest in it where you had everyone mesmerized into seeing what was in theirs? I never told you what was in mine. But it was full, full of forgiveness. It was overflowing and I couldn't even close it. And you know why?" Susan was crying now, hard.

Paul wanted to reach and touch her but how could he help someone he had punched in the stomach? How could he help her breathe?

"Because somehow I knew I had to have enough for you. Because you couldn't forgive anyone. Not the congregation for needing you too much. Not me for stepping in to coach when you couldn't. Not Jim for his almost girlfriend—yes I knew about that. Not us for letting our 20 years slip into comfort. Not us for losing interest in our story. Not Greg for his misguided interest in me. Not the kids for needing you less and less. Not yourself for anything. And God help me, I think it's used up. I think I don't have any left. And just when I need it the most. So I guess this is by way of asking you to help me."

Paul barely heard her. All her pain he felt without hearing the words. He was in his sermon, taking himself back to that beach, to that clearing. He could hear the shovel hitting the sand. He could feel the pressure on his shoulders and the strain on his forearms as he heaved heavier and heavier shovels of sand behind him, digging furiously to get to the bottom of the mystery, to hear the clunk of the shovel hitting the chest. There it was. A dull thud and the feverish scraping away of sand and dirt. The chest. It was smaller than he remembered and harder to open. It was light and he was afraid to open it. He shook it and something rattled around the inside. Relief. At least now there was something. He lifted the top and pulled out the cross his father had given him, the one that he had given to Joe for confirmation. Instead of gold, it was a deep blue glowing in the late afternoon sun.

This was the color of remorse, so strong he reached out to touch it, and in touching it, accepted it. He reached for it like it might be the comfort of the sun on his back or the freedom of wind in his hair. If he could only describe this, to offer it to all people, everyone should have it. There would be no more sorrow, just joy and faith and light. Problems would vanish. Sins were forgiven. Forgiven. The blue was forgiveness.

"But you'll help me," Paul said to the Man in White who had appeared next to hole in the sand.

"Yes," the Man said.

"You really will."

The Man nodded and stretched His arm around Paul. "Let's walk and talk," He said.

And, in his thoughts, they seemed to walk for a long time, even though all this only took a few seconds, just long enough for Susan to use her T-shirt sleeve as a tissue and compose herself. She looked at him.

"Forgive me," Paul said, the words reverberating through his chest and throat like a bodily earthquake. "I know you're wondering what she had for me that you didn't. The answer is not a thing. I love YOU. She was just an interruption in our story. Just a flash in the darkness that kept me from all I care about. It lit up for a moment but it was without comfort. It left purple dots before my eyes and a heaviness in my chest. Just the newness attracted me but it was old as soon as it happened. I knew I had committed an irrevocable act. I'd done something it would take much effort to even come to terms with much less undo. Susan, I've let us drift apart. It's me. It's been my doing. But I know I want us together like we were, a unit, a team, parents, lovers, friends. I want our story. Please. Whatever it takes. I'm sorry. Forgive me."

Susan turned and stared out over the back yard. "And you think what you want is enough."

"Tell me what **you** want, then. Tell me. What do you want to know? What do you want me to do?"

"Nothing. No. Everything. No, wait. I don't want to know. I want to understand.

But most of all, I want to be alone right now." She sunk onto the chaise and covered her face with her hands. "Right now," she repeated as though she could still hear Paul breathing, undecided as to what to do, where to go.

Paul was not satisfied. This was no solution. Not even the beginning of a solution. No closure. No forgiveness and he had asked for it. He had used the words, and they had not worked. She needed time. And he knew in his heart he was penitent. Remorse had filled him, welled up in him like an epiphany with alternating warmth and coldness. Forgiveness had come to him on that ballfield with Joe, in that lightning strike, like an undeserved but welcome gift, and he would keep it and use it and, as with all great gifts, share it. No one could ever have enough of it, nor did they know it when they had it. But oh, when it appeared, it was a strange energy, strong enough to fix everything. To survive burnout. To shepherd a congregation of midlife crises and mediocre financial contributions. To withstand the emergency and non-emergency calls during dinner and all other family and private times when you were trying to be a father, a husband, a lover, a friend. To counsel your own son from his despair. To beg your own wife's forgiveness. To continue your story together.

Paul struggled with the sliding glass door into the dimly lit kitchen and walked through the downstairs into his study. He felt wired, like he could tap into the computer network and make it sizzle and snap and do his bidding. He walked into the dark room and did not flick the light switch. The answering machine light was blinking and it was not friendly. Willie had left the computer on and the screen saver showed a celestial void that every few moments filled with tiny white lights, totally filling the screen before they abruptly disappeared only to create the galaxy from scratch once more, and then once more and then again.

The digital display on the machine indicated four messages. Paul gingerly pushed the answering machine button. He listened for the rewind, holding his breath so he wouldn't miss any of the messages awaiting his attention.

"Hi Reverend. This is Greg. I need to talk to you right away. It's about Niki." He left his and her phone numbers. The next message was from Pam. "Paul, Pam here. If you can forgive me, call."

The third message was from Jim. "Hey Paul. Just checking in. Joanie is ready to drop everything and come down there with me on a moment's

198

notice, my friend. If you want her to come, call me, or I will come alone. In fact, call anyway."

The last message was from Amy Sundstrom. Her father had broken his hip and was having surgery in the morning. She just wanted him to know. But it was more than that. Her voice, throat dry with concern, quivering with emotion, quietly cried out for him, for his presence. He would be there with her. He knew he could help and he would with his voice, his thoughts, their shared prayers. He'd call her but not tonight. He would tell Susan that Greg called, but not tonight. He would forgive Pam and call Jim but not tonight.

This strange energy was familiar. It brought youth and hope. While all around him now seemed despair, he had faith he could make it better. He could fervently try. He wished he could give some to Susan, still pacing on the deck and battling the demons he'd shown her by rearranging the furniture with a heave here and a tilt there. He had enough of the strange energy to take the next step.

———————

Joe's door was closed. Paul could hear the videogame through the thick oak. It signaled Joe's need to be alone. When in his room, he could focus on things he had learned to control with practice, practice, practice and great thumb dexterity and hand-eye coordination. Depending on the game, he could kill and maim and dribble and tackle and pitch and hit with the best of them, all through the power of continuously advancing technology.

Paul knocked. No answer. He knocked again and heard the game pause.

"Yeah?" Joe's voice sounded raspy.

"Can I come in?" Paul asked, then immediately regretted asking.

"No."

Paul felt the heat rise in his face. Damn. "I'm coming in." Paul threw open the door and crossed the threshold into his son's haven.

"Jeez." Joe turned the game back on and the beeping and buzzing was thick in the air between them.

Paul sat on the bed with Joe, not talking, feigning the same interest in the game that Joe probably was. Monsters kicking, boxing, ripping each other in two, blood gushing from torn flesh midst hacking sounds of bone-crushing kicks.

After five long minutes of this, Paul could stand no more, the tension too great, the desire for healing so powerful. But the way to begin so elusive.

"I talked to your mother," Paul offered up during a lull, hoping Joe would pause the game. It continued. "She's upset as you would expect." Still nothing. "She and I have a lot to talk about. A lot to do." The beeping and ripping intensified. Paul realized with a jolt that he needed to say this in terms related to Joe's self-centered teen age universe.

"We'll all be okay. Don't worry. We can get through this."

Joe threw the control pad on the bed and pulled his T-shirt up over his face. "Just leave me alone."

"I can't. I love you. I need to help you carry this load."

"You gave me this load."

"You can give it back."

"Yeah, right." Joe's voice was tight.

"Don't give it to me then. Give it to ..." Paul was going to say "God," but Joe broke in with "Oh, don't even start with that minister stuff."

"Joey. Joe. We've always stuck together you and me and that won't change. I've been there for you and now I need for you to be there for me. I'm sorry, son. I made a mistake and I have to make it up to everyone. I'm asking you, what will it take for you to forgive me?"

"I don't know."

"Think about it. Please."

Joe got up and walked to the door where he bumped into Willie, face white, eyes wide. "Dad, Mom's out on the deck throwing furniture around and crying." His 10 year-old senses assessed the situation. "Joe, what did you do now?"

Willie's fists were clenched and he was ready to do battle. No answer from Joe. "Something's going on."

"Come on, Willie." Paul put his hands on the boy's shoulders. "I have to tell you something."

Chapter 27

Just the Guys

On Sunday, Paul awoke to daylight flickering across his face through the mini blinds. He rolled over to see if Susan was up, then remembered just as he had every day for more than a month now. No Susan. She was probably snuggled on the sleep sofa at her mother's, taking up the whole queen size space, hair tousled with the exercise of sleeping. Was she sleeping well? Eating? He couldn't tell by the answering machine messages she left, instructions on what to do for Joe and Willie, dentist, physicals, prep for starting school next month.

Her parting words had been zingers. She'd said that he hadn't talked to her about anything important for so long why should he start now. Then she'd rolled up the cab window and ridden away into the noon sun to the airport, flying to her mother. He had learned she meant it by picking up the phone when she called and having her hang up. He had learned to listen to her voice on the machine and do her bidding with no discussion. Willie had actually designed a sign that said "doghouse" and hung it with masking tape over the door to Paul's study, and if it weren't that the dog on the sign had a tiny tear in its eye, an outsider might not even know that Willie cared that his mom was spending the rest of the summer with grandma.

Paul rolled over again and used a forearm over his face to block everything out and took a few minutes to review the day. Church. Lunch. Read the paper. Ball game at 3, a playoff with Arkport, a tough suburban competitor. The culmination of weeks of schedule juggling so he could co-coach with Greg the rest of the season—the only thing that Susan would let him do to help her as she planned her escape. Co-coaching with Greg was nothing if not awkward. Then dinner. Then homework help. Then laundry, then relaxation. Same Sunday routine since she'd left that Sunday morning. But now it was never routine. There was adjustment after adjustment to make and Paul always fell 5 to 30 minutes behind in everything.

"Dad," Willie called. "It's time." He croaked, his young voice heavy with sleep, trying to pull Paul along.

"I'm up."

"There's no milk." Willie yelled upstairs, rustling the cereal box.

"I'll get some on my way back from the park." Paul hopped out of bed and threw on his running clothes. He couldn't wait to get out and run, and breathe. He loped down the stairs to the kitchen where Willie had his travel cup full of coffee sitting on the counter by the garage door.

Paul ruffled the boy's hair. "Thanks, Will. Be back in a few. Get Joe moving, huh?"

"Aw, Dad. Why me?" Willie whined, then stopped, sobered by the answer to his question. There was no one else. "He doesn't listen to me. It won't work."

"You can do it." Paul took a big gulp of caffeine and left. Guilty now about leaving Willie to deal with Joe, about not remembering the milk, about lots of little things so they could obscure the large cloud that followed him and threatened to engulf the boys if he wasn't always careful, always vigilant.

He couldn't run as fast or as long. Too many thoughts dragged him down and cut into his runner's concentration. He was relieved to see the Fast-Go store, but once again his morning run had solved no problems. The mist on the baseball field obscured solutions, hid second base from view and put the early game on rain delay. When Paul had run by, all that met him was mist, moisture coating his coffee cup, his glasses, his face, arms and legs, coating all his pores and taking his breath away.

A few minutes on the bag wouldn't hurt. He cut across the diamond at an angle, veering toward second base. He had gone yesterday morning too. And the morning before. The canvas had become an even stronger magnet drawing him in and setting up a field of comfort where worries seemed less and control seemed better. Second base therapy had been great yesterday. He'd given the time to thinking about Joe and he'd seen that Joe's anger was about helplessness and fear of the future. Joe felt he could control almost everything else in his life, what related to baseball, school, possibly even Valerie. But not his parents, those selfish and quirky humans whom he'd almost succeeded in manipulating by reading some ill-advised book for teenagers on how to do just that. But ultimately, he'd failed in that goal, mostly because they found the book and read it and refused to let it happen. So he decided to just go back to plan A and keep to his surly self. But his parents' situation wouldn't allow it. So he has fear, resentment and anger. None of the good emotions were left to draw upon. Paul had tried to talk with him about it, but not knowing the right thing to say made that a seriously stressful experience. So he had left it to his friend, Jim, to break the ice and get things started. After Jim's visit that weekend a month ago, he had called Joe twice a week and while they talked about the things they had previously shared interest in, Jim was wise enough and good enough at it to make thinly disguised parables of their topics and indirectly lift Joe's spirits. It was a gift from God and Paul was thankful beyond measure. Paul knew the day would come when he and Joe would have another session similar to their rain-drenched one in the park and he looked forward to it, but only when Joe was ready. He would wait for the sign that he knew would come. Paul looked up to find the mist dissipating and his mood lightened with it.

The more serious issue, yet undealt with, was Joe's new found sexual freedom. Paul felt a twinge about that, knowing that the time to deal with it was immediate, that the more time and emotional distance you give a transgression, the less it feels like one. But for all the parental genetic makeup he'd inherited and for all he'd developed, Paul still felt it hypocritical to come down heavily on Joe for something he'd done himself. But maybe being a parent invited hypocrisy. The do-as-I say-not-as-I-do credo of parenting had somehow been translated into do-as-I-do-not-as-I-say. Susan, Paul thought, would say I was waiting for a luck out and maybe I am. I know I have to deal. And I will, when the time is right.

Thanking the god of baseball, he jogged toward the store to pick up the milk, feeling sorry for all who did not, or could not, allow nature to influence or reflect their soul's emotions.

Paul ran into the tiny store, focused on the refrigerator where milk was kept. He grabbed a half gallon and whirled around prepared to pay and leave with one time-conscious movement until Nicolette walked in. She too had running clothes on, a baggy dark green sweatshirt and cut-off jeans, her hair was disheveled from her run, and her skin glistened, damp from exertion.

"What a surprise," she said, touching his arm. She looked around, picked up two donuts, looked charmingly at the clerk and dropped two dollars on the counter. "Join me for a donut." She took his arm and steered him outside.

Paul moved toward the bench near the bleachers but Nicolette said, "No, over here" and pointed behind them to a patch of damp grass with a damp bench, hidden by shrubs and shadows of the seats. She sat down and Paul leaned against the bleachers.

"Willie is home waiting for milk for his cereal," Paul began.

"This won't take long." She reached in her bag for a donut. "Here."

Paul shook his head but she held it closer to him in silent insistence. He took it.

"I haven't seen you much," she said. "At least not to talk to. Not like we used to."

"I know."

"It's because of that night."

Paul nodded.

"Niki ..." Paul started again, but she held up her hand.

"You had the last word that night so it's my turn now. I have a lot to say. I was going to call and schedule a time to see you, but too many people might be talking already." She turned the donut around in her hand, almost inspecting it.

"You said you wouldn't be back and you didn't come. Not that I expected you to.

Well, I did at first but then when I thought about it, I didn't see how you could. We got kind of carried away, didn't we?" She said this as though musing about it, and finally took a bite of her donut. "Now we both have to go on. I hope you have somewhere to go from here or somewhere to go back to. I really do. I'm not sorry it happened but I'm sorry if it has caused you, no, is causing you pain because, oh, that's the last thing I'd want to do to the man who made me see things so clearly." She reached for the milk carton and Paul handed it to her. She opened it and sipped from the spout, white liquid now covering her upper lip.

"See what so clearly?" he asked when it didn't appear she was going to continue. Her eyes were bright with tears as she explained, words tumbling over each other in her attempt to get all said. "See how important Hunter is to me, and how important it is that Greg be in his life, but not in mine. How confused I was and how stupid I was to leave Hunter here in the first place. I thought I wanted more, new, different, I don't know, experiences, places, men. But after that night, the look on your face at the door, I knew it all wasn't worth it. I have been blessed. I have found it again here with my son and my ex, in spite of my whims. Greg and Hunter have had it rough because of me, because of what I have wanted and taken. And I won't do that to them again.

"Greg and I need to work out an equitable visitation schedule for Hunter; he will need that and we will, too. I have a job at Fenway Park, Hunter will love that, so I'll be moving closer to downtown. I can't stay here but will be here for them, for Hunter as he grows and Greg as he seeks to pick up his life with someone else. But I won't be here for you, nor do I expect you to be there for me. I think we'd agree."

Paul nodded. She continued and Paul listened. He heard her say how little their physical moment had meant and yet how much. What she had taken away from their talks. How that moment of passion was just a moment and that what mattered was the long haul. And he felt the same.

"I wanted you to know this because I know you're distressed," Nicolette said. "I know Susan is out of town and I think it probably has to do with me. She is kind and generous and I hope she can forgive me and maybe someday we can be friends."

That might be a leap, Paul thought as he staggered back against the bleachers, surprised by her words, and bumped his head. He lurched forward and the milk spewed forth from the open spout.

She laughed and Paul grinned.

For Paul, the weight seemed lighter, yet the invisible arm around his shoulders more firm.

"Maybe it's like that treasure thing you were talking about. Maybe you dig up the chest and open it and your most precious gift is there. And you know it and you're happy and you smile and it's some kind of peace. It's a gift of peace that you've given me and it's something I've wanted for so, so long. So I'm taking it," Nicolette said.

She said this so vehemently that Paul smiled. "And you should," he said. "I'm still looking for mine, but I have faith that I'll find it." Paul caught his breath, realizing that for the second time in a long time, he meant what he said about having faith.

"One for the road then," Nicolette grabbed the carton for one more drink.

She handed it back. "I've had enough therapy to know that I'm a taker and you're a giver. Some givers give too much and they get off balance. I know you have to give a lot, and you do. My advice? Try taking a little more." She handed the carton back, turned, made a perfect toss of the donut bag into the garbage can and jogged off into the morning jogger traffic.

Paul sank down on the grass. Mysterious ways, he thought, truly mysterious ways. You've helped me help them, he prayed, and I'm grateful. Now, if You can find the extra, help me see a way to help myself and Susan. He was suddenly hungry and ate the donut in three bites. He finished the milk in three long gulps. He stood, checked his watch, and bolted for the store to buy another carton.

Chapter 28

The Answering Machine

Willie grabbed the milk and as Paul headed up for a shower, he imagined he could hear the snap, crackle and pop of the cereal. He checked the answering machine out of habit and picked a jock strap up off the floor. A few T-shirts and stray socks caught his eye as did the empty glasses and pizza box on the cocktail table in the family room. Straightening up was never ending. Susan had said it many times, but now he knew it was true. She hadn't even whined about it, the way he was whining to himself now. She'd just encompassed it in her routine and could pick up and vacuum, pick up and dust, pick up and do laundry, pick up and prepare dinner, picking up being the common denominator in all her tasks.

In their bedroom, Paul drew the comforter up over the sheets and smoothed it out as he wondered what his common denominator was. The shower was hot, the boys having not used all the water yet. The spray enveloped him and he stood in it for a long time without moving, letting his mind wander. Maybe his common denominator was forgiveness. In everything he did, he was giving it, asking for it, explaining it. If someone called him during dinner, their first words often were "forgive me for bothering you." And he did. "Sorry for disturbing you," preceded interruptions in the office. And he graciously nodded their admittance. From the pulpit he explained how to get forgiveness. In seminars, he addressed its redemptive qualities. He tried to keep its importance in front of him in his everyday ministerial and personal life. He'd lost it for a time, but now it was back. On this day, the warm spray was baptismal, cleansing and life giving. It covered his eyes, nose, mouth, heightening his senses and awareness of his challenges. He could meet them. A few more minutes of restorative showering in preparation for his sermon and Paul grabbed for the fluffy green towel. As he rubbed himself dry, he thought of the green, the color of life and fertility. He remembered Susan wrapped in green just eight weeks ago, sitting on the floor of the bedroom, refusing his offering of peanut butter and jelly and milk in a goblet. It had been a quick road downhill from there. He shook his head at the dog who had settled onto the newly made bed.

But blessed are the peacemakers, blessed are the merciful and blessed are the pure in heart. Paul had faith that a combination of these blessings would be possible for his family. He prayed that they would.

The boys were quiet in the car, having long ago ceased griping about church-going, their behavior having been modified in some strange way by Susan's current absence. Paul was thinking about his sermon. The Lombard men piled out of the car in the church parking lot. Only Pam was there before them. The boys began jostling each other, running to be the first to hear what she was practicing, to see who could first guess the disguised song of the day. Their heels made crunching noises as they ran, kicking up stones that flew in all directions pelting the other rocks as they landed. Paul joined them but had started too late to beat them to the door. He ran up the stairs after them and leaned between them with his hands on their shoulders as they stood outside the narthex door listening. He waited for Joe to shake his hand off, but he didn't. A good sign. Pam's warmup tune was familiar to Paul, the wistful sound of the opening notes of the Beatles song. The boys strained to hear something familiar but gave up when Paul whispered, "It's Beatles music." Clueless and complaining, they shuffled toward the Sunday School hall for their most boring hours spent weekly.

"Why can't she play something we like?" Willie offered. "It makes it more interesting."

"Who knows?" said Joe. "It probably has some meaning for her or something. You know what girls are like."

"No, tell me," Willie started getting interested.

210

"Wait a year or two," Joe said, very seriously. "You don't have the brain to understand it yet."

"Oh, like you do?" Willie hissed. "Is that why Valerie's called you a million times and you don't call her back?"

"She called me? When?" Joe stopped and grabbed Willie's arm.

"A lot." Willie tried to twist his arm away. "I left you messages on the pad by the phone."

"What phone?" Joe wouldn't let go.

"The one in Dad's study."

"I never go in there. Shit, now she's probably all mad at me and it's your fault, you little wimp."

"If Dad heard you say that, he'd ground you for life. Ow. Ow!" Joe twisted Willie's arm behind him and sent him flying across the foyer, right into Amy Sundstrom. She caught the young boy on his way into the glass door and gave a helpless look to Joe's quickly departing back.

"Are you all right? Be careful. This is God's house, remember."

"Sorry, Mrs. Sundstrom," Willie said. "Joe's having a bad day. As usual."

"I'll pray for him," she smiled and hustled into the church to set up for communion.

You do that, Paul thought. Please do that. He was torn between hurrying after Joe and getting ready for the service. He took a deep breath and went to the closet for his robe.

"Quit looking for the one with no seams," Jim's voice whispered in Paul's ear.

Paul whirled around and grabbed his friend. "What are you doing here?"

"Helping you," Jim answered. "Sorry I couldn't get here early enough to run with you. Where are the guys?"

"One's in Sunday School, the other one is sulking. Care to guess which is which?"

Jim chuckled. "That's a given." Then he frowned. "How's Joe doing?"

"Can't talk right now. I've got to get inspired so I can be inspirational. Come to the house after? We'll have time for lunch and we have a game at 3." Paul reached for his robe. "How long can you stay"

"Have to leave tomorrow early." Jim placed the green vestment in Paul's hands and handed him his cross.

"It's great you're here."

"Yeah. Do you need help with the service today?" Jim reached for another robe in the closet. "I can help with communion or whatever."

"Sure. Why not? Let's team it." Paul hurried into his office for his other set of vestments. He flung open the door and strode toward the closet. The light on the answering machine in his office blinked for his attention. No time now. He was about to rush out when something made him stop and look at the phone.

The blinking light showed three messages. He tapped the button and began to struggle with getting his robe over his head when he heard Susan's voice. He stopped, tangled in the cloth, so he would not miss a word.

"Paul, I've been thinking. You know, you start out with a certain way you want things to be. Like preparing for company—when a million details careen through your head and you don't want to leave anything out. But there's always something you forget." Her voice was weepy and Paul wanted to hold her, let her bury her face in his shoulder and sob it all out. He could hear her sniffle and blow her nose, could see her in her mother's spare bedroom as flower-ridden as the female congregants had appeared just a few minutes ago. When the answering machine beeped and disconnected, Paul panicked.

He hurried to pull the robe all the way off, constrained by its softness and folds and fullness. It was a lump in his lap as he reached for his address book with her mother's phone number in it.

The second message began and Susan's voice continued. "Ran out of time. Anyhow, that something you forget, I think for you, that something was me. For me, it was you. And Paul, there are too many good things I don't want to forget about you. It's been hard this past year because you haven't let me help. You've been the manager, coach, player and spectator. You can't ..." The answering machine cut out again. Paul waited for what he knew would be her voice and she returned at the third message. "You can't be everything to everyone else and no one to the people who love you." She was really crying now. "I thought we could do this ourselves, but we need help. I want us to see someone. Please think about it because ..." She hung up. No more blinking lights.

Susan vulnerable. Susan wanting them to get help. She knew he hated the thought, felt he could deal with anything, but it was also obvious he hadn't been dealing with anything. If this was the way the game was going to go down, could he play that way? He would sincerely try. He pulled the cross over his head as he rushed out to the waiting Christians.

The church was more than half full, unusual for a Sunday in summer. Standing beside Jim at the back of the church, Paul looked for Joe. Nowhere in sight and no chance to look now. Willie was seated with his Sunday School teacher close to the front. The flowers on the summer dresses seated row upon row gave the look of a huge garden of wildflowers to the sunny inside of the church proper. If it rained, Paul thought, would they all wilt or would they be strengthened by the life-giving fluid. He had to focus now, could have gotten away with a lesser presentation if Jim hadn't arrived. Shouldn't have been drawn to that red blinking light. Had to focus. Who knew whether or not Jim had been sent by the bishop to check things out, who knew if they at the church offices had heard anything. Who knew if they knew Susan was with her mother for any surreptitious reason. No. He could trust Jim with anything. He was here as a friend.

Paul made it through the opening hymn, and let Jim handle the forgiveness of sins, the lessons and the gospel.

From his bench on the sideline of the altar, Paul watched people settle in for the sermon. Henry wrapped his arm around Rachel's shoulders and she snuggled close. Amy Sundstrom, surrounded by children, handed crayons all around and nestled in to nurse her youngest. Mr. and Mrs. Smith sat in the back where their dozing would be less noticeable. He knew important things about every person, every family in this place. He knew more than he wanted to know about their hopes, dreams, fears, pleasures. They expected a lot but they gave a lot too. Since Susan had left, Paul knew that the crowd had been restless, wondering, hypothesizing. The brave had called to wish him well, and try to ferret out some information, unsuccessfully. The cowardly had not called at all, could not make eye contact, probably had speculative phone calls daily with their fellow cowards. Then there were the in-betweeners, the ones who were church leaders who might suspect something was amiss, something that might damage their spiritual home forever, but who also were loyal to Paul, who owed him for a spiritual favor, a well-timed, well-stated prayer in time of crisis, counseling for major and minor life crises. Then there was Pam. Forgiving Pam. Still out there hustling for votes, no matter how disrespected or scorned he must feel, so loyal and true he wanted to cry again. Her music reflected her feelings, soaring, low, confused, enlightened.

An image of himself walking on the sand came to Paul, a feeling of well-being in an arm around his shoulders and a voice saying, you don't want to lose this.

He stepped up to the pulpit and looked out over the women in the flowered dresses, and their families.

"Good morning," he said.

"Good morning," they murmured back.

"Today, I want you to think about a sport where people look for a sign," he said, smiling. Then paused.

Most of the congregation smiled knowingly.

Chapter 29

The Pre-Game Show

"That was one hot sermon." Jim slapped Paul on the back. "I can't stop thinking about it."

"Let's hope they can't either," Paul said, pretending to wince under the friendly blow. "Wasn't it some manager who said something about baseball being like church. Many attend but few understand. You always just have to hope they got it."

"Yeah, I've spent many years hoping that."

Jim and Paul decided to eat at the ballpark. The concession stand was open but not mobbed when they arrived. Two hot dogs and a large soda each and they sneaked into the dugout to eat in peace before the 3:00 game. Paul looked around for the boys and saw Willie with Hunter tossing a ball back and forth. Joe was with Valerie sitting under one of the huge shade trees that provided coolness for the players during their sweaty afternoon games.

"I was right in my sermon, wasn't I?" Paul said. "Isn't everybody always looking for signs? Like a sign that you're right. Like that you're taken care of. That you can move forward.

"I guess one way or the other we are." Jim adjusted his dark glasses and pulled his pony tail tighter.

"Well, in baseball, you can count on it. There is someone taking care of you, forcing your decision. You accomplish one goal, you get to a base, then look toward the next one. You go if the coach tells you to steal and you hope you make it. It's just easier." Paul sucked the mustard off his thumb.

"It may be an easier life, playing ball, but not a better one. Baseball requires a skilled craftsman. Being a minister requires that but in a different way and more of it.

Wasn't it Reinhold Niebuhr who said to be a minister you need the knowledge of a social scientist, the insight and imagination of a poet, the talents of a businessman and the mental discipline of a philosopher?"

"You can tell who has time to read and philosophize." Paul could not hide the jealousy in his voice.

"Forget that and listen to me," Jim said. "You want my assessment of your problem? You do. And I've been skirting it, hoping you'd get to it yourself. But you're not, so here it is. Actually, this is a harangue long overdue. And I'll deliver it in language you can understand. Being the manager is part of your calling. It's how you connect. But managing the spiritual lives of the congregation was too wearing. Being the coach is really part of your make up. Do this. Try that. Good job. Work harder. This was easy to do. Just tell people and if they didn't do it, urge them to try again. But the constant urging was getting too tiring. Playing the bases required skill, traits that you continually developed over time. It required practice and more important, energy for practice, willingness to risk failure, the guts to shake it off and try again. But you ended up not having time for these. The spectators, your congregation and your family, were in the worst position. They could watch but not effect change. No matter how encouraging they were or gleeful or obnoxious, there was only so much effort you as manager, coach, and player could expend."

"So how come you don't have the same problems? You have the same positions to play."

"I choose to connect in a different way. Let me be brutally honest here, something that most ministers probably do far too seldom. You spend too much of your time coaching some of your parishioners and trying to bring them up to your speed. I let people accept me on my terms. For example, I have long hair. If they think that interferes with my ability to converse with God on their behalf and bring His word, they won't join my congregation or they don't stay. I talk a lot and my delivery is, well, unique.

217

If they like it, they're mine. If they don't, they cruise. But I want to tell you, when there is someone in need, I can help them see the problem and that has nothing to do with my ponytail or my verbosity. More importantly, I can forgive them for letting me see their weakness or their pain and then we can get on with it. They can forgive me for knowing this thing if I can make the connection that is forgiveness.

"This is the connection you've severed with everyone, Paul. If you can't forgive yourself, you're screwed. Then even if Susan can forgive you and we have reason to believe she can, hence today's phone messages, it won't work. And then there's God. Of course he'll forgive you, just ask him. Goddamn it, wallowing does everybody harm. You know the words. Ask and you shall receive. Seek and you shall find. Be truly penitent. Ask for forgiveness and it's yours. Give it up. Move on. No more wallowing." Jim stopped for a breath, took bite of his cold hot dog and flipped it into the trash. "I need more food." He got up. "Just remember you need to be the beacon here. You have been and you can be again. Whatever it was that has blown your bulb can be repaired. You are looking at the ground instead of the sky. Find the light. Look for the light, for God's sake."

Jim lumbered off to the stand, his black T-shirt billowing in the warm breeze. He had gone from presenting facts to lecturing to pleading to disgust to exasperation to starvation. Even his friends were buckling under the strain Paul felt he carried like a shedding virus.

"Hey, Rev." Paul heard Greg and Hunter arrive behind him, dropping huge bags of equipment on the ground. Look who we brought." Paul turned to see Nicolette hanging on Greg's arm.

"I'm the mascot," she offered her hand. "Greg said you needed one."

Paul tried hard not to look surprised and realized he'd failed when Greg slapped him on the back.

"With Susan at her mom's and all, I thought we could use some good female vibes." He laughed, then said, "Niki, get me a cold drink, will you?" Nicolette nodded and sauntered toward the stand. About twenty feet away she turned and yelled, "Paul, want one too?" Paul gestured no and turned to look questioningly at Greg. Greg shrugged. "She's ready to be friends, and I think I can do that now. It's like some power, you know, like that treasure chest thing you talked about in church, made her reconsider. We've been talking all week and I know we need to talk more, but it's a start. It's funny, you know. She's the mother of my son, so she is like my treasure and because she is, I can forgive her." Greg looked away. "I didn't know how much I wanted this. It's kind of overwhelming."

Paul touched Greg's shoulder. "That's great, my friend. Just great," Paul said. Profound relief was the reward for this sincerity.

They checked the roster and Greg ran out to warm up the starting pitcher. Paul was focused on filling out the score sheet when Jim returned with another hot dog and Nicolette right behind him with two drinks.

They started to talk to him simultaneously and both stopped, laughing.

"You first," they both said at the same time, laughing.

"Nicolette, meet my good friend and colleague, Jim Fuller. Jim, meet Nicolette Stone, a relatively new parishioner and first baseman's mom." Paul hoped he was doing a good job of being casual.

They were exchanging hellos when someone called to Paul from the field. He escaped into the sand and grass and turned to find Jim and Nicolette climbing the bleachers together and sitting toward the top. Paul willed Jim to look at him. Jim gave him the okay sign.

Valerie and Ashley arrived drawing Hunter and Joe like magnets to the dugout fence. Joe looked confident and in control, more manly if Paul was reading things right. Hunter was joking around and poking the girls, making them giggle.

Paul clapped his hands and hollered, 'Okay guys, let's play ball. Let's focus now." And I will too, he thought.

The umpire was having a bad day and they had some bad calls early on. The pitcher couldn't put anything in the narrow area the ump had established as the strike zone for their team and because of walk after walk after walk, Paul's team was down three runs.

Joe on second was ready for anything. It was a good thing because it all came to him. A line drive to the second baseman. Scooped up and nailed to Hunter, stretched out at first. A diving stab at one trying to go through the hole between second and first, stopped by Joe and lobbed to Hunter. Two outs. A high pop fly and Joe was taking no chances. He backed up, put his glove in sun-blocking position and caught it, never a doubt.

"Show off," Willie yelled proudly to his brother. Greg ran out to welcome Joe and brought him to the bench, arm around his shoulders like a special friend and confidant.

"Got to forge ahead, guys," Jim yelled.

"Let's get 'em," Nicolette hollered standing and shaking her fist with great passion.

Top of the final inning, and the first two players on Paul's team walked. It was obvious the opposing pitcher was tired. He was looking at the coach like kids do, pleading, asking to be removed. The coach called time and walked to the edge of the field to talk to him. Paul could see the boy straighten his shoulders and take a deep breath as instructed, as he had been instructed so many times himself. He felt for the boy. The top of the order was up next. It would require much concentration to forget that and just pitch.

This was the beauty of the game. This was where the rush came in. You're at the plate in position to be a hero or a goat and you had only yourself to rely on. All you've learned to this point, all you've absorbed, everything you've practiced came into play now. You had to call it all up and you had to reach down to find that collection of things that would let you connect.

Joe, the team's lead-off hitter, got into position. Runners were on first and second. The first pitch came in low and away and Joe let it go by. "Good eye. Good eye," the crowd offered in unison. Joe stepped out of the box and tapped the dust off his shoes. The agony on the pitcher's face was painful to see. Joe moved back into position and swung at the next two throws. Now the agony was on Joe's face. Full count and a chance to be a hero. The crowd was silent. As quiet as communicants queuing up to receive the sacrament of Holy Communion. As quiet as a solitary walk on the beach.

The pitch was outside and Joey lunged for it, hungry for the hit. It went hard and fast past the ear of the third baseman and continued to the farthest corner of the ballfield. The two runners were in already and Joe was burning it around the bases. He ran past third knowing he was the tying run, then hesitated, must've seen the ball over his shoulder out of the corner of his eye and dove back to the protection of the canvas at third. Wise, Paul thought, yelling supportive comments, wise but not gutsy.

The pitcher straightened up, having gotten a reprieve, and threw the ball to the third baseman three times, pinning Joe to the base. Hunter was at bat. The goat or the hero took a new shape. Paul turned to Greg to say something supportive but Greg was gone. Nicolette was gone too, and Paul found them standing shoulder to shoulder by the fence, Nicolette yelling at Hunter to keep his elbow up. Hunter was pale but determined. He let the first ball go by. Strike one. He swung weakly at the next pitch and sent it foul down the right baseline. Strike two. Jim was now leaning on the fence on Nicolette's other side. They were all quiet. No one wanted to be the one to distract Hunter or otherwise give the pitcher the edge.

Susan would have been muttering, "I hate this. I hate this. I hate for it to come down to this." And Paul would have had to remind her all over again about the beauty of baseball, but not right at that tense moment. Perhaps he would have on the way home.

And sure enough, it was one of those slow motion plays where Hunter hit the ball hard and it sailed and sailed and sailed out, out, out to the center fielder who had to go back, back, back and lean over the fence to snag the ball. Which he did but then couldn't hold onto it. It dropped to the ground. The crowd went wild. Nicolette and Greg were beside themselves. The team was all over Hunter, who could not stop smiling, not for a minute, looking at his mother and father, looking at Ashley, looking at Paul.

"Wish Mom could have been here," Joe whispered to his father after tagging home. "She would have gone nuts."

"She will when you tell her," Paul tried

"It won't be the same. We'll be going to some playoffs now, you know."

It was like a warning, a word to the wise. Get her back, he was saying. Do anything to get her back. He turned and swaggered toward the waiting Valerie and they strode holding hands over to the victory mass of boys getting pieces of pizza and pop as their just rewards.

The sun was going down, the warmth of the day turning to an evening coolness. It had been a long one, today had. Full of hope and fear and disappointment and pride.

Nicolette and Greg picked up the equipment and left, talking about the wonders of Hunter. Jim fell into step with Paul outside the dugout. "Great game," he said. "Something for everyone."

"Please don't draw any parallels to my current situation, " Paul groaned. "I can't withstand another theological assault without a beer in hand."

"Don't worry. I'm done. If I haven't gotten to you by now, I'm not as good as I think I am," Jim said, flashing a rather serious smile.

They walked a ways before Paul turned around to look for the boys.

"They're in line for more pizza," Jim said. "Let them enjoy this. Let's sit here and wait." He pointed to the bench by the garbage can.

"No more lectures?"

"Promise."

"I need a beer real soon though," Paul said.

"I could go for one too." Jim sunk back onto the slatted bench and waited a moment before saying, "She's an interesting woman. But needy. Enough said."

"I've decided what I need to do next," Paul said. "No more lectures, okay? I've called an emergency executive committee of the council for Thursday evening. Jim, I need to take the first step. Can't keep going on like this."

"So you are going to confess," Jim said. "I really do need a beer or something. You realize this means you might be done here and possibly everywhere."

"I know. But, I can't keep going on like this. I thought this has been all about me and it isn't. Look what I've done to my family. I have to salvage what I can. And I don't know what's next."

"I don't know what to say, and for me, you know that's rare," Jim said. "But I have been thinking about one thing. If this calling has become overwhelming for you, after all these years, why don't you try to do the thing that has been dragging you away from it. Reinvent yourself. Try baseball."

Paul looked surprised. "Too late. Too old," he said.

"Not playing. Involving yourself some other way. Coaching. High school or college coaching. Maybe even at one of the Lutheran colleges if you can't quite give up the religious aspect. I've watched you these weeks that Susan's been gone, helping Greg with the team. You look happier that I ever have seen you. Go toward that happiness, my friend." Jim squeezed Paul's shoulder. Paul looked up at him. "Go toward that happiness."

Chapter 30

The Confession

Friday morning's run to the ballfield was liberating. So much to think about.

First, just last night at a special meeting, Paul had told members of the council executive committee that he was submitting his resignation. After much thought he had accepted that he needed to take the first step. Susan would want that, and he found he did, too. Whatever comes, he thought. Henry Jensen, council president, Mr. Ginker, Mr. Knox, Mrs. Zorn and Mrs. Gurney were in attendance. Paul had asked Henry to call the meeting saying he had something important and highly confidential to discuss. This guaranteed the entire committee would be there. No coffee and cookies ready to go for this meeting. Paul had quickly gotten to the point. It had been rough.

"Friends," he had begun. "As your pastor, I have done something that I am truly sorry for, something that has affected my relationship with this congregation and with my wife and family. He had paused. "So to get my head and home in order, I need time and space. Therefore, for everyone's sake, I am resigning at year's end to give the council a chance to call and interview a new pastor." He had paused. He looked around at the group. "I'm so sorry," he said.

Both of the ladies had made a small gasp of disbelief. The men had cleared their throats.

"I'm sure you are aware that Susan is not currently here in town and that's why. We are trying to work things out." He had paused again. "I can't imagine after this that I will continue to be your pastor or that you will want me to. I wanted you to hear this from me, instead of the whispers in the hallways and phone calls and however else these events officially are transmitted to everyone. I assume the council will report this to the Bishop and we'll go from there." He looked around.

"Well, Paul," Henry had said, looking directly at him. "I wasn't sure why you called this special meeting. Of course, it's usually about the budget when something comes up emergency. However, I wouldn't be honest if I didn't say there has been some talk about your behavior recently, things feeling a little off, you being a little off, not like the minister we know and love."

The others nodded.

"Have you all noticed something or had someone say something to you about my work or behavior?" Paul asked.

They all looked at each other and nodded.

"Frankly," said Mr. Ginker, "we've been waiting for it to pass or for you to come to us, but I don't think any of us thought this is what you would tell us. We all have times when things are a bit rocky; often we talk to you about those things. Who do you have to talk to?"

"I have been getting help and support from the Rev. Jim Fuller."

"No one at the main church office knows yet?" Henry had asked.

"No. Not yet. At least I don't think so," Paul had said. "There is a certain way these things have to be approached and I think you need to find out how we begin."

"I feel like we should have a general meeting of the congregation so everyone knows what is happening. The Bishop may even want to be here for that; I'll make some calls tomorrow," Henry said. The others nodded in agreement. "You know, I can't even imagine what people will think, but I am fairly sure they will take you at your word and want you to leave. This is something that will be hard to comprehend. Now that this is part of your story, I don't see how you can continue to be our leader no matter how much we each individually may have benefited from your time here, and you should know that some of us really have."

225

"I know," Paul had said. "Whatever happens, I just hope eventually you all can forgive me for this disappointment." He stood and looked at the group. They looked at him. Paul did not ask for questions because he didn't want to answer any. He wasn't sure what more he could or would say.

Second, there was Susan and the boys. Susan seemed ready at least to talk. He knew what he had to, wanted to say.

Last, what Jim had said about reinventing made sense. Paul could not see himself getting, or wanting, another congregation even if the church rules would allow that. The idea of teaching, coaching was very attractive. He had a call in to Wilhelm to see if he thought that even was feasible. The more he thought about it, the more fervently he prayed it was.

Chapter 31

Joe's Approach

Paul sat in his study across from the blank screen on the computer. It was Sunday night, his performance over. Church had gone fairly well. Joe's team had won the right to go to the playoffs two weeks away. And Susan had called and left **him** a message, actually addressed her words to **him**. She was willing to try a way out of this. On this night, he didn't need to write anything or prepare anything. He leaned back in his chair enjoying the crinkle of the leather, even in the sticky hotness of this summer night. His second bottle of beer sat on the baseball coaster on his desk, condensation from the glass forming beads that would eventually soak into the pressed paper of the coaster containing Mickey Mantle's face and batting average.

"Well, Mickey. A little time to myself to think about things, without the pressures. A luxury," Paul whispered.

He looked at his watch. Just past midnight and waiting for Joe. If he came home anytime in the next 15 minutes, Paul would forgive him the time past his midnight curfew. Later than that, they'd go head to head once again. Paul got up to pace around the room, straightening books on the shelves, rearranging his notebooks full of baseball cards. He turned off the brightest lamp and went outside on the deck to look at the night sky. Darkness was sporadic in this suburban neighborhood with front yard lights and porch lights dotting the flatness as far as he could see. If you could look beyond that, way up, up, it was dark black; a void, restful, non-confrontational, soothing. Like the cosmos should be. A place where man can look for his inner self and find peace. Carl Sagan's hypnotic voice filled Paul's head, remembered from many years of PBS programs on the universe watched in the darkness of his room.

A rustling of the shrubs interrupted his thoughts and Paul wondered if a skunk or racoon or rabbit had found its way onto the Lombard property. He wasn't in the mood to deal with a critter tonight and started to go back inside, when Joe came up the steps.

"I'm here," he said, righting one of the Adirondack chairs Susan had thrown aside that night a month ago, and left there by the men in her family as a monument. He plunked himself into it.

Paul grunted assent. It was as much an invitation from Joe to talk as he'd had in weeks. He walked to the railing and gazed over the back yard, seeing nothing.

"What did you do tonight?" slipped out, causing Paul to wince as it did.

"Went to the soda shop with Hunter and a bunch of the guys. Walked Valerie and Ashley home. Stood around and talked for a while after."

"Great game today. You guys played as well as I've ever seen you."

"It just came together. You know, Mom always says there's some magic when that happens, stuff she can't explain but it's there and everybody knows it. It sort of felt like that today."

"I miss her too, Joey."

"Then do something."

"It's not that easy."

"Make it easy."

"She's really mad and hurt, you know, because of what I..."

Joey lightly pounded the arm of the chair with his fist and heaved a sigh. His voice seemed deeper and more mature as he said, "You guys don't make sense. You don't do what you tell us to do. How many times have you told me never to go to sleep angry? Don't hold grudges. Forgive and forget. Talk about it. All that stuff I'm supposed to do and you never do." The words were pouring out, staccato, like knives thrown at a man on a wheel in a circus act.

"What do you want me to do?" Paul asked.

"Talk about it."

"Your mother hasn't wanted to talk to me. I've been giving her some space and only today she left me a hopeful message that we might talk."

"She'll talk to you. I know she will. I feel it. But someone has to go first." Joe extended his legs and put his feet on the railing next to Paul. "It's like you always tell Willie and me. It's not right here without her, Dad. It just isn't."

"Yeah. I know."

"Then do something."

"Yeah. I wish I knew how, what."

Joe got up to stand close to Paul, leaned on the railing close to him but not touching. "Say you're sorry," he said.

"I've done that already. It didn't go over too well."

"Maybe I could help you. Maybe I should invite her to the playoffs."

"You could try."

"When she calls tomorrow, I'll give it a shot."

"Good deal, Joe." Paul put his arm around his son, like he used to before all the distance had grown between them, and Joe didn't move away. They stood together, looking at the stars for a long quiet time, then Joe did move out from under Paul's arm, rubbing his hands through his hair like he did when he was much younger and was frustrated or nervous. He went inside and Paul heard the refrigerator door open and the fizz signifying the opening of a can of soda. Then Joe came back out and leaned his back against the railing and took a long slug of the drink. He cleared his throat, turned to lean on the deck railing once again and looked at Paul.

"Dad. About Valerie." Joe readjusted his elbows on the railing. "I'm not sorry."

"Okay."

"Don't tell Mom."

"Okay." Then Paul added "I won't, for now. But be careful.

"Okay." Joe said. Then he stood up and brushed twigs and pine needles from his shirt. He stood shoulder to shoulder with Paul, staring into the night. "You know, I've been waiting for about an hour for you to come out here," he said.

Tears came to Paul's eyes. Why are You so good to me, he asked the stars.

"Going to the ballfield for a while," he whispered.

"Gotcha," Joe said.

After 8 weeks. To hear her voice and respond to it. She'll call tomorrow like she usually does and I'll pick up the phone, Paul thought as he jogged to his safe place.

Chapter 32

The Story Continues

One morning a few weeks later, Paul was again in the same position he'd taken on second base for many months. He was lying on his stomach with his head was on the bag, right cheek down. His right hand, fast asleep, was under the base in the same way as it so often found its way under his pillow. He rolled over, carefully, not wanting to give up the base just yet.

He thought about how he'd answered the phone several weeks ago according to his plan instead of letting it go to answering machine the way Susan had been preferring it, and he and Susan had been talking ever since. First week was talking about the boys and school and sports physicals, then the second week about how they were sleeping, eating, and the third week about how they were missing the two of them together, parents, Dad and Mom. Their talks got more personal and soon Paul found himself lying on the couch with his feet propped on the back of the sofa just as he used to settle in for late night calls with Susan in their courtship phase. They had talked about everything then, held nothing back, knew each other's political leanings, he Democrat, she Independent, not surprising. Family back stories, both good and bad and skeletons in the closet they had shared. Discussion of Paul's next step had peppered their dialogue. They had sorted out important issues in those phone calls.

And now they were doing it again. After almost 20 years together, they were in the prologue to the next chapter in their story. He had told her that.

"I guess you could call it that," she had said softly.

She had asked how things were at church.

"I'm glad you brought it up," he said. "Susan, I talked to the Church

Council and tendered my resignation effective the end of the year to give them time to find a replacement. You know it takes several months."

"Oh," she said, surprised.

"I had to. I told them that some personal things were keeping me from being the pastor they needed, and I truly believe that."

"I believe that, too. But what now?"

"Well, I've been thinking that the living the total pastoral life is not for me anymore."

"Ya think!?" Susan said. "After what we have been through? Are still going through? Sorry, I couldn't resist."

Paul had chuckled. Almost like the old Susan, he thought, but with an air of maybe sadness, and all Paul knew then, lying on the couch, was that he wanted to make that go away. He told her his thoughts for the future, including both religion and baseball. "I'm thinking of trying to coach baseball at a college, maybe a religious college, and teach there as well."

"I can definitely see that," she had said.

In these nearly nightly phone calls, Paul felt there was something larger at work than the connecting they had done back then. And this something larger allowed him to begin to talk about the Nicolette situation. It was after all the elephant in the room. They talked about emotions, betrayal, and how Paul could ask Susan to forgive and how she could accomplish that. These were the most difficult conversations of their lives together, but neither wanted to, nor could, stop talking. As Susan said, she felt the story they were writing together was not over yet. They both felt the truth in that.

That morning, there was an early morning haze on the infield, thicker than he'd ever seen. The mist rolled out of the swampy pond water, a pale white cloud. The herons were there, barely visible, but Paul knew they were there. He shook his head to clear it and focused on the sounds of the girls from the softball team positioning themselves for early morning practice on the other baseball diamond across the muddy field. The coach's whistle cut through their waking up sounds and the girls moved jerkily towards their stations, the bases, the mound, the outfield where their jolted movements would become fluid and spare and purposeful when the ball came their way, if they could see it.

The peace that passes all understanding was somewhere in this dampness, hidden by moist droplets, a screen of liquid obscuring most everything, shapes barely discernable, making it necessary to really focus to see who was out there. His automatic focus on second base kicked in and he watched the increasingly visible female shapes out there move gracefully from side to side. From waiting to hoping. From tense preparation to brief relaxation. From catching to leaping. Then the crack of the bat. The second base player had it. The ball was hers. She tagged the base and leaping, tossed the ball to first. Paul heard the smack of leather on leather immediately before he heard the crunch of flesh and bone on gravel and saw her complete her leap by connecting with the cool stones of the infield, a huge and painful thump.

He could see the puffs of breath from the other girls' lips as they ran to her assistance. "You all right?" "Can you walk?" "You're going to have a doozy of a bruise." The young girl lay still, just rubbing her thigh, her friends running for ice. Their bodies were growing more and more visible and real with every ray added to the sun's increasing power. They were less mysterious now and defiant. They were worried and some were tearful. The mist hid vulnerability and promised power. That was how it should be.

And as she got up and brushed herself off, Paul saw her as a younger Susan, looking toward a younger Paul alone on the bleachers, her chin up, head high, no tears, just defiance for that part of the game that might cause pain, willing to risk it. And the younger Paul applauded silently through the soft white air, knowing she was the one, now even more certain.

He looked toward first base, and it seemed like he saw Willie, trying to pay attention to his very important position, socking his glove to make the pocket stronger and deeper. Placing his foot just aside the bag and stretching as far as he could to the right. Doing all the things he'd been taught even though he didn't truly understand why. This was the way it should be. Blind faith. Just do it. If the ball always went where it should, he'd be covered and able to cover. It was the ball's and the body's unexpected responses to the laws of physics yet unlearned that brought chaos to Willie's game.

Paul rolled toward third base and it seemed like there was Joe. Tough and ready. He knew the physics of the game and played the properties of velocity, mass and trajectory well. But he wasn't quick and sometimes he wasn't all there. Were the girls watching? Could they see his biceps when he flexed them under the auspices of warming up? Did his uniform fit to flatter his best features? Should he move in for the possible bunt or take a chance on the double play?

And it seemed Susan was in the dugout. Hair mostly tucked into her cap with wisps falling free here and there, blowing in the breeze. A hand reached out of the haze to tuck her hair back up. Paul saw himself, a young man, virile and confident, meeting her eyes with the promise of a future doing what they loved with both passion and intellect. She peered into the haze, searching the cloud. She could see the kids and waved them into position, calling some positioning directions for the next batter as she continued to search. She pulled her cap and shook her hair loose, still straining to see something or someone. The vision ended as Paul blinked and really focused his eyes on the dugout.

Susan really was there. She was looking toward second base, and when she saw Paul, she walked across the muddy infield and stood over him, blocking the rays of the sun at the same time framing herself in a halo of ultraviolet glory.

"I thought I'd find you here right now," she said. She was a shadow against the light, an image with the outline clearly seen and the interior a secret still. She crouched down to say, "Joe called me to tell me about the team's big win. I felt like I needed, no, wanted to congratulate Joe and the guys in person so here I am. And I needed, wanted to talk to you face-to-face."

"I just had a dream or maybe daydream, I think it was, a dream about you, and Joe and Willie. In the part about you ..." Paul heard himself whisper so softly she had to crouch down to hear. "You were a young girl playing ball and you dug it out for the double play and fell completing it. It must have hurt like hell but you didn't cry."

"I'm tough," she said, not sounding that way at all. "I can take it."

"You shouldn't have to." He stood up. The barely perceptible weight of a comforting arm around his shoulder helped Paul dare reach down for Susan and help her to stand. He put his forehead to hers and held it there. She did not pull away.

"Are you alone here?" She asked.

"Yes." Paul said. It was a question.

"Is there someone else here I mean?" he heard Susan murmur softly.

"Only you," he said out loud. Just you. I see it so clearly. Just you.

"Boys doing okay?"

"We are doing okay. They miss you. They want you home. We want you home."

"You know, being with my Mom these past weeks has been enlightening," Susan said, stepping back so she could see Paul's face.

"I had a hard time listening to her advice when I lived at home. She was always taking the opposite approach from me on most everything, but now, she makes sense." Susan paused.

235

"Go on," Paul said. "What kind of sense?"

"Well, we've been talking a lot and she's been warning me not to, as she says, 'Take such an aggressive posture.' I guess she meant leaving so quickly and continuing to avoid you. Said there are two sides to every story and I knew that but I wasn't ready to listen to yours or tell you mine. You know, I was uncomfortable being with you when I left but now I realize it's more uncomfortable without you."

"I kind of feel the same. I know you want us to go talk to someone together, and I know I have always resisted that. But now I see your point and agree we need help going forward. I think what I am saying is, we are worth it. After something like I have forced us to experience, after something like that, I think a relationship can't stay the same. I think it either is damaged or grows stronger. I feel with some help our story will continue stronger. I hope you can forgive me and I hope you feel the same."

"It may take me a while, Paul, but my heart is open to forgiveness. Forgiving you doesn't make it hurt less right now, but maybe it can over time. You can't pay lip service to forgiveness. It has to be really, true, meaningful. With some work, I think we can get there. I know I am willing to try. Paul and Susan's story needs to continue. I want it to," Susan said.

"That's all I can ask."

The mist was mostly gone as Susan and Paul walked toward home, shoulders touching, enough for now.

THE END

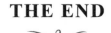

OTHER TITLES BY KATHY JOHNCOX

THE LAST GENERATION OF WOMEN WHO COOK

These stories—all about food—delight the senses and satisfy our hunger for a good narrative. Worth reading. Bon appétit!

-Gail Hosking, author of Snakes's Daughter:

The Roads in and out of War

WHAT A KISS CAN DO

"What A Kiss Can Do" takes you to the most unusual holiday party you'll ever attend. Once it's over, you can't stop reading until you finish Rita Jensen's romantic ride— starting with a kiss tat launches and adventure no one could have predicted. A fun, romantic read!

-Deborah Benjamin,

author of The Death of Perry Many Paws

ABOUT THE AUTHOR

Kathy Johncox, fiction writer, communications professional, world traveler/army brat, coffee-loving Norwegian, daughter, wife, sister, mother and a pretty darned good cook, was born in St. Louis, Missouri. She gathered material in two foreign countries and seven states before settling down to write at her current home in upstate New York. She has published a number of short fiction pieces in local newspapers and magazines, and has published two books both in hard copy and Kindle—one, a collection of short stories entitled *The Last Generation of Woman Who Cook* and the other, a romance novel entitled *What A Kiss Can Do*, both available on Amazon. She considers herself an eclectic writer, so it's anybody's guess what will be next!

Books available in print and on Kindle at www.Amazon.com.
www.kathyjohncoxbooks.com